The End of Time

Gavin Extence

HODDER &
STOUGHTON

First published in Great Britain in 2019 by Hodder & Stoughton
An Hachette UK company

1

Copyright © Gavin Extence 2019

A CIP catalogue record for this title is available from the British Library

Hardback ISBN 978 1 473 60542 8
Trade Paperback ISBN 978 1 473 60541 1
eBook ISBN 978 1 473 60543 5

Typeset in Guardi 10/16 pt by Palimpsest Book Production Limited,
Falkirk, Stirlingshire

Printed and bound by Clays Ltd, Elcograf S.p.A.

Hodder & Stoughton policy is to use papers that are natural,
renewable and recyclable products and made from wood grown in
sustainable forests. The logging and manufacturing processes are
expected to conform to the environmental regulations of the
country of origin.

Hodder & Stoughton Ltd
Carmelite House
50 Victoria Embankment
London EC4Y 0DZ

www.hodder.co.uk

For Siân, Kara and Ciaran –
at its heart, a story about siblings.

PART 1

The Mediterranean Sea

The Crossing

So there we stood, on the stony beach beneath the forest and the mountains and the stars. The land across the water was now only a smudge in the moonlight, and the crossing looked so very much further than it had on Google Maps.

I remember this moment clearly. I was afraid. I turned to my little brother Mohammed and said, 'We don't have to do this. You know that, don't you?'

My brother's eyes shone briefly in the darkness.

'God above, Zain!' he hissed. 'Don't be such a pussy.'

He did not use those actual words, of course, because we were talking in Arabic. But in this instance, I have translated his phrasing very closely. The same anatomy was referenced in both cases. My little brother can be extremely insulting when he chooses to be.

'Our mother would not want you speaking that way,' I rejoined.

'Well, Mum's not here, is she?'

There was not much I could say to this, so I said nothing at all. I just looked at him and tried to imitate the expression our father would have made in this situation. Calm, patient and still in control. An undertone of quiet disappointment. You were raised better than this, young man.

It is possible that the many shades of my intention were lost to the darkness. Mohammed made an obscene gesture with his fist.

'God give me strength,' I said beneath my breath, but loud enough that he could hear.

Mohammed shrugged then. Or he attempted to shrug. The life jacket made the movement awkward. It was too big for him, even after I had knotted the straps twice over to tighten the fit. This was one of the many things that continued to occupy my mind.

I turned back to the sea and, stepping forward, let the waves run over my bare feet. It stung straightaway, and it felt far colder than it probably was. You have to bear in mind that we'd been walking for much of the day, over bare rock and baked, rutted ground. My feet were blistered and swollen, and that first shock of cool saltwater felt like needles in my flesh. Nevertheless, I tried not to react, or not in any way that would be obvious to Mohammed. I waited, instead, for the pain to diminish to a dull throb, allowing my feet and ankles to become used to their new environment. By logic, I knew that the sea, in August, was not much colder than the night air; it might even have been a little warmer. And it was, essentially, the same sea I had swum in for much of my life, just a little further west. It was not something to be feared.

'How far do you think it is?' Mohammed asked me.

'Two kilometres. Three at the most.' I could not, in good conscience, lie about this, however much I wanted to. Because of the time we'd spent hiding from the police, who patrolled the roads and beaches closer to town, we'd not covered as much ground as we'd hoped. We had not been able to get to the narrowest point in the channel, where little more than a kilometre of water separates Turkey from the Greek island of Samos. But there was no chance now of continuing over land. We might spend another three hours stumbling along in the darkness, our energy failing, and with nowhere to refill our water bottles. So the choice we faced was simple: accept defeat and turn back, or attempt the swim from here.

But I was never going to be the one to make the final call. When it came down to it, I could no more command my little brother into the water than I could tell him to leap into a fire.

It was he who broke our silence, by summoning a large quantity of phlegm into this throat and spitting it into the sea. A fourteen-year-old's act of defiance.

'Let's do this,' he said.

We drank the last of our water and then discarded the empty bottles on the beach, where they lay as a small sacrilege in the moonlight. Most of our belongings, such as they were, we'd left at the hotel in town. A change of clothes, some toiletries. In terms of material possessions, there was no longer much to abandon. Everything else – everything essential – had been sealed in waterproof bags and squashed into our backpacks.

Let me ask you to imagine this. You're going to attempt to swim across the sea to a whole new continent. Everything you can take with you has to fit into one small backpack, and every gram you pack will be a gram acting against you, a gram seeking to pull you down beneath the waves.

So what do you take?

Some things are obvious. You take your shoes and sunglasses, and one set of lightweight clothing, and not only because you do not wish to offend your new host nation with your nakedness. You assume that in the morning you'll have to walk many miles under the hot Greek sun.

You take your money and your phone, which you've double-bagged for extra insurance.

You take your passport because it is proof of your nationality – proof of your desperation. In case swimming across the sea does not, in itself, prove that you are desperate.

These are the practical things I had packed into my backpack, along with two more items for the benefit of my soul. The first was a photograph of my parents, taken before the war began; and it was stowed within the pages of the second, which was a copy of my holy book. This was a hardback English-language edition of *The God Delusion* by Richard Dawkins, which I'd concealed in the dust jacket from Charles Dickens's *Great Expectations* so that no one would know I was an apostate. But I'm sure I'll get to that later. It's not so important right now.

After some experimentation, and many adjustments, Mohammed and I had managed to secure the shoulder straps of our backpacks under our life jackets, which we now inflated; and we stood for only a moment in this state, like two fat blue-black turtles poised at the edge of the world. Then Mohammed started to wade forward into the surf, and I was at once pursuing, until in several clumsy bounds I had drawn beside him, waist-deep in the dark Aegean Sea.

'Whatever happens,' I told him, 'whatever happens we stay together, side by side.'

For once he did not object to this plan. He just nodded.

I started counting, very slowly. 'One . . . Two . . . Three . . .'

Together we plunged into the water.

The First Attempt

This was not our first attempt to get into Europe. The first time, we'd tried it the conventional way. We paid the smugglers one thousand euros each for a place on an overladen dinghy with a malfunctioning outboard motor. We were told when we handed over the money – half of everything we had – that we'd be travelling in a small group with perhaps fifteen to twenty other refugees.

A cattle truck picked us up just after midnight and drove us to the coast. Inside were fifty-seven other refugees – men, women and children. I know because I had plenty of time to count them; and having done so, I was quick to reassure myself that this situation would not last. I did some elementary mathematics and spent the rest of the journey with the naïve hope that there would be at least three boats waiting to ferry us to Europe.

The journey to the coast took three hours. We sat on the wooden floor with our fifty-nine bodies all squashed together, roasting in the darkness. Sometimes a child would cry and a parent would respond with comforting noises, but other than that, nobody spoke. The truck stank of animal faeces and sweat and fear.

We were stopped twice during the journey. Both times, the engine was left running, but over its noise I could hear swift words being exchanged in Turkish. Each encounter lasted no more than three minutes, and the back of the cattle truck was never investigated.

Bribery was occurring. Perhaps I don't need to spell this out, but I'm not sure. If you're reading these words, you're probably from the West – and people from the West don't always understand the way the rest of the world works. This is not a criticism, just an observation.

After the second stop the roads got rougher. For maybe thirty minutes we were bounced and jostled and ground together like peppercorns in a mill. It might have been dangerous, but for us being packed in so tightly; there was not far to fall. Then, at last, the truck stopped and the engine cut out.

We were unloaded at the end of an unlit dirt track, and allowed no more than ten minutes to stretch our limbs and drink from our water bottles and savour the free air. After that, we were herded by torchlight to the sea. Our herders were two men armed with rifles. They looked cold and intimidating. They looked the way armed men always look.

The ground was hard and uneven, and the only path was the one that had been trampled by previous footsteps. There were men carrying small children and women carrying babies. There were people who had recent injuries, and people who were sick or malnourished. And the pace set by the armed Turks was not a gentle one. Several people stumbled or fell, and when others went to their aid, they were shouted at in a foreign language.

The whole time, Mohammed remained silent and kept his eyes to the ground. The sight of him filled me with remorse. I regretted putting us in this terrible situation. And in truth, I doubt there was a single person in our group who did not harbour feelings similar to mine. If not now, then certainly later. Later, we all had our regrets.

On the beach, two more Turks were waiting with the boat – the single dinghy – which had already been inflated and was resting on the stones not far from the water's edge. I'd estimate it was about five metres long by two metres wide, and was probably designed to hold a maximum of fifteen adults. The shouting started almost at once, and it was then that I realised why our hosts were armed. Before, it hadn't made much sense. After all, we were all here of our own free will; we'd each paid a thousand euros for the privilege. So my hypothesis had been that the guns were in case we ran into the police or the coastguard or a rival criminal gang. It was only on the beach, once the shouting began, that I understood. The guns were to protect the smugglers from us, from the inevitable riot that would otherwise have ensued.

Despite the guns, one of my braver companions stepped forward and addressed the Turks in halting, broken English. 'You can't think us to get on this boat!' he shouted. 'We do not pay our money for this!'

The Turk who seemed to be in charge smiled at this point. It was the first time I had seen any of them smile, and it was in no way reassuring. He stroked the barrel of his rifle, then gestured with the beam of his torch at the sea. 'Europe is that way, my friend. But if you prefer,' he pointed the torch back the way we had just come, like a flight attendant pointing to the emergency exits, 'the road is that way. Is about two-hour walk to town.'

There was a long and awful silence. Then the Turk nodded to himself, still smiling. 'Who else speak English here?'

After a moment, a few hands went up, then a few more. Mohammed nudged me in the ribs. I don't know why. Maybe he thought my superior command of English might win us a better seat. With much reluctance, I also raised my hand.

The Turk swung his torch beam across us in an arc. I was holding my breath, and I think I was not the only one. A second later, the torch beam settled just to my left, on a tall man of about forty years. I noticed, then, that this man's raised arm was not shaking, as I'm sure mine was. His expression was completely neutral.

'You, my friend,' the Turk said. 'You are going to be our pilot. You know what pilot is?'

The man in the torch beam nodded.

'Good. You come with me.'

I thought at first that this was a joke, but it soon became evident that it was not. The man who had just been volunteered to steer us to Europe was taken over to the back of the dinghy, where one of the other Turks began to instruct him on how to work the outboard motor.

Meanwhile, the rest of us were left to put on our life jackets, and in many cases, to say our prayers. Most of us had brought life jackets with us, because you could buy them cheaply in Turkish supermarkets. These days, you could buy a life jacket pretty much anywhere in western Turkey. People sold them on unfolded blankets all along the seafronts. But if you'd somehow managed to miss all these opportunities, the smugglers were also happy to provide them for one hundred euros apiece.

We were soon hustled into a queue at the water's edge, where we waited. Fifty-nine men, women and children, holding in our arms the bags that contained everything we now owned. Apart from the sound of the waves, there was absolute silence.

'I'm not sure we should do this,' I whispered to Mohammed.

He gave me a look that said *What choice do we have?*

I suspect it was what everyone else on that beach was also thinking. Apart from the very young children. They were probably thinking only that they wanted to go home.

It took all four Turks and some men pulled from the queue to launch the boat. Then we had to wade nearly up to our waists and climb in. The families with children went first, and lots of the children were crying. People had to sit on their bags with their children in their laps to free up space, and there still wasn't enough. The boat filled from the centre outwards as the Turks held it steady in the water, and the seating got ever more precarious, with the last men to board having to perch on the outer edge of the dinghy. You wouldn't have thought it possible, but somehow everyone got on; and the boat was so low in the water that every wave threatened to flood us.

The Turks guided the boat further out to sea, then instructed our 'pilot' to activate the outboard motor. It sputtered to life and we started to move, ever so slowly, out onto the open water. At this point, the smuggler who seemed to be in charge started to wave at us, with much theatricality. 'Goodbye, my friends! Safe travels! A great future in Europe is waiting you!'

His body diminished in the darkness, and within moments, he was gone.

Europe was not visible yet, not even as points of light on a dark shore. So our boat was heading out to sea with only a smuggler's promise that we were going in the right direction, which is a guarantee not even as reliable as blind faith. Several of my travelling companions seemed to agree, and within seconds of setting out, a number of smart phones had appeared from pockets and waterproof bags, the light from their screens cutting the darkness. I followed this example and, switching on my GPS, saw that we were indeed moving towards Europe. We were heading to the Greek island of Lesbos. I measured the distance on the map with my thumb and it was about eight kilometres.

Mohammed and I were squeezed toward the back of the boat, not far from the motor. This, it turned out, was an especially bad place to be, on account of the noise and the smell of burning petrol. Crammed in near us were a heavily pregnant woman and her husband, and the woman was holding a scarf across her nose and mouth in a futile attempt to block out the fumes. Neither of them was wearing a life jacket. It was possible that they'd spent the last of their money to be on this boat.

It was after half an hour or so that the engine started making troubling noises, and five minutes after that, it died completely. The petrol fumes vanished, but an unmistakable smell of scorched electrics remained.

Within seconds, there was chaos.

Men and women were shouting on top of each other. Children were crying. Another man was battling with the pilot for control of the rudder, trying to hold the boat face on against the waves. And amidst all this, the pregnant woman began to scream and attempted to rise to her feet. Her husband quickly threw an arm around her, but she kept on screaming and fighting him, and every time she lurched upwards the whole boat rocked and there was even more screaming as water rushed over the sides and swirled around our feet.

Then Mohammed also started getting to his feet, and I had to assume that he too was hysterical, even though his face was set in a grim and resolute frown. I tried to manoeuvre myself against the crush of all the other bodies, but before I could take any meaningful action, I saw in a flash my little brother's intention. Looking completely calm, he began releasing the straps on his too-big life jacket, one by one. Then he slipped his head and neck free from the harness and presented the empty jacket to the pregnant woman and her husband, never saying a word.

Most of the people on board our tiny vessel could not have seen this action, so the general shouting and rocking continued as before. But the pregnant woman, at least, did stop screaming. She sank back to the wet floor of the boat, sobbing and clutching the life jacket to her chest. The husband looked like a man who'd been given an electric shock, and to me his dilemma was obvious. He didn't want his wife and unborn child to drown, and neither did he want to be responsible for the death of a fourteen-year-old boy. So I did the only thing I could in this situation, having been put to so much shame by my little brother. I, in turn, wriggled out of my life jacket and placed it over Mohammed's shoulders.

'It's okay,' I shouted to the husband in Arabic, trying to propel my voice above the general din. 'I am a strong swimmer. The strongest in all of Syria.'

I do not know if he heard me or not, so I tried to mime with my hands a fish gliding through the water. He may not have understood this either.

The boat did not capsize. After a while, people stopped panicking and started talking, until it was concluded that the only good option was to phone the Greek coastguard and give him our

GPS coordinates. Several passengers had had the foresight to look up and store the number before we left Turkey. Not one of us spoke Greek, of course, but it was soon discovered that I had by far the best English of anyone on that boat. When I say it was discovered, what I actually mean is that Mohammed volunteered this information.

'You should let my brother speak,' he declared, while two other Syrians were arguing over who should take the responsibility for the phone call. 'He is a student of English Literature at Tishreen University. It's likely that he speaks the language far better than either of you.'

Mohammed has never been reluctant to voice his opinions, even in adult company.

So I made the phone call and the Greek coastguard also spoke good English, because, as you know, it is the second language of most European professionals.

I explained the situation in brief, and, as you can imagine, it was a situation that the Greek coastguard had experienced many times before. There was a short wait after I gave him our GPS coordinates, and then he informed me that our boat was not yet in Greek waters. We were still, at present, Turkey's problem.

I asked him if he intended to leave us in the middle of the sea – me and my little brother and the pregnant woman and the many crying children. He replied that of course he didn't, and he'd be calling the Turkish coastguard the moment our conversation was finished. Someone would be there to pick us up as soon as possible.

I thanked him and hung up.

The rest of the boat looked at me expectantly.

'We're going back to Turkey,' I said.

The shouting started once more, and now it was all directed at me.

I'd guess it took another hour. The shouting ceased, the boat bobbed up and down on the waves, and we all tried to stay as still as possible. Someone with a phone turned on the torch and shone it into the darkness periodically, like a tiny lighthouse.

When the Turkish coastguard arrived, he swiftly made the decision that there was no hope of towing us back to shore. Instead, a small ladder was lowered and one by one we were loaded onto the much larger boat. Blankets and towels were offered to anyone who was thought to be in shock, which was most of us, and then we headed back to the nearest port. The dinghy was left as it was, bobbing silently in the darkness.

At the dock we were turned loose. If this surprises you, then you have not been to Turkey recently. There are millions of refugees there, most of them from my country. And I don't know exactly how many of us were trying to escape to Europe every single night, but my guess is thousands. The point is that no one needed to ask where we'd come from or what we were doing in a rubber boat in the middle of the sea in the middle of the night. They already knew, because our situation was completely unremarkable. So nobody needed to investigate us, and nobody wanted to detain us, and there was nowhere else they could send us. So we were turned loose. Immediately.

On the dock, we were approached by the husband of the pregnant woman. He handed Mohammed's life jacket over to me, and then he kissed me on both cheeks. Then he kissed

Mohammed on both cheeks. This is not a homosexual act where I come from. It is a sign of deep friendship or gratitude.

There was a small silence, after which he patted Mohammed's shoulder a couple of times, and then returned to his wife, who was sitting on the ground huddled in a blanket.

I've often wondered what happened to the two of them. In all likelihood, they never made it to Europe. If they were lucky, their baby may have been born in a tent in an overcrowded refugee camp.

'What you did was extremely brave,' I told Mohammed later. 'Our parents would be proud of you.'

He looked at me like this was the most embarrassing thing he'd ever heard.

'I'm proud of you too,' I told him.

'For God's sake, Zain!' Mohammed rolled his eyes at me. 'What else was I going to do? That woman was fucking crazy. She was going to tip the whole lot of us into the water. If I hadn't acted, all of our stuff, all of our money, would be at the bottom of the sea right now!'

I thought about this for a while. 'So you gave her your life jacket because you were worried about our *stuff*. Is that what you're telling me?'

'Damn right it is!'

There was a small, strange silence.

'I'm still proud of you,' I said.

Mohammed stomped around in the dirt for a few moments, letting out another string of expletives. Then he suddenly started to laugh. He dropped to his knees and hugged his chest, shaking uncontrollably.

'What is funny?' I asked.

He looked up and pointed at me, still shaking, and then flexed his small fourteen-year-old's biceps. 'I'm the strongest swimmer in all of Syria!' he declared.

It was a terrible impression, but it made me smile. I launched myself at him and tried to put him in a headlock, but he managed to elbow me in the ribs and wriggle free.

After that, we sat together on the grimy pavement and looked at the boats in the harbour. We were in a coastal town somewhere in Turkey, but apart from that, I had not a clue.

'So, what now?' Mohammed asked.

The Middle of the Sea

The world had shrunk to a pool of pale moonlight, no more than a few metres across. Mohammed was to my left and just slightly ahead, since I was determined to keep him in my sight at all times, and we were both doing a slow, energy-efficient breaststroke, since this is the only stroke you can attempt while wearing a life jacket and a sodden backpack. Beyond our moonlit pool, there was only a wall of impenetrable blackness.

Yet it did not feel dangerous at first. I should stress that. Compared to the journey with the smugglers, it felt almost peaceful. While we were still close to the shore and we still had our energy, while there was still the possibility of turning back, it was not all that different from swimming in the sea off the coast of Latakia. The familiar rhythm of limbs and muscles and breaths working in harmony. Tuck, breathe in, stretch, breathe out. Repeat.

It was only later, after maybe an hour of swimming, that things became difficult. In the middle of the channel, the water was colder and more turbulent. The waves were a metre high and the current had started to shift so that we were being pushed off our straight-line course. And, by then, the straps of my life jacket and backpack had started to bite into my shoulders. Progress was slow.

But I kept my eyes fixed on Mohammed. I kept my eyes fixed and my arms and legs moving, and so did he, and we edged closer and closer to Europe.

It was then that something unfathomable happened. Our pool of light was suddenly contracting and dimming, and within moments the darkness had swallowed everything. Mohammed disappeared. The whole world disappeared, and I was left alone and sightless in a vast, incomprehensible abyss.

You are probably like me. You've probably lived your whole life in a city and have no experience of what true darkness is like. So let me tell you: it's terrifying, especially when it descends in already threatening circumstances. This is why I reacted as I did.

I stopped swimming with a gasp and swallowed a mouthful of seawater. Then I started coughing uncontrollably. It was this that made me realise I was not yet dead, which had been the wild thought surging in my mind. That this was the infinite blackness of death, and soon I would be judged, and surely found wanting.

Something grabbed my arm, just below the elbow. It took a moment to identify it as a human hand.

'Mohammed!' I shouted. 'Mohammed, please tell me it's you.'

'Who else would it be?'

His voice was as breathless as mine.

'God, what happened? Where did you go?' Even as I asked this, the light started to return. I thrust my shoulders and neck back as another wave lifted me, and as I did, I saw the blazing moon re-emerging from behind a cloud. Beyond this, there was a clear streak of sky in which hundreds of stars were spread like glitter. I thought it was the most beautiful sight I'd ever seen.

'Are you okay?' Mohammed asked me.

'I panicked and swallowed some seawater.'

'You're okay now?'

'Yes, I'm okay now.'

'We need to keep swimming.'

'Which way?'

'To Europe!'

'I mean which *way*? I've lost all sense of direction.'

'Swim against the waves. Keep the moon over your left shoulder.'

He tugged at my arm, and then pushed once more into the waves.

It was fortunate that at least one of us was keeping his wits.

We swam and we swam. My arms ached and my legs ached and my mouth was as dry as ashes and my lips stung like they'd been rubbed with sandpaper. The flesh of my neck and shoulders and armpits had been flayed by the life jacket, and every stroke was an act of self-torture.

I had to assume that Mohammed was also feeling all of this and more. His pace had slowed, and even over the waves and the blood rushing in my ears, I could hear him panting with exertion.

Time had ceased to have any meaning, but I knew that we were more than halfway now. We were still battling the current that was pulling us off our original course, but the waves were no longer working against us. They were coming in diagonally behind us. I would have feared that we'd somehow been turned around, but the moon was still there over my left shoulder. And soon, pinpricks of light became visible ahead, like tiny fireflies blinking into existence.

'I can see Europe!' I shouted. 'I can see the lights of Europe!'

Mohammed didn't respond. He just kept swimming.

The black shore was rising in front of us when he finally stopped moving. I don't think it was a conscious decision he made, not when we were so close to our goal; he just had nothing left to give. He slumped upright in the water, with his life jacket holding his head just clear of the small waves. He had his eyes closed and when I slapped his cheek he was unresponsive.

So I did the only thing I could. I took hold of his life jacket with my left hand, and with my right I continued to swim. It was like pulling a lead weight through the water, and there wasn't a muscle in my body that wasn't screaming, but I just kept going and going. I clawed at the water, and in tiny increments, we moved forward.

I think I hear the throb of an engine as we approach the beach, but it's impossible to be sure. When you're utterly exhausted, the line between reality and imagination disappears.

I heave my brother's limp body onward, and then, as I kick out, my foot makes sudden contact with sand and stones. I lurch forward against the shelving seabed, dragging myself and Mohammed into the shallows and towards our salvation. And then he is ripped from my grasp.

There's no longer enough water to hold him up, so I have to get my arms under him, and somehow, against a rush of dizziness, I manage to haul him out of the sea and stagger a few paces up the beach.

I try to lower him gently onto the rocks, but my knees give out and we both collapse to the ground.

I'm aware of cold stone pressing into my cheek. I'm aware of warm blood in my mouth. I'm aware of Mohammed's chest still rising and falling, rising and falling, against my pinned hand.

This is the last I am aware of.

My mother's voice is an urgent whisper. She tells me that I need to leave now, repeats it for the third or fourth time, and all the while she holds me in a tight, tight embrace, unable to let go. I don't want her to. I want her to say she's changed her mind. We should stay together, me, her and Mohammed, whatever the cost.

It's a hot evening in early August, not long after sunset. The sort of evening where people stay out late, eating in seafront restaurants, enjoying the sights and sounds of summer. That's what I might be doing in different circumstances. A quiet coffee shop or café, easy conversation with friends. As recently as two weeks ago, life was relatively normal. There's been fighting to the north, where the Free Syrian Army and various Islamist militias are gaining ground, but Latakia itself is a government stronghold. We're one of the last cities in Syria to remain completely under the regime's control.

Mum's phone buzzes against the kitchen counter. She can't ignore it. She releases me and wipes her eyes with her sleeve.

'It's the car. It's outside.'

Simple words, but spoken like a death sentence.

'Mum, I don't know if I can do this. I'm not—'

'You can do this. You have to.'

I want to tell her again that I can't. I'm nineteen years old, and I've never been away from home for more than a few days. I'm scared, terrified.

She rests her hands on my shoulders, forcing me to look her in the eye. 'Zain, you have to take care of Mohammed. You're the only one who can.'

I take a breath, then nod, not trusting myself to speak.

Mohammed is in his room. Mum asked him to wait there a moment so that she could talk to me alone. He's hardly said a word all day, but when I saw him last, his eyes were rimmed red. Despite everything, he still won't let anyone see him cry.

'Zain, if there was any other way . . .' Mum trails off, closing her eyes for a moment. When she opens them again, her look is fierce and determined. 'Your dad . . . I have to stay here if I'm going to help him. I have to try. You understand that, don't you?'

'Of course.' I nod once more, as firmly as I can. 'I'll look after Mohammed. I'll make sure he's safe.'

Mum doesn't say anything. She hugs me again, and I can feel her heart pounding against my chest.

The moment stretches, and then the phone cuts the silence a second time, horribly loud and insistent. The driver. We don't know much about the man who will take me and Mohammed to the Turkish border; a friend of a friend gave us his details. But we were told he's made the trip at least a dozen times before, and when he spoke to Mum, he claimed there was little that could go wrong. We'll pass several checkpoints on the sixty-kilometre journey, both government and opposition, but he's never met a soldier who'll turn down a bribe. Mum emptied her savings account a week ago, before the regime could freeze her assets, and thinks *there'll be enough to get us all the way to Western Europe. Everything's been prepared, and now there's no turning back.*

'You're going to be okay.' She repeats it like a mantra. 'You're going to be okay.'

She touches my cheek, one last time.

Resurrection

I came round with fingers poking me in the neck. The fingers belonged to a man who was clearly not a European. In the grey predawn light, I could make out mottled skin that appeared somewhat darker than mine, and white hair and an unkempt white beard, and large thick eyebrows, that somehow had managed to stay black. He was wearing a life jacket identical to mine. They might have been bought in the same supermarket.

I blinked my eyes fully open and croaked the first thing that came into my head, which was this: 'As-salāmu alaikum wa rahmat-ullah.' Peace be upon you, and God's mercy. It's a formal and polite way of greeting a Muslim. I don't know if you have anything similar in the Western world. You seem to get by using nothing more elaborate than 'Good morning.'

If I'd hissed like a snake, the man I was greeting could not have leaped away faster. He slipped on the loose rocks and he ended up on his buttocks a little further down the beach, yelping a curse of which my brother would have wholly approved.

He started laughing.

'*Bismillah!*' he exclaimed 'You're alive!'

'Yes,' I rasped. 'I am alive.'

I tried and failed to push myself to my feet. My right arm, it turned out, was still pinned under Mohammed's chest. I managed to slide it free. It was so numb it might have belonged to a mannequin. Mohammed groaned, rolled, and stayed asleep.

Attempt two: I manoeuvred myself until I was kneeling, then pushed against the rocks with my one good hand. My legs wobbled in protest; I was so weak I could barely stand. In a moment, the man had scrabbled over the rocks and had an arm under my shoulder. 'Easy, boy,' he warned. 'It looks like you've had a tough night.'

His accent was Iraqi. His face was deeply lined and he had a couple of teeth missing. I estimated his age to be between fifty-five and seventy-five. It was hard to tell because he looked as if he'd been recently blown up, which was not outside the realm of possibility. He smelled, very strongly, of alcohol.

'Are we in Europe?' I asked.

'So I'm told,' he replied.

I glanced around the beach. Apart from the three of us, it was deserted.

'I don't think you should be standing yet,' the old man said. 'I checked your pulse, but I couldn't find it.'

He started chuckling again.

I didn't know what to say, so I said nothing as he helped me back into a sitting position. It was then that I noticed he wasn't wearing any shoes, and that he was also missing two fingers on his right hand. The index and the third finger; they ended in stumps just below where the knuckles should have been.

'Where are your shoes?' I asked. This seemed the politer enquiry.

'Ha! My shoes! Where are *your* shoes, boy? Where are your clothes? What in God's name happened to you?'

I was not naked. I should point that out. I was wearing swimming shorts, as well as the life jacket and my backpack, which I hoped still contained the rest of my clothes. It took me a couple of attempts to unstrap the life jacket and toss it onto the beach. It was extremely painful because my shoulders had been rubbed raw, but I was eager to be rid of it. I didn't feel too bad about abandoning it here, since the beach was already littered with several hundred other life jackets, as well as a number of inflatable boats which had been punctured and dragged onto the rocks.

I upended the backpack and was relieved to discover that my waterproof bags had remained unbreached. I removed my trainers from one of the packages and held them, one in each hand. The old man was staring at them like I'd just pulled a rabbit from a hat.

'I'm sorry,' I told him. 'I don't have any spares.'

'What happened to you?' he repeated. 'Did your boat sink?'

'No. No boat. We swam.'

'From *Turkey*?'

I shrugged and gestured at Mohammed. 'It was my brother's idea.'

Mohammed had started snoring. I gave him a small shake, then a more vigorous shake, and he swiped his arm at me, as if trying to swat away a fly.

'Mohammed, wake up. We have company.'

He groaned.

The Iraqi grinned widely, showing off his missing teeth. 'Typical teenager, yes?'

I started to laugh.

And it may sound strange, but let me tell you, I felt so damn good in that moment. Because despite everything – despite being exhausted and weak with hunger and thirst, despite the aches and sores that I could feel all over my body – in that moment, I knew we were alive. We were alive and we were in Europe, and for the time being, at least, we were safe.

It took a lot more shaking before Mohammed woke up, and when he did, he was every bit as disorientated as I had been. He spent some time patting his still-inflated life jacket while eyeing the Iraqi with great suspicion.

'Who's the old man?' he said eventually.

'You'll have to excuse my brother,' I said. 'He's also had a difficult night.'

The Iraqi was waving away this apology even as I was making it. 'The whole world's going to hell anyway. If there was ever a time for plain speaking, it's now.'

'What happened to your fingers?' my brother asked.

'Mohammed!'

'Ha! The boy calls the one-eyed man one-eyed, doesn't he?' He looked at Mohammed for a moment, then said: 'Al-Qaeda happened to my fingers.' He held his good hand flat and made a chopping motion against his stubs.

I didn't say anything.

Mohammed didn't say anything.

'Can you guess what my crime was?'

He looked at us expectantly. Even so, it took me several

moments to realise that this wasn't a rhetorical question. He really did want us to guess.

'Was it . . . blasphemy?' I asked.

'Theft,' said Mohammed.

'My crime was smoking a cigarette,' the old man told us. 'Can you believe that?'

'Yes, I can believe that,' I said.

He nodded a couple of times.

And then, because there was another silence, and because I was determined to mind my manners, even if the whole world *was* going to hell, I introduced us. 'I'm Zain,' I said, 'and this is my brother Mohammed. We're pleased to meet you.'

The old man did not respond to this for a long time. He was staring at the sea, apparently lost in thought. I cleared my throat, and was just about to repeat my introduction when the Iraqi suddenly turned to face us once more, a huge grin splitting his face.

'You may call me Isa,' he said. 'Isa al-Masih.'

He slapped his thigh and started cackling.

Isa, I should tell you, is the Arabic form of Jesus, and it's not an uncommon name in Islamic countries. Al-Masih means 'the Messiah'. Going forward, it will be simpler if I just refer to the Iraqi as Jesus – or 'Jesus Christ' – since this was the essence of his joke.

He continued to cackle as I helped Mohammed out of his life jacket, which I then discarded on the beach next to mine. Jesus was almost certainly drunk. That was my strong hypothesis, given the smell and his general behaviour. But I still had no idea where he'd come from, or what had happened to his shoes.

My swimming shorts were damp, but not soaking, and since

I was reluctant to strip off in front of Jesus, I thought it better to leave them on. I pulled on my plain grey T-shirt followed by my socks and trainers. Mohammed put on his FC Barcelona shirt, which he had worn every day since I bought it for him in a Turkish market. For the price we paid, it was certainly a counterfeit, but neither of us thought you could tell. On the back, it had a large number '10' and the name 'Messi' in bright-yellow letters.

Jesus had managed to stop laughing by now, and once we were fully dressed, he hopped over to us and placed one hand on my shoulder and the other on Mohammed's.

'You boys look like you need some breakfast,' he said. 'Follow me.'

He scrambled towards a tiny headland where the beach curved back on itself. He moved surprisingly swiftly, like a startled animal.

Mohammed turned to me. 'I don't think we should follow him,' he said.

'Why not?' I asked.

'Why not? *Seriously?* He's completely fucking bat-shit crazy!'

Mohammed did not use those exact terms, of course. He used an Arabic idiom, likewise strewn with expletives, which carries much the same meaning. He raised a reasonable point, but at the same time, I couldn't see that we had any better option available to us.

'He must be going somewhere,' I pointed out. 'He didn't just spring out of the ground. It's possible that he actually has some breakfast for us . . .'

My brother scoffed at this. 'It's also possible that he lives in a cave and paints the walls with his own shit.'

'Many things are possible,' I acknowledged.

31

Jesus had stopped fifty metres up the beach and was jumping up and down on his chicken-thin legs, waving frantically that we should follow.

'Come on,' I said. 'I'm fairly sure he's harmless.'

Mohammed groaned loudly but raised no other objection.

We shouldered our backpacks and followed the Messiah up the beach.

The Missing Shoes

We walked for maybe ten minutes, our legs aching and our mouths desert-dry and our shoulders still raw from the swim. Despite his lack of shoes, Jesus was able to cover the ground far quicker than us, so he stopped and waited periodically, always waving us on and shouting words of encouragement. We rounded the small rocky headland as the sun was coming up over the sea, and as it did, my heart leapt. On the beach below us, in a small clearing amidst a thousand discarded life jackets, there sat a group of around twenty people. Women and children, mostly. The grey carcass of an abandoned dinghy was still bobbing in the shallows just behind them.

Jesus was waiting for us with a fat smile. 'Here are some of your countrymen,' he said. 'There were more, but I guess some of them left straightaway.' He gestured at a dirt track at the far end of the cove. 'Town is that way, I'm told. It's a twenty-kilometre walk, so it makes sense to get moving before the sun gets too hot.'

Mohammed frowned at this information. 'If town's that way, then why were you wandering off in the opposite direction?'

'Ha! That's a good question. I thought I was just taking a walk.'

'Just taking a walk?'

'That's what I thought. Now I'm not so certain.' Jesus scratched his white beard for a moment. 'I have a different theory now. Would you like to hear it?'

I said yes at the same time as Mohammed said no.

'Shut up, Mohammed,' I said. 'If you ask the question you should be prepared to hear the answer.'

'*You* shut up!'

'Go ahead,' I told Jesus.

'I no longer want to tell you,' Jesus said. 'I fear you will laugh.'

'Of course we won't. We won't laugh, will we, Mohammed?' My brother rolled his eyes and shrugged, which was as good an affirmation as I ever got from him. 'Go ahead, Jesus,' I repeated.

He was staring out to sea with a look of intense concentration, as if trying to calculate a complicated sum in his head. Mohammed and I waited expectantly.

'I think I chose to walk in that particular direction because two boys had washed up on the beach. They obviously needed my help. That's what brought me.'

I looked at Mohammed. Mohammed looked at me. Neither of us laughed because neither of us knew what Jesus was trying to say. I wasn't sure Jesus knew what he was trying to say either; but he'd started nodding to himself, very slowly, as if he'd uttered some profound piece of wisdom.

'I'm sorry, Jesus,' I said after a moment, 'but I'm not certain you understood my brother's question. He wanted to know why you were walking away from town, in the first place. On your own, in the opposite direction . . .'

'I came to help you boys. You needed my help.'

'Yes, but you didn't know we were there. Unless . . . did you see us from further up the beach? From up here? Is that what you're saying?'

'Pah! How could I see you from up here? It was dark, and I have an old man's eyes. I didn't see you until I was almost on top of you.'

'Right. So . . .'

'What you're saying makes no fucking sense!' Mohammed interjected. 'You didn't know we were there, so you couldn't have been coming to help us? Do you understand that?'

Jesus smiled patiently. 'But I *did* come to help you. Don't you see? It makes perfect sense to me now.'

'It makes no sense!'

Jesus shrugged. 'Maybe God sent me.'

Mohammed swore again, then put his fingers to his temple and mimed blowing his brains out with a handgun.

'Jesus,' I said, as gently as I could. 'I think perhaps you're reading too much into this situation. Why would God send you to us?'

He thought about this for some time, regarding us both through squinting eyes. 'You boys are very young to be in a strange country on your own,' he said. 'Perhaps you need a guide.'

'We don't need a guide,' Mohammed retorted. 'We have Google Maps.'

'Google Maps will only take you so far,' Jesus said.

He said it the way you might utter the words of an ancient proverb. Mohammed looked like he was about to snap again, so I decided it was time to kill the conversation, which was clearly getting us nowhere.

'Shall we go?' I asked.

A couple of minutes later, we were approaching the people assembled on the beach. Several of the women shot disapproving looks at Jesus. This did not surprise me.

'They swam from Turkey,' he said, by way of introduction. 'I found them half drowned.'

'We were *not* half drowned,' Mohammed complained. 'We were resting.'

'You're Syrians,' one of the women stated. She was also Syrian; it was clear from her accent. She was about thirty-five years old and had two little girls with her. I estimated the older of the two to be around five years old. She was half hiding behind her mother's shoulder. The other girl looked to be no older than two or three. She was asleep in a blanket at her mother's feet.

'I am Zain,' I said, 'and this is my brother Mohammed.'

'It's just the two of you?' the woman asked, very gently.

'Yes.'

She didn't press the point any further. No one did. This was something that had become pretty standard since leaving Syria. The real question – where are your parents? – never got asked, but always hung there in the background, as visible as the black smoke from a bomb blast.

The woman spoke a couple of words over her shoulder to her older daughter, then came over and gave Mohammed a hug. I'm not sure how he felt about this. The women we met along the road often wanted to mother us, and I never had a problem with it. But as you know, Mohammed was fourteen, and the world's biggest tough guy. He usually met any display of kindness or affection with a stiff-bodied silence. I thought I caught him wincing slightly, but that was probably because of the swim. If his shoulders were as bad as mine, he'd need some time to recover.

The woman did not seem to notice his reaction. Once she'd finished with Mohammed, she came to me and placed a warm hand on my cold cheek.

I am not the world's biggest tough guy. I'm sure, by now, you realise this as well. Most of the time I manage to hold it together – because what else can I do? – but on this occasion, I could feel myself starting to unravel. Slowly, I reached up and removed the woman's hand. She looked a little upset herself, so I tried to give her a reassuring smile. But I doubt it was very convincing.

'You must be exhausted,' she said. 'When did you last eat? Have you had anything to drink?'

At once there was a general commotion as people started producing bottled water and chocolate and dried dates and flat-breads from their bags. This was everything they had left, everything they'd brought to sustain themselves and their families until they reached civilisation, and they were practically throwing it at us. Such is the nature of human beings sometimes.

My hands shook violently as I lifted a water bottle to my lips. It was the finest breakfast I've ever had.

The woman who wanted to mother us was called Sabeen. Her older daughter was called Aida, as in the famous Italian opera, and the younger was called Rihanna, as in . . . well, as in Rihanna. We also have Rihanna in Syria. I didn't ask about her husband for the same reason she didn't ask about our parents. In a situation like that, you have to assume the worst.

We talked a little, while Mohammed ate and ate, and every so often someone would interrupt to ask if we really had swum all the way from Turkey. Jesus stayed away from the main group, smoking and muttering to himself. He held his lit cigarette between the stubs of his amputated fingers. Every so often, another of the women would shuffle over and whisper in my ear that I should be wary of that man; he was a drunkard, and unpredictable.

'He says his name's Jesus Christ the Messiah,' I whispered back to them, one by one.

There was a lot of tutting and head-shaking at this revelation, but no one had an alternative name to offer. Indeed, no one seemed to know a thing about him, aside from his being a drunkard, which everyone had gleaned. He had been the only Iraqi on a boat full of Syrians, Afghans and Pakistanis, so it was generally surmised that he was travelling alone. He had spent much of the boat journey drinking from a litre bottle of whisky, until, at some point, he had managed to get into a fight with one of the young Pakistani men. The Pakistani ended up throwing the whisky overboard, and Jesus started hitting him with his shoes, which he wore on his hands like boxing gloves. These had swiftly followed the whisky into the Mediterranean Sea, at which point, the men had been separated and Jesus was restrained for the rest of the short voyage.

I had been on one of those terrible boats, as you know, so I could well imagine the utter hell of sharing that cramped space with a belligerent drunk. I could appreciate the danger such a person would pose. I could picture, clear as crystal, Sabeen and the other mothers trying to shield their frightened children from the developing spectacle. And yet – despite all these things – I still felt sorry for Jesus. He may have been an awful travelling companion, but he was also the man who had held me up when

I was too weak to stand, who led me and my brother to food and water. I didn't like to see him as he was now, alone and maligned, and I suppose this is why I reacted as I did.

In general, I don't like upsetting people with stories of brutality, because most of us don't need reminding about such things. But in this case, it felt necessary. So every time one of the women related a new detail of his appalling behaviour, I responded with the same bald fact.

'Al-Qaeda cut his fingers off,' I told them.

It had the intended effect. Word quickly spread and people started looking at Jesus with gentler eyes. Later, one of the Afghan men went over and offered him a sandwich.

The sun was a handspan above the sea when two large vehicles rumbled down the dirt track. A battered pick-up truck and an old, dust-streaked Land Rover. Several people recoiled at the sight of them, and some of the younger children started crying. None of us associated the arrival of such vehicles with any positive outcome.

Then engines cut out and two doors swung open. I squinted against the glare from the windscreens and managed to make out the two figures walking towards us. They did not look very threatening. It was a middle-aged Greek man and his middle-aged Greek wife. They were carrying water and bread.

Let me tell you: you could feel the relief and gratitude sweeping through our small congregation of the desperate. It was so tangible you could have reached out and touched it.

The man held up his hand and said a single word, which I assumed was hello in Greek.

'Any you speak English?' the woman asked.

As always in such situations, Mohammed elbowed me in the ribs, not waiting to see if I'd respond without coercion.

'Yes, I speak English,' I said; and then, as if further proof were required, I added: 'You are a sight for sore eyes.'

She exchanged a confused smile with her husband. 'We bring you food and water,' she said. 'And we have transport for . . . ten, fifteen peoples. As many as we get in.'

I translated this into Arabic, and the Greek woman was soon swallowed by a sea of overwhelmed mothers babbling their heartfelt thanks.

Later, after the food and water had been dispensed, the vehicles were loaded with passengers. Obviously, the young children were prioritised, and they couldn't be separated from their parents, so they were prioritised too. Then there was the man with the terrible limp, and the man with diabetes; they were also squeezed into the back of the pick-up. As for Jesus, well, he was old and drunk and shoeless, and in an ideal world, he too would have been afforded a place in one of the vehicles. But by the time the rest of the needy had been dealt with, there was nowhere to put him. I can't imagine the other passengers were too displeased with this outcome.

Mohammed, in contrast, was glowering. He had glimpsed our immediate future, and he did not like it at all.

'I think we should ditch Jesus,' he told me in an angry whisper.

'We're not ditching Jesus,' I whispered back. 'Forget it.'

'He's out of his mind! He doesn't have any shoes! It's going to take all fucking day to walk him to town!'

'Forget it, Mohammed. And stop swearing.'

'Look at his feet! We'll be lucky if he lasts five minutes!'

Unfortunately, my brother raised a valid point.

I walked over to the Greek woman who was just about to leave in the Land Rover. I tapped on the window and she wound it down.

'I'm sorry to bother you again,' I said. 'You've already done so much for us, but I was wondering if your husband has any spare shoes?'

I couldn't ask the husband because he spoke no English. Of course, the wife didn't speak a lot of English either, but with repetition and lots of pointing at Jesus's feet, I was able to convey the essence of our problem.

The woman got out of the Land Rover and conferred with her husband for a few moments. She returned shaking her head. 'Very sorry,' she said.

'It's okay,' I told her, 'you've already been very generous.'

She didn't get back in the car. She had her lips pursed and was frowning very intently at Jesus's bare feet, which were already cracked and smeared with dried blood. She started talking to herself in rapid Greek, then, after a short pause, she shrugged and removed her own footwear, which was a pair of pale-pink flip-flops. 'This is best I can do,' she apologised. 'Is better than nothing, yes?'

'Yes, absolutely.' I gave a small bow. 'Thank you very much.'

She got back in the Land Rover and drove away, with Aida and Rihanna waving from the boot. Sabeen's wave was more hesitant, and came with an apologetic smile. She had already expressed her concern and regret that there was no room for us in either of the vehicles. I tried to convey, with a small shrug, that it was no big deal, and certainly nothing to fret about. We'd get to town eventually.

I walked back to Jesus and handed over the flip-flops. 'These are for you.'

Jesus stared at them dumbly while Mohammed roared with laughter.

'I hope they're not too tight,' I said. 'They have an open back so you should be able to squeeze into them.'

Jesus took the flip-flops without comment and put them on, and it was then that the miracle occurred.

I had spent quite a lot of time looking at Jesus's feet, for obvious reasons, and they had never struck me as unusually small. Likewise, I assume I would have noticed if the Greek woman's feet were freakishly large. But when Jesus put those pink flip-flops on, it seemed to me that they fitted him to the millimetre. You think I'm joking, but I assure you I am not. My rational mind was screaming *How can this be?* Mohammed had stopped laughing and looked dumbfounded. Jesus looked entirely unsurprised.

It was just like Cinderella.

A Walk in the Sun

Google Maps told me that Jesus had been correct about the distance. We had to walk twenty kilometres through the mountains to get to Samos Town, which was where we could get registered and processed as refugees. It was fortunate that we now had some fresh bread and plenty of water to sustain us. With Jesus to manage, we'd be lucky if we made it to town any time soon.

We set out all together – me, Mohammed, Jesus, and the half dozen other men who'd been left behind – but before long, the group started to separate. This wasn't surprising. Some of the men had wives and children they needed to reunite with, and none of them had sufficient patience to cope with Jesus, who had to stop every few minutes to remove stones from his flip-flops. The dirt track had become a road, of sorts, but it was steep and full of holes and strewn with rocks, so even without the frequent stops, progress would have been slow. Slow and painful. Having left most of our possessions in Turkey, our backpacks were light, but the straps still bit with every step. And, of course, it was getting hotter all the time. We climbed higher into the mountains, and the sun climbed higher in the sky, and by the time we'd lost the last of our companions, you could see the heat shimmering off the pitted tarmac.

Given the temperature, it would have made sense to walk in silence and conserve moisture and energy, but Jesus would not shut up. Some of the time he was clearly talking to himself, and some of the time he was incoherent, but there were also long stretches when he was lucid and bombarded us with questions. Mohammed soon stopped responding, so it fell to me to sustain our half of the conversation.

'Do you speak very good English?' Jesus asked.

'Yes, I speak good English,' I told him.

'I speak only five words,' he said. 'Yes, no, fuck, shit, blocks. I learned them from an English army man.'

'Blocks' was the obvious anomaly; I made Jesus repeat it several times to make sure I hadn't misheard.

'It means testicles,' he told me. 'The English army man said it very often.'

'Are you sure?'

Jesus nodded, cupping his hand suggestively.

'It must be army slang,' I said. 'It's not a word I've ever come across.'

'Who taught you to speak English?' Jesus demanded.

'My mother when I was very young.'

'Ah. This makes sense. Your mother would not teach you about blocks. Your mother is English, correct?'

'No, she's Syrian too. She's a teacher.'

'A teacher of English?'

'No, primary school. Seven- and eight-year-olds.'

'Is she an attractive lady, your mother?'

'She's my mother!'

'Syrian women are very beautiful, but also very bad tempered.'

'You probably shouldn't generalise.'

'Do you read English as well as speaking it?'

'Yes.'

'What does it say on this boy's shirt?' He jabbed his finger at Mohammed, who was walking several paces ahead of us.

'It says Messi,' I told him.

Jesus's eyes widened at this news. 'Al-Masih? This is a strange coincidence!'

'Messi. He's a football player. FC Barcelona.'

'Yes, it's a football shirt. We have football shirts in Iraq. The strange thing is that it would say al-Masih.'

'It doesn't. It says Messi. *Meh-see.*'

'God keeps sending us his signs, doesn't he?'

'No, he doesn't. It's not a sign; it's a problem with your hearing.'

'Does your brother believe this football player is the Messiah?'

'Yes, he does. But that's beside the point. It's just a name.'

'A nickname?'

'No. It's his actual name. He's Argentinean.'

'Argentinean? And yet his name is Arabic!'

At this point, Mohammed turned around and screamed. 'It's *Messi*, you donkey's dickhole! MESSI!'

His cry echoed all around the mountains.

Jesus looked extremely impressed. He started jumping up and down in his pink flip-flops and whooping at the sky.

I thought there was little chance of us getting to town before nightfall.

*

Jesus was difficult when he was drunk, but he was even worse when he started to sober up. After an hour or two of walking, with his whisky lost at the bottom of the Mediterranean Sea, it became apparent that he was on the turn. He stopped talking and started grunting. Considering that he'd managed to get to Greece from Iraq, I suppose you'd have to call him a *functioning* alcoholic. But he was barely functioning. This was getting clearer with every minute that passed.

Back in Syria, my family owned a very old air-conditioning unit, which was continually on the verge of breaking down. Every summer seemed destined to be its last, and every autumn we found ourselves astonished that it was still with us. Honestly, the noises it made! Coughs and wheezes and rasps, choking sputters and long metallic groans.

Well, this was what Jesus was like as he slowly sobered up. That he kept going was another minor miracle.

I called a halt when the sun was not quite overhead. We sat in the patchy shade of a citrus tree and ate some bread and drank some more of our water. We'd each taken a two-litre bottle from the Greek couple, but this was disappearing quickly, and I didn't rate our chances of replenishing our supply any time soon. So far, Samos was something of a ghost island. We'd passed some terraced farmland, but no farmhouses. According to Google Maps, the nearest village en route to Samos Town was still eight kilometres away. A couple of cars had passed us on the road, but none slowed down. Jesus had tried to get their attention by raising his hand, but most of the drivers did not even make eye contact. Those that did, looked furious.

My initial suspicion was that they were angry at us simply for being in their country, but I later learned that the hand gesture

Jesus kept making – arm extended and palm held flat – was considered extremely offensive in Greece. It is called the *moutza* and means 'I rub shit in your face.'

After he'd drunk most of his water, Jesus removed his pack of Turkish cigarettes from his tatty shirt pocket. His howl of dismay told us that he'd run out. He leapt to his feet, crushed the empty packet in his hand, and threw it into the withered grass at the roadside. There was already a lot of rubbish there. Empty bottles and crisp packets and cans. We were not the first to walk this route.

Jesus's breaking point occurred not long after we'd resumed our journey. He stopped walking and sat on his bag in the middle of the road, and no amount of cajoling could persuade him to move.

'Let's at least find some more shade,' I said. 'You can't stay here. You'll roast.'

'You go on, my young friends. I am finished.'

'You are if you stay here. Come on. Let's get you off the road. Mohammed, help me.'

Mohammed took his own bag off and slung it at the roadside. 'I'm not carrying him,' he spat.

'It won't be for long. We just need to get him to some shade.'

'You heard him – he said we should keep going without him.'

'Yes, and we're not going to. He'll die.'

'We can send help.'

'God will help me, my friends. I am placing myself once more in his almighty hands.'

Having said this, Jesus lay down on his side, using the bag as a pillow. I don't know how he managed it; the tarmac was like a hotplate.

'Jesus, I think you need to get up,' I told him.

'I think we need to keep walking,' Mohammed said. 'I'm not going to stay here and die with him.'

'No one is going to die – not if we get out of this sun.'

'I'm not carrying him. Do it yourself.'

'Mohammed, one hand does not clap.'

This is an old Arabic proverb. It means: we need to work together to achieve a positive outcome.

My brother ignored me.

'Mohammed, get your lazy arse over here and help me!'

Silence, broken only by the electric screech of the insects in the bushes and trees; and then a distant humming sound, getting slowly louder.

It was a car, small and white and gleaming. It had no choice but to slow down as it approached, on account of the road being very narrow and Jesus lying in the middle of it. The driver was a young woman, whose age I estimated to be between twenty-five and thirty years. She sounded her horn once, twice, three times before pulling to a stop. She didn't look angry, just irritated. I mouthed an apology. Jesus raised his good hand in greeting, palm flat.

Now the woman did look angry. She gave one more blast on the horn, then backed up so that she could start manoeuvring around us. It was tight, but with two of her wheels in the dirt at the roadside, she was able to pass without crushing Jesus's feet.

She accelerated fifty metres down the road, then screeched to a halt and started reversing again. She stopped the car barely a metre from Jesus's motionless body, wound down the window, and leaned out, gesturing briskly at the back door.

'A thousand thank-yous!' I said in English.

'Just get in!' she snapped. 'Quick, before I change my mind.'

With some difficulty, we managed to cajole Jesus into the back of the car, where he promptly fell asleep. Mohammed got in next to him, dumping his and Jesus's bags between them on the seat. I think he did this as a precaution. Jesus was slumped diagonally with his mouth hanging open. Without the barrier of bags, Mohammed would have certainly become a pillow at some point.

I got in the front and put my seatbelt on. Our driver had half-turned in her seat and was looking at Jesus over the top of her sunglasses.

'What's wrong with the old guy?' she asked. 'Does he have sunstroke?'

'No, I'm afraid he doesn't.' I coughed delicately. 'He may be a little hung-over.'

She said something in Greek, which I deduced was a curse word. 'He's not going to be sick, is he?'

'I have euros. If he's sick, I will pay to have your car professionally shampooed.'

'You speak good English.' She put the car in gear and pulled away. 'So who is he? Your grandfather?'

'No, we are not related. My brother and I met him on the beach. His name is Isa – Jesus. That's what he calls himself, anyway.'

She snorted at this. 'Jesus?'

'Yes, Jesus.'

'Ha! Is he Christian?'

'I haven't asked, but I think it's unlikely. Jesus is also in the

Qur'an. He is one of our most important prophets, second only to Mohammed.'

'I didn't know that,' she said.

I took this as an invitation to educate her further.

'We don't believe exactly what the Christians believe about him,' I told her. 'We don't believe he is the son of God, but there are lots of other things we do agree on. We believe that his mother was a virgin. We believe he was chosen as a messenger to reveal the word of Allah. We believe that he will return at the end of time, and that his coming will herald the Day of Judgment.'

The Greek woman gave me a strange look. 'Well, as long as he's not sick in the car . . .'

Let me tell you: this Greek woman was called Effie, and she was on her way to the supermarket. This was her day off, but usually she worked serving drinks to tourists in a beachside bar. This was why her English was very good. She also spoke German, Italian, Spanish and a small amount of French. My mother would have liked her very much.

Now let me tell you something about Effie's car. It had air conditioning, and it worked far better than our air conditioning in Latakia. I felt as if I had ascended bodily to paradise. And when I looked over my shoulder at Mohammed, he was smiling peacefully. It was the first time I had seen him looking peaceful in many weeks.

'Thank you for stopping,' I said to Effie. 'It's a hot day to be walking.'

She laughed at this. 'Yeah, well I *almost* didn't stop. Your friend Jesus needs to watch what he does with his hands.'

This was when she explained about the *moutza*.

'I don't think Jesus knew what he was doing,' I told her.

'No, I guessed that.'

'But it may explain why we had no success getting any other cars to stop,' I reflected. 'I think Jesus has given the *moutza* many times this morning.'

'It can't have helped,' Effie told me. 'But . . . well, lots of people wouldn't have stopped anyway. They'd be too scared to.'

'They're scared of us?' I could not quite believe this. I glanced at Mohammed in his FC Barcelona shirt and Jesus with his gaunt face and white beard and wrinkles. Jesus was snoring loudly. 'How can they be afraid of us?'

'It's not you,' Effie said. 'Or it's not only you. The police have put out notices. They say that if we pick up illegals we'll be prosecuted for people smuggling.'

'But we're already here!' I pointed out. 'I'm just a passenger in your car. How could anyone mistake this for smuggling?'

'They couldn't. They're just trying to intimidate us. It's meant to be like . . . I can't think of the word. When you make threats to stop bad behaviour.'

'A deterrent?'

'Yes, deterrent! The authorities – the police, the local government, they don't want us to make life easy for you. That will only encourage more of you to come.'

We didn't need any encouragement. That's what I might have said in other circumstances. Most of us had seen our home country blown to pieces. Many of us had lost our families. Some of us had had our fingers chopped off by terrorists. Basically, you'd have to make life in Europe pretty fucking awful before we decided it wasn't for us. But I wasn't going to say any of this to Effie. She was nice, and I didn't want to ruin her day by talking about death and torture.

'Listen,' she said, after a while. 'You'll find lots of good people here. You'll find people who want to help you anyway, whatever the official rules say. But don't expect too much from Greece. Our country has no money, and we need the foreign tourists to keep coming, the Germans and the English. Otherwise . . . well, otherwise we're all up Shit Creek. You understand?'

I did understand, because I have watched American TV and movies and have a good command of their idioms.

There was silence for a minute. Then I asked: 'What will happen if the police do stop you? What's the punishment for helping us?'

'No idea. I'm like everyone else in Greece: I don't have any money to pay a fine. I guess they might take my car or something.'

'I'm afraid I don't have enough euros to buy you a new car,' I told her.

Effie laughed at this. 'Well, fuck it . . . They're not going to stop me from acting like a human being.'

My father would have liked Effie too. He would have told me to propose to her.

It took thirty more minutes to reach the supermarket on the outskirts of Samos Town. Jesus's eyes snapped open the moment the engine stopped. He looked very confused, glancing first at the supermarket and then at Effie. Then his face split into a grin.

'*Allahu akbar!*' He shouted. 'We are saved!'

'What did he say?' Effie asked.

'He said thanks for the lift,' I told her.

'Tell him thanks for not vomiting in my car.'

'She says you're welcome,' I translated.

'One more thing,' Effie said. She held her thumb up to Jesus. 'Next time you're hitch-hiking, try this. It might work better.'

Jesus stared at her raised thumb for a moment and then howled with laughter, slapping both his thighs.

'This is not a good gesture to use in the Middle East,' I told her. 'It means I am going to shove my thumb up your anus.'

Effie quickly lowered her thumb.

The Law

We needed basic supplies, so we went into the supermarket with Effie. I shopped, while Mohammed was responsible for making sure Jesus didn't fall over or break anything. You may think me extremely naïve, but these were the only problems I anticipated. I'd never had to take an alcoholic shopping before.

I bought some more water and sandwiches, and some oranges and dried apricots, because my mother would have worried that we weren't getting enough vitamins. I bought some special moisturising balm for our sunburn. I bought aspirin for our aching muscles and Jesus's hangover. The supermarket didn't sell shoes, but I did find sunglasses, which Jesus also needed. It wasn't sensible to be walking around Southern Europe without them. Still, I was conscious of our tight budget, so the pair I chose for him cost only a few euros. They were wraparounds, since I thought this style was less likely to fall off, and the lenses were large and thick to minimise the amount of sunlight he had to cope with, which would benefit us all. They weren't fashionable sunglasses. I didn't think this style of sunglasses had been fashionable since the 1980s. But I assumed, correctly, that Jesus would not be too concerned by this.

I rounded up Mohammed and Jesus. We said goodbye to Effie, who had more shopping to get. We paid. We left.

At the far end of the car park, Jesus stopped and removed two thirty-five centilitre bottles of whisky from the back of his trousers. I guess that he had tucked them into the waistband, or possibly into his underpants, one bottle braced against each buttock with his shirt concealing the necks.

'Jesus!' I shouted.

Mohammed groaned and slapped his forehead.

Jesus ignored us. He had put one bottle in his bag and was busy opening the other. He held the bottle to his chest with his right hand and used his left – the one that was fully operational – to unscrew the cap.

'Jesus,' I repeated, 'we are guests in this country! Your behaviour brings shame to all of us! It brings shame to the entire Iraqi nation!'

Jesus shrugged like this was nothing new.

I turned to Mohammed. 'You were supposed to be watching him!'

'I was watching him!'

'He managed to get two bottles of alcohol into his underpants. How is this watching him?' I paced a small circle. 'What are we going to do?'

'What do you mean, "What are we going to do?" We're going to get the hell out of here before we're arrested and sent back to Turkey!'

'We need to pay for this, Mohammed. We will not be accomplices to a theft.'

'Ha! You've got to be fucking joking? It's bad enough that you buy him sunglasses. You're not going to spend our money on getting Jesus drunk again!'

'Do you prefer him sober?'

'I'd prefer him gone! He's a fucking liability!'

'Mohammed, he's standing right here!'

'You're a fucking liability!' Mohammed told Jesus. 'See? He doesn't even care.'

This appeared to be true. Jesus absorbed our exchange with utter placidity. He just kept drinking.

I wasn't going to take the alcohol from him, because I'd heard what happened to the last person who tried that. But neither could I bring myself to walk away.

'I'm going to go and pay for them,' I said.

'You're not serious? What the hell are you going to say?'

'I'll say that my friend forgot to pay.'

'Ha!' Mohammed did his nasal impression of my voice. '*My friend forgot to pay*. Enjoy jail, Zain. A pretty boy like you will do well in there.'

He raised a valid point: there was no sensible way to go about this. But I still intended to pay for the alcohol.

'Watch him,' I told Mohammed. 'Don't let him go anywhere.'

'Where's he going to go?'

This was a fair point too. Jesus didn't look as if he intended to run away. With nobody threatening his alcohol, he looked perfectly happy to stay put.

I walked back into the supermarket. Near the doors was a charity collection box which I'd noticed first time round. I put a twenty-euro note in it and returned to Mohammed and Jesus.

'Okay. Let's get out of here,' I said.

'You're such a faggot,' Mohammed told me.

'You should eat some apricots,' I said. 'You too, Jesus. You need the vitamins.'

On a good day, I'd imagine the port of Samos Town is a very pleasant place to take a stroll. The harbour is a wide natural cove filled with deep-blue water and surrounded on three sides by forested mountains. It reminded me of the main harbour at Latakia, but without the giant oil tankers and cargo ships. The boats on the marina at Samos were small and wooden. Fishing boats and sailing boats – the kind of boats you could have put on a postcard. Along the seafront, there was a broad promenade lined with benches and trees and cafés and souvenir shops. But these souvenir shops had become like the ones in Turkey. Instead of postcards of the pretty boats in the pretty harbour, they were mostly selling tents and sleeping bags to the haggard men and women who'd made it across the Mediterranean in the last few days.

There were hundreds of us. The benches were packed with tired families and every inch of shade was occupied. There were wet clothes and bags strewn across walls and fences and the branches of trees – anywhere that could be used as a temporary washing line. It looked as if someone had blown up a launderette.

I didn't need Google Maps to find the police station because it was unmissable. It had an entrance that opened onto the promenade and a queue coming out of it that was at least a hundred people long. We weren't going there to turn Jesus over for his criminal activities, I should make that clear. It was where we needed to register as asylum seekers. Like every other person who had made it across the sea, we knew exactly where to go and what to do because this information was readily available online. Personally, I liked to prepare well in advance, so I'd memorised the key points on our itinerary before leaving the hotel in Turkey. It was like revising for an exam.

I queued outside the police station for about half an hour, while Mohammed was again responsible for Jesus. Then, when this became too much for Mohammed to cope with, we swapped positions so that he queued while I listened to Jesus's drunken ramblings. After another hour, we all queued together, and we edged closer and closer to the front. Jesus started on his second bottle of stolen whisky, and lots of people frowned at us, and the mothers and fathers pulled their children closer to them.

'Jesus, your behaviour is making people uncomfortable,' I hissed. 'Is there any chance you could stop drinking?'

He responded by clutching the bottle tight to his chest. His eyes were extremely wary.

'I'm not going to take it away from you,' I clarified. 'You shouldn't have stolen it, but . . . Well, that's not the main issue right now. You need to consider other people. There are children present.'

He looked at Mohammed, then gave a small nod. 'You are worried about your brother. Is this correct? You fear my actions may corrupt him.'

Mohammed let out an exasperated sigh. 'He's not talking about *me*, you idiot. I'm not a child.'

Jesus ignored this. 'Mohammed, you must not start drinking. Ever. It will not make you happy.' He turned back to me with a broad grin, as if expecting a pat on the back.

I decided it was time to be firm. 'Listen, Jesus. Do you want to keep travelling with us or not?'

'Of course. You are good company. You are good boys, I think.' With his free hand, the mutilated hand, he touched his 1980s wraparound sunglasses. 'These have made the day far easier. I am very grateful. Many of the people I have met have not been kind to me. There was a man on the boat who *stole* from me. He—'

I cut him off. 'We know about that. Please try to listen. If you want to stay with us there have to be some rules. You have to make some compromises. Do you understand?'

He nodded enthusiastically. 'It is good to have some company. Most of the people I meet, they do not want to know me. They—'

I spoke over him for a second time. Mohammed had his head in his hands and had started grinding his jaw.

'Jesus, listen. We are going into a police station. You cannot drink in the police station. You need to put the whisky back in your bag.'

It came as a shock when he actually complied. He put the whisky in his bag, folded his arms across his chest, and grinned like the Cheshire Cat.

Mohammed jabbed a finger in my ribs and then tilted his head angrily, drawing me to one side. 'We're not really going to keep travelling with him, are we?'

'It won't be forever.'

My brother glared daggers at me.

'Mohammed, please. You heard him. He's on his own. No one else is going to help him.'

'No one else is stupid enough to try!'

'Mum and Dad would help him. You know they would.'

'Mum and Dad aren't here.'

There was a silence, as always. I sighed heavily. 'Let's just get him registered. We can figure out what to do with him after-wards.'

Mohammed groaned with suppressed rage.

The policeman we finally got to see had lost all his hair apart from two strips above his ears. His face was very red, despite the small fan that was whirring at the end of his desk. He looked about fifty, and extremely tired.

His English was not good, but it was adequate, and he was able to process me and Mohammed in very little time. We showed him our passports and he filled out a form for each of us in Greece's strange mathematical alphabet. He took our photos and our fingerprints. He asked us why we were seeking asylum in Europe, so I began explaining to him that my family had had some difficulty with the Syrian government recently, and that, in addition, I was at an age where I was in danger of being conscripted into the army and asked to kill my fellow countrymen, which I wanted to avoid if at all possible. But he cut me off before I could get to the end.

'I will just write "war", okay? This is plenty.'

Getting Jesus processed was not so easy.

He had no passport. He had nothing at all that could prove his identity or nationality. Given the state of him, I suppose it was a miracle that he still had the clothes on his back. His bag contained only some soiled trousers, a pair of rolled-up socks, and the whisky, which the policeman eyed suspiciously.

'I think you people don't drink?' he said. He meant Muslims.

'We vary in how far we follow the letter of the Qur'an,' I told him.

'You please speak slower,' he said.

'Some Muslims drink,' I told him. 'It depends on the country.'

The policeman frowned. 'It's difficult to process this man,' he said. 'He should go to detention centre. There is translator there. She ask him more questions.'

'If you ask the questions, I can translate,' I told him.

'Yes, but he have no documents. He need to be keeped here on Samos. This is law, you understand?'

He waited a moment. I thought he was probably waiting for a bribe, so I started to delve in my pocket for my euros. I hoped Mohammed was not following the conversation. His English wasn't great, despite our mother's best efforts, but if he'd been paying close attention, he'd probably have known what was going on.

But the policeman started talking again before I could get my money out.

'Listen,' he said. 'You see how many refugees we have here. We have no more room. So you tell me he is Syrian like you. You tell me he is Syrian and we fill out this form and get you out of here. You understand?'

'This man is a Syrian,' I said. 'He is my Syrian uncle. He is sixty years old and also fleeing from war.'

The policeman smiled at this. It was the first time I had seen him smile. 'Good. You smart boy. Now we just need name and photographs and then we finish.'

'His name is Isa,' I said. 'I-S-A.'

The policeman transcribed this into Greek letters, then asked: 'He have other name?'

It may have been the policeman's non-standard English that caused me to misinterpret his question. 'Yes,' I said. 'In Christianity, he is called Jesus.'

61

'Jesus?'

'Yes.'

He was frowning again. 'This man's name is Jesus Isa? First name Jesus, second name Isa. That what you tell me?'

'No his name is Isa al-Masih,' I clarified. Jesus grinned; Mohammed groaned. 'But in English this means Jesus Christ.'

At this point, the policeman sighed at length. He handed me the pen and told me to write al-Masih on a scrap of paper so that he could spell it in Greek.

Once I'd finished, he took Jesus's photograph and fingerprint. Then he brought out three slips of white paper which gave us permission to travel freely in Greece for the next thirty days. He told us we should get on the ferry to Athens, which left the following morning, and once there, we should report to the refugee centre for further processing.

I was about to take the white slips from his hand, but he moved them away at the last moment, holding them just out of reach.

'A second, please,' he said. 'I do big favour for your friend Jesus Christ, you understand?'

I nodded, even though it wasn't exactly true. My impression had been that the policeman was mostly doing a favour for himself, by trying to reduce his workload.

'We have two police officers in this building,' he told me. 'Two police officers to write forms for maybe two, three hundred refugees. Some speak English, some don't. Not many speak good English as you.'

He tapped his pen on the desk a couple of times. I already thought I knew where he was going with this.

'You stay for rest of day and translate, like you do for your friend Mister Christ. You help me, you help others outside, and I help you. I get you food and drink and good chair to sit in. Here in this room, not outside in hot sun. We make a deal?'

Normally, I would not have hesitated. And it wasn't just that I had no idea what would happen if I said no. More than this, it was the chance to be inside. It was the possibility of a chair. It's surprising how quickly these things can become the most wonderful luxuries.

'What about my brother and Jesus?' I asked. 'I can't leave them.'

'I find cell for them to stay in. We have two cells that is used to keep the women safe, the . . .' He gestured a bump around his stomach.

'The pregnant women?' I asked.

'Yes, pregnant women. Women with very young babies, just weeks old. Your brother and your friend Jesus share a cell with them women.'

'That's kind of you,' I said, 'but I don't think that's the best idea, do you?'

'Is best idea I have,' the policeman told me.

I pointed to the corner of the small office. 'They can rest over there. My brother slept on the beach last night, for maybe two hours. Jesus has had less than an hour of sleep, earlier today. If you let them lie down there, I guarantee they will not be a problem.'

The policeman looked sceptical, but eventually he shrugged. 'Fine. You translate, and I let them stay here. I even find blankets to lie on. This is the deal, yes?'

'I need to charge my phone. Can I do that too?'

'Okay, but this is last thing.'

'Jesus also needs shoes,' I said.

The policeman peered over his desk at Jesus's flip-flops. He stared at them for the longest time. Then he closed his eyes and shook his head. 'Okay,' he said. 'When we finish, I take you somewhere to get shoes. This is everything, yes?'

'We have a deal,' I told him.

So for the rest of the afternoon, I translated. The policeman – whose name I never discovered – fetched a spare swivel chair and the promised blankets, and then he set me straight to work. And it was relentless. Person after person, family after family. The majority were Syrians, but there were also Iraqis and Iranians and Afghans and Yemenis and Sudanese and Somalians and Eritreans. Representatives of every failed or failing state within a thousand kilometres of Greece. We managed to get by using a mixture of Arabic and broken English, except for one Afghan family, for whom I had to pull an additional translator from the queue. At that point, the office became rather crowded. We had an Iranian translating the Afghans' Dari into Arabic, which I then translated into English, which the policeman wrote down in Greek. Jesus and Mohammed remained asleep in the corner the whole time, with Jesus again snoring loudly. Every so often, one of the other refugees would nod at the corner while throwing me a questioning look, and I would raise my eyes and shake my head, which, as you know, is the universal sign for *Don't ask*.

People came and went all afternoon. They gave their names, they showed their ID if they had it. They had their photographs and fingerprints taken. They told their horrendous stories. I allowed them to talk as much as possible, to give their reasons for seeking asylum in the European Union, because sometimes people just need to talk. They need to feel that someone is listening. But before they could get very far at all, the policeman would get irritated and ask me: 'War or persecution? Which one?' I didn't blame him because this was his job. Every day he had to clear a queue of desperate, traumatised people, knowing that tomorrow it would reappear, and it would be more or less identical. It must have felt like some horrific magic trick.

It isn't often that you get to see someone else's perspective, someone else's life up close, but I think, that afternoon, I did. My conclusion was that this policeman may have seemed impatient and unsympathetic, but he was not a bad man – not like the police in my country. He was just doing his best in an impossible situation, like a fireman battling an unstoppable fire.

When we were finally done for the day, I slumped in a weary heap in my chair. The wall clock showed it was seven thirty in the evening, but it felt like midnight. The policeman clapped me on the shoulder.

'You do well today,' he said. Then he gestured at Mohammed and Jesus. 'Come on. We go get your friend Mister Christ some shoes. Then maybe some hot food.'

And that is what we did.

The Hotel Room

The policeman took us to a small warehouse near the harbour. It was a very small warehouse – more of a storage shed, really. Inside were three more Greeks, two women and a man. They didn't look much older than me. They might have been students, I guessed. They were sitting on cardboard boxes and were surrounded by more cardboard boxes. Lots of cardboard boxes.

There was a barrage of rapid Greek, and the policeman pointed first at me, then at Jesus, then at Jesus's feet. Three pairs of eyes looked down in perfect synchrony, and three lips were immediately bitten. This was getting to be a familiar response. Of course, we all knew what was going on in that moment, even Jesus. He shrugged briefly, then performed a quick drunken tap dance, which he managed with surprising dexterity. I suppose it helped that those flip-flops really did fit him like a glove.

All three of the seated Greeks howled with laughter. Even the policeman was smiling, though he was shaking his head too. Mohammed rolled his eyes. I put my hand on Jesus's shoulder and said: 'This is Jesus. He needs some new shoes.'

It was a simple statement, but it caused a second explosion of laughter.

One of the women had tears streaming down her cheeks; the other panted that Jesus's shoes were already perfect. The man managed to pull himself together and hopped down from the box.

'Okay, Jesus,' he said. 'Let's find you some shoes. This way, please.'

We followed the Greek man to one of the cardboard boxes towards the back of the storage shed. Inside were at least twenty pairs of men's shoes. A mixture of trainers, sandals and walking boots. Jesus started holding them up to his feet, one by one, and soon we had a pile of half a dozen contenders. During the next five minutes, he rejected every pair. He complained that they pinched or rubbed, they were too tight or too loose – or 'too heavy'.

Eventually he picked up the flip-flops again. 'I think these are the best,' he said.

'Jesus,' I told him. 'We may have to walk many more kilometres when we get to the mainland. You need to find some shoes that are a bit more . . . robust.'

Jesus shrugged and slapped the flip-flops against the side of another cardboard box with an impressive *thwack*. Then he held them up for me to inspect. 'These shoes will not be destroyed easily, my friend.'

I took a pair of white trainers from the discarded pile. From what I'd been able to discern, these were the ones that had provoked the least grumbling. 'We'd like to take these ones,' I told the Greek man. 'But if it's okay, Jesus would also like to hold on to his flip-flops. Just in case.'

The Greek man smiled and nodded. He had a reassuring smile. 'No problem. You need anything else? We have clothes, sleeping bags, toiletries – you need these things?'

I could have wept.

We spent another ten minutes going through various cardboard boxes and replenishing much of what we'd had to leave behind in Turkey. I found spare clothes for me and Mohammed, though there was little chance of him taking off the Messi shirt at any point. I knew this from experience. I also found some cargo shorts and a light-tan shirt which I thought would fit Jesus. I persuaded him to part with the soiled trousers in his bag, which the Greeks assured me they could wash and recycle. All the clothes in the warehouse had been donated by the islanders, as had the sleeping bags and tents – though they had now run out of the latter. Obviously, they were in high demand. There were also toothbrushes and toothpaste and deodorants and razors and female sanitary products that had been donated by local shops and pharmacies. There were boxes of nappies and children's toys.

When we were done, the policeman conferred briefly with the other Greeks, then nodded a couple of times.

'You go with these people,' he said to me. 'They take you where you get hot food.'

'Thank you,' I said.

'Where you sleep tonight?'

'I don't know. Somewhere in the port, I suppose. At least we have sleeping bags now.'

He frowned for a moment, then shook his head. 'Listen. I phone my sister. She has small hotel. Very small, and never any free rooms at the moment. You understand why. By afternoon, all rooms is gone. But if I ask her, she maybe find space some-where. In lounge or restaurant, I don't know.'

I wanted to hug him. If he'd been Syrian, I'd have kissed him on both cheeks. But of course I didn't; he did not strike me as the sort of man who would appreciate such a gesture. 'Thank you,' I said. 'That's very kind of you.'

He waved his hand dismissively. 'Bah! You just make sure Mister Jesus is best behaviour. Okay?'

'Okay.'

So he made his phone call, and within a couple of minutes, we had a room for the night. The policeman told us it was just a small store room that was usually used for spare bedding and vacuum cleaners and that sort of thing, but his sister had some roll-out mattresses that we could use. It would be a tight squeeze, but she thought we'd just about fit.

'I give address to these people,' the policeman said, gesturing at the other Greeks. 'They take you there after food.'

Shortly afterwards, he left without ceremony.

He was a good man.

We walked back along the promenade in the direction of the police station. I was talking to the young Greek man, who was called Andreas. He was wheeling a small trolley of sleeping bags because there were bound to be people who needed them, espe-cially now the sun was going down. The two women, Hana and Alyx, were walking on either side of Mohammed, and every time they tried to talk to him, he blushed the colour of a sun-dried tomato. Because he was a fourteen-year-old boy and they were two pretty Greek women who insisted on calling him Lionel Messi, which I could tell he secretly loved. The only problem

69

was that every time they said Messi, Jesus assumed they were talking about him and demanded that I provide simultaneous translation. I refused, and he spent the next ten minutes grumbling and looking at his flip-flops, which he still refused to replace. Every so often, he took a long drink from his whisky bottle.

'Is Jesus not a Muslim?' Andreas asked me after the first such incident.

So I explained that I didn't actually know *what* Jesus was because we'd only met sixteen hours ago, and he'd spent much of this time asleep or incoherent. Added to this, different Muslim nations varied in their attitudes to alcohol, and I really didn't know what the situation was in Iraq at present. I only knew about Syria, which had a secular constitution and a liberal stance on alcohol, and Saudi Arabia, which was a theocracy, and completely dry. Of course, everyone knew Saudi Arabia was dry, but we knew it better than most in Syria; before the war, it was not unusual to see Saudi businessmen passed out on Latakia seafront or stumbling through traffic or falling into the harbour. Trust me: outside of their own country, those dry Saudis drank like they were staging a personal jihad against alcohol and would not be happy until every last drop had been eradicated from the Middle East.

At some point during this explanation, I realised that I was rambling, which I have a tendency to do when I'm tired. But Andreas was still listening intently; he seemed interested, and even amused, which was gratifying. Nevertheless, I was certain that I'd strayed from my original point. So I concluded with a shrug, telling Andreas that Jesus was just Jesus; he followed his own rules.

And it seemed a reasonable statement to make. Even though I'd only known Jesus for a few hours, a lot had happened in that time – enough that I felt I could generalise about his basic character. At this point, Jesus still seemed to me a simple creature to understand. He drank, he muttered, he made life difficult. What else was there to know?

We walked on in silence for a few minutes, with just the sound of the trolley wheels squeaking, and then Andreas asked me: 'Will you keep travelling with him – Jesus – when you reach the mainland?'

'Fate has thrown us together. That's what Jesus seems to think, anyway.'

'What do you think? Do you believe in fate?'

'I don't know . . . I believe sometimes we don't get the freedom to make the choices we want to make. There are bigger powers that choose for us. But you'd believe that too if you'd lived in Syria. I don't know if it's the same as believing in fate.' I glanced back over my shoulder. Jesus was still following a few paces back, mumbling to himself. I shrugged again, and turned back to Andreas. 'Perhaps we will go our separate ways soon. That would be the sensible thing to do. But . . . you've seen how things are with him. He's not a well man. He's on his own, and he only speaks Arabic. No one else is going to help him.'

Andreas nodded thoughtfully, scratching his stubble, and I think I probably mirrored him a bit, scratching my own stubble. His was the kind of trendy stubble that's probably been carefully shaped and groomed. Mine was because I'd not had access to a razor for a while, and it was thick and itchy. When I got to the hotel that night, one of the first things I planned to do was find a bathroom and have a shave. I would shave and I would wash

71

my face in warm water and then I would sleep. I would sleep somewhere that wasn't the cold hard ground. It was a notion that had been playing in my head on repeat ever since the policeman had promised to phone his sister. And, I might as well tell you, it was not a notion that was destined to last very long. But while it did, it was wonderful.

Andreas interrupted my thoughts by asking me what I planned to do when I reached Athens. He didn't think I should even bother reporting to the refugee centre for further processing. There was no point.

'Our government can't provide anything for anyone,' he told me. 'You've seen what it's like here on Samos. All we can afford is two policemen to stamp your forms and get you moved on as quickly as possible. Most of the people want to help, but all they have to give are recycled clothes and maybe some vegetables from their gardens. And Athens is the same as Samos, only worse. There's no money, no jobs, no future. We can't afford to look after our own people, so what hope is there for anyone else?'

Andreas shrugged and looked briefly at the sea, as if surveying a vast flattened city. 'So you will do what everyone does,' he told me. 'You'll head north to Germany or Sweden. Go to the part of Europe where you at least have a chance to rebuild your life. Am I right?'

'Yes. I mean, you're almost right.' I glanced at Mohammed; each of the Greek women had taken hold of one of his arms and he was now the exact same colour as the sunset. 'We want to go to the UK,' I said to Andreas. 'I think it makes more sense for us. I speak the language. Mohammed has enough English to get by. Neither of us knows a word of German.'

Andreas gave a small frown. 'I'm sure you could learn German quickly enough. And the UK . . . Well, the UK is a difficult country to get into. It's like a fortress compared to the rest of Europe. They have the sea as their moat and they've pulled up the drawbridge. Do you understand?'

'They have a train that goes under the sea,' I said. 'My mother told me about it when I was a young child. I've always wanted to ride it.'

'Ha! It would be nice if it was that easy.' Andreas looked at me for a few moments as if trying to work out how serious I was. I suppose I'd made myself look quite naïve by talking about the train under the sea, as if Mohammed and I could just hop aboard in Paris and get off in London, no questions asked. I wasn't that naïve; I realised that you couldn't get into the UK without a valid passport.

'Listen,' Andreas said after a while. 'I spent a year in England when I was a student. You know how many times I saw the sun? Maybe twice, I think. Seriously, have you heard what nuclear winter is? Well, that's the UK. It's like they had a secret nuclear war with Ireland and ruined their skies forever.'

I smiled at this, undeterred. 'I was studying English before we left Syria. The UK would be the best place for me to finish my studies. It would be the best place for Mohammed to go to school.'

Andreas shrugged again. 'Well, what can I tell you? I'm trying to put you off, but only because the path you've chosen is the most difficult one. If you're still determined to get to the UK, then I wish you good luck. You will need it.'

We kept walking, and we talked a bit more, about nothing I can remember. But I do remember that I felt very relaxed, despite everything. I could almost have imagined I was walking along the promenade in Latakia, watching the same red sun sink into the sea.

My thoughts were interrupted by the sound of a woman calling my name. This was extremely incongruous, as you can imagine, and for a moment I assumed it was an hallucination brought about by tiredness. Then the woman whistled. It was Sabeen. She was sitting on a bench with Rihanna curled up in her lap and Aida still trying to burrow into her shoulder. We walked over to say hello.

'You made it,' Sabeen said, her eyes flicking to Jesus – first his face, then his flip-flops. 'Did you walk the whole way?'

'About halfway, I think. Then Jesus lay down in the road and a Greek woman stopped and picked us up.'

'Oh . . .' Sabeen was obviously looking for something else she could add to this response, but found nothing.

I introduced Andreas and Hana and Alyx, and everyone started speaking all at once. I had to translate at first, but after everyone had slowed down, it turned out that Sabeen had enough English to get by. Soon Hana and Alyx had abandoned Mohammed in favour of Sabeen's girls and had managed to coax them out of their shells using a combination of smiles and chocolate. Then, at some point, Andreas was asking Sabeen if she needed sleeping bags for the night, and she said yes, that would be very kind, which made me throw a look at Mohammed, who immediately shot me a look back that said *Don't you dare*, which I of course ignored.

'Sabeen, do you have somewhere to sleep tonight?' I asked.

She gave a resigned smile and gestured with her open palm at the bench.

'Mohammed, may I have a word with you in private?' I said.

We shuffled away up the promenade, Mohammed's face like a thundercloud and Jesus following the two of us like a bemused shadow.

'No way,' Mohammed said. 'Absolutely not!'

'Mohammed,' I told him, 'I'm going to give you a choice. Either you accept this and do the right thing, or you can be the one to explain things to Sabeen. You go over there and tell her why you think you deserve the room more than her two little girls.'

For a moment, he looked like he was genuinely considering it, but I think it was mostly an act at this point. He was just trying to make me sweat. Or that's what I hoped. But before I could say anything else, Jesus stepped forward and placed a fatherly hand on Mohammed's shoulder.

'Your brother is right, Mohammed. You know this to be true.'

'Fuck off, Jesus! You don't get to lecture anyone about morality.'

'Thank you, Jesus,' I said. 'That's extremely decent of you.'

Mohammed kicked an apple core that had been discarded on the promenade and it exploded in a shower of pips and juice. He swore at me for some time; his exact words are difficult to translate, but an approximation would be: 'Fuck you, Zain, fuck you and your fucking conscience. I hope you get struck by a dick.'

I took this as a sign of consent, and went over to tell Sabeen the good news.

At the far end of the harbour was a large stone jetty, about a hundred metres long by twenty wide. It had iron mooring posts evenly spaced around its perimeter and a strip of street lights running down its centre. This was where we slept. There were perhaps a hundred other people there with us, mostly clustered around the lights. Everyone who had no better option – no hotel room or bench or patch of grass or dirt on which to lay a blanket.

It probably goes without saying that it was not the most comfortable night I have ever spent, but neither was it the worst, for a number of reasons:

1. We were safe. We were not hiding from an armed militia or border patrol. We were not alone in an unfamiliar forest. We were not in a cattle truck or a smugglers' boat. We were not in the dark Mediterranean Sea.

2. We had full stomachs. Andreas had taken us to a restaurant where more volunteers were distributing hot meals. The queue for the toilet was out the door, but I did not see anyone complaining. Given what many of us had been through recently, we might have been queuing for the gates of paradise.

3. Jesus had been pacified with cigarettes and alcohol. Obviously, this was not an ideal situation, but even Mohammed agreed that the alternative would have guaranteed a terrible night and a worse ferry ride tomorrow. For us and everyone else. So we'd found a late-night shop and bought enough whisky and tobacco to last for the next twenty-four hours, and in return I extorted some basic promises: Jesus would be answerable to me, and to a lesser extent Mohammed, at all times; he would be as discreet about his drinking as possible; he would stay away from families with children; he would not steal. I thought that there might be a time in the future when we could address Jesus's alcohol problem in a more satisfactory manner, but for now, a combination of bribery and blackmail would have to suffice.

4. Our hardship was not pointless. As I lay on the cold hard ground, I could at least know that our being here meant that

Sabeen and her girls didn't have to be. She had started crying when I offered her our room for the night. She had cried and she had hugged me and she had hugged Mohammed, who had finally had the good grace to blush and mumble that it was the least we could do. So when I woke in the night with my whole body aching, I at least knew that the pain was serving a greater good. Suffering is far more tolerable when it has a purpose.

5. I was completely and utterly exhausted. Once I lay down in my sleeping bag, with my backpack as a pillow, I'd guess that I was asleep within seconds; and for most of the night, my sleep was blessedly free of dreams.

The thing that eventually woke me was the ferry docking. It wasn't as noisy as you might expect, but I suppose there was part of my mind that was still on high alert, a finger of awareness reaching out into the dark for sudden changes to my surroundings. When I opened my eyes, its bow was gliding into my field of view like an apparition. It took me several moments to understand where I was and what was happening. My hands and face were cold. *The God Delusion* was poking into my neck.

I retrieved the phone from my pocket and checked the time, which was a little after five a.m. Jesus and Mohammed had not stirred. They were both cocooned up to their necks in their sleeping bags and as far as I could tell were asleep. Silently, I got up.

I walked the short distance to the empty ticket office where the jetty met the main promenade. There were figures asleep against the closed doorway, so I kept going until I'd found a spot where I could be alone. Here, I sat down on a low wall and took out my phone again.

I opened WhatsApp and looked at the message I'd sent to my mum over the restaurant's Wi-Fi the previous evening. It read: Are you there?

There was no reply, just as there'd been no reply to the identical message I'd sent before we left the hotel in Turkey.

I took a couple of breaths, then I dialled the number for our apartment in Latakia. There wasn't even a dial tone anymore. I got an automated message telling me the number was no longer in use.

Had I expected anything else? No, not rationally. But I still felt as if my insides had been ripped from me.

Sometimes, hope can override rationality.

I got up from the wall and I walked back to Jesus and Mohammed, who still appeared to be sound asleep. I got back into my own sleeping bag and shut my eyes, willing myself to drop again into that deep well of unconsciousness that I'd attained earlier in the night. That was all I wanted right then. I wanted nothingness.

But tired as I was, sleep would no longer come.

I lay there in the dark and I thought about my mother.

The Calming of the Storm

The ferry to Athens was called *The Poseidon*; it had its name painted in huge white letters across the hull, both in English and Greek. Poseidon, as I'm sure you know, was the ancient Greek god of the sea, so there were probably a thousand Greek ships called *The Poseidon*, and beach bars and hotels and swimming pools too. Because this is what happens to gods when they are no longer taken seriously: people name swimming pools after them. I've never seen or heard of any tourist attraction called Allah the Gracious, the Merciful – but in a few hundred years, who knows? In time, all things become possible. Certainties become implausible, fact becomes fiction, magic becomes technology.

To the ancient Greeks, I'm sure that *The Poseidon* would have seemed a vessel that no mortal hand could have created. *The Poseidon* was 192 metres long by 27 wide; it had various decks and levels climbing as high into the air as our low-rise apartment block back in Latakia. On the main stairwell, there was a schematic showing the ship's dimensions and capacity. It could accommodate 1,600 passengers and 750 cars – though for this voyage, almost everyone was a foot passenger with a single backpack carrying all their worldly possessions. If any of them owned cars, they were likely abandoned on the streets of Damascus or Aleppo or Homs, covered in the dust of exploded buildings.

Let me tell you: after the past week, the opulence of *The Poseidon* was astonishing. The ticket price included not just transport, but a superior aeroplane-style seat, well padded and reclining. There were lounges and bars, two restaurants and a gift shop. The toilets, unsurprisingly, were a major attraction. Under usual travelling conditions, I'm sure the facilities would have been more than sufficient, but during our twelve-hour voyage, there was a permanent queue snaking out of every toilet door. The sinks were the hardest to get to; plenty of people were taking the opportunity to wash their hair or shave. After some consideration, I decided that this was one luxury I'd have to forego. My hair had received a decent rinse during the swim; and as for shaving, it seemed simpler to let nature take its course.

For a while, I stood up on the top deck with Jesus and Mohammed. Jesus wanted to smoke, and I could tell from Mohammed's face that he appreciated being out in the open air. The sky had become cloudy overnight, and there was a strong breeze, so it was pleasantly cool compared to the previous day. And there was something satisfying about being out on the deck, watching Samos disappear at the horizon as *The Poseidon* sliced through the water.

What drew me away, eventually, was the need to plan. I told Mohammed that I was going downstairs to use the free Wi-Fi and that he would have to supervise Jesus.

'What am I supposed to do with him?' Mohammed scowled.

'You don't have to do anything with him,' I said. 'Just watch him. Make sure he doesn't fall overboard. And don't let him anywhere near the gift shop.'

My brother rolled his eyes and snorted angrily. In an ideal world, I would have had a second supervisor in place to supervise Mohammed's supervision of Jesus, which I did not entirely trust. But the world was not ideal, and I would have to make do.

'Listen, Mohammed,' I said. 'All you have to do is keep an eye on him. It's not a big deal.'

'Then why don't you do it?'

'Because I have to figure out what we'll do when we reach the mainland.'

'He's at least twenty years older than Dad. He can look after himself.'

There was a small silence, while we both regarded Jesus, who was leaning against a railing, happily oblivious to our discussion. In all honesty, it seemed unlikely that he was going to cause any significant trouble. His drinking had reached a kind of equilibrium across the course of the morning, and while I wouldn't describe him as sober, neither was he inebriated. He probably wasn't going to fall overboard or attack anyone with his flip-flops. He looked as if he'd be happy to chain-smoke for the entire journey. Nevertheless. The horror story of his last boat trip was still fresh in my mind. It made sense to be cautious.

Mohammed hadn't stopped scowling; I resorted to bribery, using the only reliable currency I had.

'I'll let you have some time on the phone later,' I told him. 'You can play games. Maybe even watch some YouTube. The internet connection's pretty good.'

'I want four hours,' Mohammed demanded.

'Don't be ridiculous. You can have one hour.'

'Three.'

'One.'

'That's not fair! You have to negotiate.'

'I'm not letting you run the battery down to zero.'

'We're on a ferry! They have electricity.'

'Have you seen the queues for the sockets?'

'Okay, two hours. That's as low as I'm going.'

'Ninety minutes.'

'Ninety-five minutes.'

'Done.'

I went downstairs, feeling tired but satisfied. It was a steep learning curve, but I thought my parenting of Mohammed was certainly improving.

I spent about half an hour researching Athens, familiarising myself with the significant parts of the city. This did not include the Parthenon or the Temple of Zeus, obviously. The stops on our itinerary would include the port and the bus or train station, possibly via the refugee centre. I say 'possibly' because the more I read, the less worthwhile this detour seemed. Legally, we were required to register our arrival in Athens. Legally, we were forbidden from leaving Greece. But everything Andreas had told me the previous evening was borne out in the online forums: the reality was that Greece had no means to help us. There were lots of stories of yet more pointless queuing, followed by the pointless stamping of forms, after which people would be returned rudderless to the streets. Reports suggested that the public parks were full of tents; they had become permanent camps for those who'd spent the last of their money getting to mainland Europe. Everyone else, everyone who could afford it, was heading north to Macedonia.

Needless to say, the Greek authorities were doing everything they could to ignore this mass exodus to the border. It may have been illegal for us to leave, but there wasn't an official in Greece who thought we should stay. The Macedonians, meanwhile, were just as determined to keep us out, and had deployed their army to patrol all the main crossing points. And further along the migrant route, Hungary was busy constructing a razor-wire fence the full length of its border with Serbia. It was nearing a hundred kilometres long, and on schedule to be finished within a week.

It was this ticking clock that finally convinced me we should waste no time in Athens. We needed to cross the Hungarian border before it became impossible. Everyone knew that Hungary was the gateway to the rest of the European Union. Once you were in Hungary, you no longer needed to show your passport to travel. You could hop on a train in Budapest and get off in Munich; from there, you could travel on to Brussels or Stockholm, or Paris or Calais, no questions asked. If you made it to Hungary, you had, in effect, made it to the West.

Reading all this had given me a headache, a dull throb that seemed to be located at the precise midpoint between my eyes. I was still very tired, I suppose, having slept little in the past few days; but more than this, I felt a certain *weight* pressing down on me, one which I hadn't really noticed while everything else had been going on. It was a heaviness that had only become apparent now that I was on my own – away even from Mohammed – and in a situation of relative comfort. At the time, I couldn't put a name to what I was feeling, but I worked it out later on.

It was the weight of responsibility, which, believe me, can feel as heavy as a mountain, especially if you're not used to it.

I took a couple of aspirin with a mouthful of warm Coca-Cola. The phone battery was down to forty per cent. This was my next concern. It may have been enough to honour my debt to Mohammed, but I wanted to be certain. If I failed to deliver the ninety-five minutes I'd promised, or delayed their delivery, it would weaken my position in any future negotiations. At the very least, I thought I could check the queues for the sockets again.

I went through to the closest lounge where there were half a dozen power points scattered around the room; you could locate them instantly because that's where everyone was clustered. The queues were like the ones you get in a barber's shop, with three or four people seated around each double socket. Since leaving Syria, I had gained extensive experience of queuing for electricity, and in my assessment, these queues were not at all bad; I estimated a wait time of an hour. It could be longer if someone was charging from flat, or had a very old phone, but the risk of this could be lessened with some basic reconnaissance.

Not long afterwards, I had taken a seat at what I'd deduced was the shortest queue. It consisted of two middle-aged men whose phones were almost charged, a middle-aged woman in a niqab, who appeared to be sleeping, and a man called Tariq, who had started talking to me as soon as I'd sat down. He was twenty-three – only a few years older than me – but if I'd had to guess before talking to him, I'd have put his age closer to thirty. He had that sort of bearing – a kind of cynical worldliness that made me feel like a child. He wore a battered leather jacket and a sarcastic half-smile, as if he knew something – many things – that I did not. In all honesty, he was the sort of man who made me feel instantly uncomfortable. In English, you'd probably say he was a bit *rough*. But what could I do? We were in the same phone queue, and there was no getting away from him.

We talked for a while about our immediate circumstances. Tariq told me that he was travelling alone and was heading to Sweden, where his cousin was already claiming asylum. I told him that I was travelling with my brother Mohammed, and Jesus, who we'd met on the beach, and that we were heading to the UK, where I planned to finish my studies. It was at this point the conversation deteriorated.

'England's a bitch to get into,' Tariq said. 'I had a friend who went there a couple of years ago. It took him, like, ten attempts. He hid for two days in the back of a refrigerated lorry.'

'Oh. That must have been . . . cold.'

Tariq generously ignored this remark. 'I'd like to go to the UK some time, too,' he told me. 'They have some of the finest women in Europe.'

'And the finest universities,' I added.

Tariq laughed as if I'd said something hilarious. 'Seriously, though. The English girls are *loose*, especially when they're drunk.'

'Well . . . You probably shouldn't generalise.'

'It's a well-known fact.'

I shifted awkwardly in my seat, and, of course, Tariq detected my discomfort at once, like a dog smelling fear. He gave me a look, stern and suspicious. 'You're not . . . bent, are you?'

At this moment, the woman in the niqab, who was sitting opposite, snapped her eyes open. Her eyes were knives. The only option was to mirror her outrage. I moulded my reddening face into what I hoped was a clear demonstration of shock and anger. 'Of course I'm not *bent*,' I said. 'Quite the opposite!'

Neither Tariq nor the niqab woman was convinced; I could tell that straightaway. It was time for Plan B: a suitably humiliating version of the truth.

'I'm a virgin,' I said, lowering my eyes. 'It makes me uncomfortable to discuss sexual matters.'

The transformation was instant. When I looked up, I could see that the niqab woman was now *completely* on my side. She had turned her dagger-eyes on Tariq, who looked deeply embarrassed on my behalf.

This seemed my best chance to escape. I rose from my seat and walked away, with as much dignity as I could muster. Charging the phone would have to wait.

I needed some time by myself. Not long; I wasn't going to leave Mohammed with Jesus indefinitely. But since it had been a couple of hours already, ten minutes more was neither here nor there.

My headache was still lurking, and to make matters worse, I'd started to feel sick. It wasn't just the conversation with Tariq, which had left a familiar hollowness in the pit of my stomach. It was the motion of the ferry, too, which had become more noticeable since I'd sat down to charge the phone. I guessed the waves must be bigger now that we were away from Samos and in the open sea. They'd have to be much bigger to be noticeable on a boat as big as *The Poseidon*.

I walked back to my seat with my stomach lurching. Sitting helped, and so did closing my eyes. There were small blinking lights that continued to bother me, but it wasn't as bad as the strange imbalance I felt when I tried to focus on anything – not quite dizziness, but a milder sense of misalignment, as if the world was not quite in synch with itself. I tried reclining my seat to see if this made a difference, but it was hard to tell. All I knew was that I still needed a few more moments to rest. Just a few more moments . . .

It barely seemed that I'd closed my eyes before I was coming round with a guilty shudder. Mohammed was shaking both my shoulders, and the world continued to lurch unpredictably.

'Zain? Zain! Wake up, you stupid fuck!'

My eyes snapped fully open. 'Mohammed, you mustn't swear. It reflects badly on our family. Where's Jesus?'

'You need to come with me. He's gone crazy. Crazier! I think he's going to kill himself!'

I sprang out of my seat and immediately stumbled forward several paces. I might have fallen over, but Mohammed managed to grab my arm as I passed him. It wasn't just that I was confused and disorientated. The rolling motion of the ferry had become much worse, and walking was problematical. When I looked around, I saw that almost every seat had now been filled, and most of the other passengers looked as ill as I felt. It seemed as if mere minutes had passed since I sat down, but obviously it had been much, much longer. My brother tugged at my arm. He was completely drenched; his hair was plastered to his forehead and his Lionel Messi shirt clung to his skinny frame as if it had been glued there.

'Where is he?' I said. 'Not still out on deck?'

'He's either out on deck or in the sea,' Mohammed told me.

We ran to the main stairwell, the floor shifting like a seesaw below us. The few people we passed in the aisles and corridors were holding on to chairs or tables, or braced against walls – whatever they could do to steady their footing.

Outside, the rain was pounding the deck like heavy artillery.

There was no one else out there – no one but Jesus – and it was obvious why. It wasn't just the rain; the rolling of the boat was more pronounced here too, the rises longer and the falls bigger and more sudden. The wind was blowing in sharp gusts, and overhead, the sky was a sheet of unbroken grey.

Jesus was near the front of the ferry, just off to one side. At first, I thought he was floating, at least half a metre off the deck, though still appearing to sway ominously with the motion of the ship. It was only after I'd wiped the rain from my eyes that I saw the truth. He had managed to climb up one of the side railings and had both feet planted on the metal bar that formed their lowest rung.

I felt a surge of relief when I realised he wasn't *trying* to kill himself, which was how I'd first interpreted Mohammed's warning. To be fair, this was not my brother's fault. He'd not had time to explain the situation fully, and had merely told me that Jesus was *going* to kill himself, which was still a distinct possibility. The pink flip-flops could not have provided much of a foothold on the wet metal of the railing, and I had no idea how well he could grip with his mutilated right hand. As for his grip on reality, that had long since fled. He was soaked to the skin, and his hair was like a hundred white rivers cascading down the back of his neck. Every time *The Poseidon* plunged from a wave, a jet of seawater exploded over the front of the ferry. With the biggest waves, the sea rose before us like a wall of frosted glass, suspended for an instant, then shattering into a million pieces of liquid shrapnel. Jesus, meanwhile, stood rooted to the railing as if he were a human sacrifice, an offering to appease the angry sea. He had his head thrown back and was howling with wild laughter.

'HOW LONG'S HE BEEN LIKE THIS?' I shouted at Mohammed.

'I DON'T KNOW,' Mohammed shouted back. 'MAYBE TEN MINUTES? IT STARTED VERY SUDDENLY!'

'HAS HE BEEN DRINKING?'

'NO MORE THAN USUAL. I SUPPOSE HE'S SWALLOWED QUITE A LOT OF SEAWATER, TOO.'

'YOU SHOULD HAVE GOT ME STRAIGHT AWAY!'

'WELL, I COULDN'T LEAVE HIM, COULD I?'

This was a fair point, I supposed. There must have been a moment when the balance tipped, when not leaving him became more dangerous than leaving.

'JESUS!' I bellowed. 'JESUS!'

He didn't look around. Instead, he released the railing with his left hand – his *good* hand – and waved at us.

'JESUS, YOU NEED TO GET DOWN FROM THERE. IT'S DANGEROUS!'

'I HAVE FACED GREATER DANGERS, MY YOUNG FRIEND,' he shouted. Or I thought that's what he shouted. He still had his face turned up towards the sky, and some of his words were lost to the wind.

'PLEASE, COME DOWN,' I pleaded.

'YOU SHOULD COME *UP*,' he told me. 'THIS IS TREMENDOUS. I FEEL SO *SMALL*!'

As if to emphasise this point, another jet of seawater arched across the boat and slapped him square in the face, like some monstrous tentacle. Jesus spluttered, briefly, then whooped with delight. I decided it was time to intervene.

'STAY WHERE YOU ARE!' I yelled at Mohammed, who had started moving as soon as I did. 'IF HE FALLS OVERBOARD,

89

YOU NEED TO ALERT THE CREW!' I had no idea what the crew could do in such a scenario – not much, I supposed – but that was not the point. The point was to keep Mohammed where he was. To keep at least one of us safe.

I edged towards Jesus slowly, keeping both hands on the railing. He seemed unsurprised when I touched his arm, gently, so as not to startle him. When he turned his face to me, he was grinning broadly.

'YOU MADE THE RIGHT DECISION, MY FRIEND. JOIN ME. THIS IS SOMETHING YOU DON'T WANT TO MISS.'

'IT'S VERY IMPRESSIVE,' I screamed.

'*ALLAHU AKBAR*!' Jesus roared.

'*ALLAHU AKBAR*!' I agreed. 'PERHAPS WE SHOULD GO BACK INSIDE NOW?'

'BAH! WHY ARE YOU AFRAID? THE STORM WILL NOT LAST MUCH LONGER. ENJOY IT WHILE YOU CAN.'

Another wave broke over the front of the ship; another plume of water whipped down towards us. For a moment, I was blinded. Jesus disappeared in a flash of white spray, and I had the image in my head, as clear as if I'd been watching it on a cinema screen, of him tumbling over the railing, the grey sea rushing up to meet him. But the next instant I was blinking the water from my eyes, and he was still there, head thrown back once more.

'JESUS, I DON'T WANT TO DIE!' I cried.

'NO ONE'S GOING TO DIE,' Jesus told me. 'HAVE SOME FAITH. THE STORM IS ENDING.'

'HE'S COMPLETELY FUCKING CRAZY!' Mohammed shouted.

'YOU WATCH YOUR LANGUAGE, MOHAMMED!' I shouted back. But it was hard to disagree with the sentiment.

Jesus *was* completely crazy. That much was obvious. With him perched as he was, the highest bar of the railing was not even level with his waist; all it would take would be the slightest loss of balance, an unusually large wave, and he'd plummet into the sea like a lead weight.

But even as this thought came to me, I realised that something had changed. The sea spray was no longer crashing over the deck with every wave, and although I was still gripping the side rail with both hands, it was no longer a fight to keep my footing. The light was changing too – a rapid brightening from grey to white – and when I looked up, it was as if a hole had been punched through the clouds, as if *The Poseidon* were suddenly floating at the bottom of a vast well of light.

The rain stopped, like someone had switched off a tap. The deck and railings sparkled.

It sounds impossible – I realise this. But I'm not here to tell you what is or isn't possible, only what happened.

When I glanced back at Mohammed, he wasn't gaping exactly, but the look in his eyes told me that he, too, was struggling for an explanation.

Jesus sprang down from the railing like a gymnast dismounting his apparatus; the pink flip-flops made a wet slap as they struck the deck. It was like a whip crack, calling me and Mohammed to attention.

'I think I shall go back down now,' Jesus said. 'I might try to sleep. I'm quite tired.'

With that, he walked back towards the main stairwell as if nothing at all had happened.

'What the fuck was *that*?' Mohammed hissed. After all the shouting, his voice seemed barely a whisper.

91

I shook my head in dumb silence. The whole boat was steaming in the sunlight, making it appear that Jesus was again floating, his feet lost in the rising mist. High above him, a bright rainbow stretched from horizon to horizon.

The sky behind the boat was still grey, and the waves had not abated entirely. It seemed like nothing, compared to what had gone before, but the continued rolling motion did something to reassure me.

'The weather can be weird at sea,' I told Mohammed. 'It can change very quickly. We both know that.'

'Not that quickly,' Mohammed said; then, after a few more moments had passed: 'He *knew*. He said the storm was about to end. He said it and it happened.'

'It's a coincidence,' I told him, but Mohammed did not look convinced. 'Well, I don't know . . . Maybe he could tell before we could. He was up on that railing. Maybe he felt the waves getting smaller before we noticed.' Mohammed nodded slowly, as if this was at least possible.

'Look,' I said. 'It doesn't have to mean anything. I'm not even sure anything happened, not really. The mind distorts things when you're afraid.'

'I wasn't afraid!' Mohammed protested. 'Speak for yourself!'

'Fine!' I told him. 'You weren't afraid. But I was, and whichever way you look at it, it was an extremely stressful situation, so the basic principle still stands. Just because something's out of the ordinary, it doesn't mean it's . . .'

I trailed off. Mohammed was frowning at me, and I could find no sensible way to conclude my thoughts.

We stood on that steaming deck for some time, neither of us saying a word.

PART 2
The Borders

Along the Train Tracks

We sat on a bus bound for the small town of Idomeni at the Greece–Macedonia border. It was the middle of the night – some time around two a.m. – but I was wide awake; my body clock had been ruined over the past week. Mohammed was awake too, but probably for different reasons. He was staring out of the window, as he had been for the last hour, even though there was nothing to see out there. Just darkness and road and the occasional passing vehicle. Every so often, he glanced across the aisle to where Jesus was snoring, a suspicious frown on his face. The frown wasn't new exactly – he'd been frowning at Jesus ever since we'd met him – and yet something had shifted, quite subtly, since the ferry. Since the storm. My brother looked less irritated than he had, and also far less certain.

We'd talked about it, very briefly, after boarding the bus, when Jesus had fallen almost immediately asleep. Mohammed didn't believe in the supernatural any more than I did; and unlike me, the closest he'd ever come to religion was his unwavering worship of FC Barcelona. Yet it was clear that he was having great trouble processing what had apparently happened on the boat.

'He said the storm would stop and it did, just like that. Within *seconds*.'

'Mohammed, you don't need to exaggerate. It wasn't that quick.'

'Within seconds,' my brother repeated. 'It's like he told it to stop.'

'Don't be absurd. That isn't what happened.'

'He's like some . . . weird drunken sorcerer.'

I scoffed at this. 'Coincidence! It was just a freak storm, and a freak coincidence. A complete one-off.'

Mohammed shook his head and mumbled something.

'What?' I asked. 'If you have something else to say, then you should say it.'

'I said that it might not be a one-off. There was another time too.'

'What are you talking about? What other time?'

My brother looked at me with a strange mixture of embarrassment and defiance in his eyes. 'In the supermarket,' he said. 'When he stole the whisky . . . well, I'll admit that I wasn't watching him like a hawk, but still. I *was* with him the whole time. I still don't know how he managed it . . .'

'Well, somehow he did, obviously.'

'Zain, the man doesn't even have all his fucking fingers!' Mohammed said this loud enough that the woman in the seat in front looked around disapprovingly. He ignored her. 'Most of the time he struggles to walk in a straight line. We're not talking about a master criminal here.'

I shook my head, but kept quiet. It went without saying that

96

Jesus was not a man over-endowed with manual dexterity; but neither was Mohammed a competent watchman, however much he protested. It was far easier to believe a lapse from my brother than . . . whatever the alternative was. That Jesus had somehow magicked the whisky into his underpants. I was about to raise this point, but Mohammed leapt in first, his voice now an ominous whisper.

'Listen,' he hissed. 'What do we even know about him? Has it ever occurred to you that him being here makes no sense?'

'What do you mean?' I whispered back.

'It makes no sense!' Mohammed repeated. 'Why is he even in Europe? What's he doing here?'

'The same things as us – obviously. The same things as everyone else on this bus. He's trying to—'

My brother started speaking over me, still not loudly, but with much urgency. 'It cost us a thousand euros each to get on one of those smugglers' boats. A thousand euros, Zain! Think about it. Do you think it cost Jesus any less?'

Usually, my brother could not be described as a very deep thinker, and subtlety has never been one of his strengths. But he isn't an idiot; and here he had perceived something that I had somehow missed. If Jesus had ever had a thousand euros, it seemed unlikely that he'd have spent it on a boat ride across the Aegean. There was only one thing he was likely to spend his money on. The realisation came as an eerie shock, but my brother was absolutely right. On a fundamental level, Jesus being in Europe made no sense at all. He may have had good reasons for leaving Iraq, but why leave Turkey? Why not stay and spend his thousand euros on alcohol?

Neither Mohammed nor I said anything after that. He realised that he'd made his point and turned his face to the window. I spent the next hour deep in thought.

Some of what my brother had said was easy to dismiss, at least in theory. I didn't have to open up *The God Delusion* to know what Richard Dawkins would say about the strange occurrence on the ferry. That it *had* been a strange occurrence, I was willing to concede. It may not have been a matter of seconds, as Mohammed claimed, but that storm had disappeared quicker than seemed possible. And Jesus had . . . guessed that it was about to end, which seemed equally improbable. But coincidences *do* happen. Perceptions can be tricked, especially in stressful situations. That is what Professor Dawkins would have said. He would have pointed out that an improbable event is not the same as an impossible event, that we should never confuse a mystery with a miracle.

In short, Jesus was certainly weird, and indisputably a drunk, but he was not some kind of sorcerer. He could not see into the future, and he could not command the weather.

It was reassuring to look over at Jesus as I processed these thoughts. He did not look miraculous; he looked the exact opposite. He was slumped across both seats with his flip-flopped feet protruding a small way into the aisle – enough to be an inconvenience to anyone who wanted to pass him to get to the toilet. He was still snoring and his lips were very slightly drawn back in the hint of a snarl. Every so often, he twitched. In all honesty, he reminded me of a stray dog that used to live outside our apartment block in Latakia. That dog also looked like it had been recently blown up; it had patchy matted fur, and walked with a pronounced limp. Yet, whatever misfortune it had suffered, it was still a strangely friendly and trusting creature. It would often pad up to me as I left the building, its tail wagging, and a pat on the head was enough to ensure that it would follow me to the shops and back. To me, Jesus had a similar demeanour – an animalistic honesty and straightforwardness. It might sound odd, given that he also stole and withheld significant personal information, such as his real name, but there you go. I can't explain it any better. When I looked at him sleeping, I was reminded of that stray dog, and I felt the same pity.

There would come a time when I'd have to ask him some of the questions my brother had raised, but for now, it seemed an unnecessary complication.

With this resolved in my mind, I soon fell asleep.

I was woken by the low sun glaring through the window. The clock on the phone showed that it had just gone six thirty; Google Maps showed that we were about fifty kilometres from the border. Outside was flat farmland in various hues of green and gold and brown.

Mohammed had also fallen asleep at some point, with his head against the window, and I was unsurprised to discover that Jesus was still snoring. In my short experience of the man, he was extremely good at sleeping. It didn't seem to matter where or when. His feet were still poking out into the aisle; as far as I could tell, he'd barely moved a muscle in the last six hours.

The bus we were on was owned by a company that usually ran excursions for tourists. But there weren't many tourists this year. There were refugees, instead – all wanting transport to the Macedonian border. We'd been approached by a broker selling tickets almost as soon as we disembarked from the ferry in Athens. At fifty euros each, it was a little more expensive than the public bus service, but this was offset by the fact that it went directly to the border and departed at midnight. The alternative was probably another night spent at the port, or in a public park. With its onboard toilet and climate control, the tourist bus was, by comparison, a hotel on wheels.

Mohammed and Jesus were both awake by the time we pulled to a stop, on a dusty and deserted road just outside of Idomeni town. There was a small roadside shop where I bought water and fruit and sandwiches and whisky for our breakfast, and because I'd left Mohammed outside, I didn't have to endure his disapproving looks. After that, we walked the short distance to the train tracks, which crossed the border a kilometre to the north. The bus driver had advised us that the Macedonian army was allowing refugees through at this unofficial crossing. We didn't need to worry about walking on the train tracks because all trains to Macedonia had been temporarily suspended; when I asked him why, he told me it was because of all the people walking on the train tracks.

So we headed north, at the back of a procession of about fifty other refugees. There was birdsong and the noise of insects in the tangled grasses along the embankment, but no one spoke. For once, Jesus didn't moan. The day was still cool, and we were rested, and soon we'd be crossing into another country, apparently without impediment. There were at least ten minutes when I felt extremely optimistic.

When we got to the unofficial checkpoint there were several hundred people already waiting. Maybe as many as a thousand. The crowd was large and dense enough that I couldn't see what was happening at the front.

I climbed a small tree. From its lower branches, I could make out half a dozen army trucks, parked just beyond some temporary wire-mesh fencing which I assume marked the border. The railway track was blocked by a line of at least twenty men wearing army fatigues. The refugees at the front of the crowd were mostly sitting on the ground, which suggested they'd been here a while. Some were lying down, their heads resting on backpacks. There were more people here than I'd first thought.

'What's going on?' Mohammed asked from the foot of the tree. He looked as if he was also considering climbing it. Jesus hadn't followed us. He had sat down on the train tracks, his face unreadable behind his 1980s wraparound sunglasses.

'I'm not sure what's going on,' I told Mohammed. 'I'll go and ask someone. You stay with Jesus.'

He gave me the normal glare upon receiving this instruction, but I jumped down from the tree and headed for the crowd before he could protest too much. No one at the back had any idea what was happening, which was unsurprising, since most of them had arrived at the same time as us. I squeezed further forward, murmuring apologies and rebutting accusations of queue-jumping. It was easier once I was past the standing group; after that, I just had to thread my way through the seated until I was face to face with one of the border guards. I smiled, and he stared at me without expression.

'Do you speak English?' I asked.

He shook his head, somewhat paradoxically.

I tried again.

'Are we going to be let through?' I asked.

'You wait here, please.' This was the next guard along, gesturing back towards the crowd.

'How long will we have to wait?' I asked him.

He made the shooing gesture again, and someone shouted in Arabic that I was wasting my time; the guards weren't interested in answering questions. It took me a moment to identify the speaker. It was a man not much older than me. He was sitting among a pocket of people a few metres away, wrapped in a tattered blanket.

'Do *you* know what's happening?' I asked.

'Nothing's happening,' he said. 'Not for the last few hours.'

'How long have you been here?'

'Since last night.'

'Last night?'

He shrugged. 'We thought it would be easier to cross at night.'

'I thought they were letting people through?'

'They are. A few hundred at a time. They're prioritising families with young children.'

I frowned at this unwelcome news. Even with Jesus pretending to be our uncle, I doubted that we'd meet the selection criteria. It would have helped if Mohammed wasn't the toughest fourteen-year-old on the planet. A few tears on his part would surely have benefited us here. Maybe I could persuade him to rub his eyes raw while we waited? No, he'd probably just end up looking angry . . .

I thanked the man I'd been talking to and headed back through the crowd.

'So what do we do now?' Mohammed asked, after I'd told him and Jesus the bad news.

'I suppose we just wait,' I said. 'There's not much else we can do.'

Mohammed swore and started kicking the rocks at the side of the train track, and Jesus watched him for a while, apparently fascinated by the outburst. I went back to the tree I'd climbed and sat with my back against its trunk.

The day grew hotter and the crowd swelled as people continued to trickle in from further down the train line. I tried to get some more sleep but couldn't, so I spent some time studying the border on Google Maps.

A few hours later, there was a small riot.

I climbed my tree again, not out of cowardice, but because it wasn't clear what was happening at first. There had been movement in the crowd ahead of us, and then lots of angry shouting in English and Arabic, and some other languages that I didn't recognise. From my new vantage point, I was able to see most of what was transpiring. The guards had let some more people cross the border – there were a few hundred further along the train track, some walking north and some facing back to see what the shouting was about. The problem was that the Macedonians were now trying to staunch the flow and reseal the border. The crowd was surging forward in response, and more guards had appeared from somewhere, wearing full riot gear over their army uniforms. They started to form a barrier with their shields, and for a few moments it looked as if that was going to be the end of it. But then a group of young men on our side charged forward and managed to break through the line at several points. I'm using the term 'our side' in a geographical sense, not to suggest that I suddenly felt part of a faction in this conflict, though I suppose I was, by default. Either way, there obviously weren't going to be any winners in this situation; it would be a shitty outcome for everyone. In my limited experience, most conflicts end up this way.

The guards started striking out with batons, and the men on 'our side' responded by throwing punches and hurling rocks. Before long, tear gas was being fired into the crowd, followed by stun grenades. Even from my position, a good hundred metres back, the flashes were bright enough to momentarily blind, and the noise was thunderous. The branch I was on started to shake, and it took me a moment to realise that this wasn't from the concussive force of the explosions. It was my brother scrambling up beside me. He looked excited rather than scared. His eyes shone with what I took to be a wild blood lust.

'I think this might be our chance,' he yelled.

'Forget it, Mohammed. We're not getting involved in a riot.'

'People are getting across. Look!'

He was right. Amidst the general confusion, a handful of people had made it past the police line, but many more were retreating, lots of them bloodied or temporarily blinded.

'I'm not letting you get tear-gassed. Forget it. We're staying right where we are – all three of us.'

I looked down to confirm that Jesus was not doing anything crazy. He wasn't. He was standing on his tiptoes, trying to get a better view of what was happening, but his face remained placid. Obviously, he was not gripped by the same battle madness that had Mohammed, who was again insisting that we should make a dash for the border.

'They're Europeans,' he reasoned. 'They're not going to shoot us or anything like that. The worst they can do is hit us with their sticks. It's better than waiting here another ten hours.'

I ignored him, and not just because he was talking nonsense. The line of guards was clearly firming up, and most of the crowd

had started to fall back. If there had been some limited opportunity to get across the border, it had now passed. What was left
was plenty of evidence that we shouldn't go anywhere near those
Europeans with their 'sticks'. Many of the people who'd been
involved in the rush forward were now nursing cuts and bruises.
Parents were trying to comfort their crying children, and one
man was screaming in Arabic that we were not animals and the
guards had no right to keep us penned in here. The guards'
faces, meanwhile, displayed a mixture of grim determination,
anger and shock, as if many weren't sure what had just happened.
A lot of them were no older than me.

My brother had stopped ranting by now. I gave him a pointed
look before I dropped down from the tree. He followed a moment
later, and we both walked back to Jesus. We all stood side by
side in silence, surveying the carnage.

'Well? What now?' Mohammed asked. 'I don't think they'll
be letting anyone else across any time soon.'

For once we were in complete agreement.

Mohammed pointed an accusing finger in the direction of the
guards. 'I don't want to stay here with these sisterfuckers,' he
said.

He was upset – though he'd never admit it – so I let the
obscenity slide.

'Jesus, what do you think?' I asked.

He thought about it for a good five seconds. 'I think Mohammed
is correct,' he said. 'These are the sort of men who would fuck
their sisters without a second thought.'

'Okay . . . What about the rest? Do we stay or do we go?'

'The wise man chooses his battles carefully,' Jesus told me. 'I
think, for now, we should retreat.'

Mohammed nodded vigorously. 'There must be other places we can cross. They can't block the whole border.'

As you know, I had studied the map, so I already had a tentative back-up plan in mind. I'd identified a crossing point that was less likely to be policed. 'There might be another way,' I told them. 'But . . . well, it's not entirely straightforward. It involves a little bit of walking.'

Mohammed shrugged. 'As long as it doesn't involve any swimming.'

'It involves hardly any swimming,' I told him.

The Two Towns

We walked back along the train tracks and on into town. It was hot now, and it took a long time. We stopped to rest periodically, but with the sun overhead and barely a cloud in the sky, there was very little shade to be found. The surrounding area was all thirsty farmland and drooping orchards, pancake-flat except for some blue mountains rising hazily at the horizon.

Idomeni itself was tiny, and its narrow streets were deserted. We walked between uniformly whitewashed and shuttered houses without seeing a soul. Apart from the rhythmical slap of Jesus's flip-flops, there was no noise at all – no background traffic and not a breath of wind. In the central square, the Greek flag hung limply from its flagpole.

'Where is everyone?' Mohammed asked, his voice disconcertingly loud. 'It's like they've all been abducted by aliens.'

'I think they are hiding from the sun,' Jesus said.

This was also the explanation I favoured. Idomeni was like an oven; no one with any sense would be walking its streets at this time of day.

In the square, there were two buildings which stood out from the rest. One was a church, plain and white and not much larger than the surrounding houses, but distinguishable by the large cross affixed to its roof; the cross was studded with light bulbs, and there was an improbable bell tower that looked to have been improvised from an old electricity pylon. The other building was the largest in the square by some way, and I was almost certain it was some kind of small hotel or hostel. It didn't have a sign – at least not in English – but there were some tables and chairs outside on a small raised terrace, and another Greek flag was on display, drooping from a first-floor balcony. The doorway was small and obscured by hanging beads, so it wasn't obvious if the premises were open or closed, but it looked to be our best hope for escaping the heat for a while. The church could be our back-up option.

Beyond the tightly woven beads, the door turned out to be open, but the space beyond was as dark as a cave. Removing my sunglasses did nothing to alleviate the temporary blindness. I stopped abruptly, and felt Mohammed bang into my back, followed by Jesus banging into *his* back. The blackness slowly lessened, and I found myself in the world's smallest, dingiest bar. A couple of chairs and tables resolved amidst the gloom, followed by three seated figures. Three very old Greek men with eyes like fat black buttons. Mohammed muttered something idiotic about vampires, which drew no response; unsurprisingly, the Greek men did not speak Arabic. They didn't speak English, either, but using rudimentary sign language, I managed to establish that we were allowed to come in and sit down. The man whom I assumed was the landlord mimed drinking from a bottle, and I nodded enthusiastically and ordered three Coca-Colas and, after a short conference with Jesus, a glass of beer. The landlord served them with ice and lemon and a small dish of olives on the side.

Let me tell you: it was the finest Coca-Cola I have ever drunk, and in other circumstances, I would have happily stayed in that bar for the rest of the day. As it was, we stayed for maybe an hour. I ordered more drinks, charged the phone, and went over the plan with Mohammed and Jesus a second time. It was much easier to show them the map here, away from the glare of the sun, but there was still a lot of guesswork that had to be done. The landlord's lack of English meant that we couldn't ask him about the river, and unfortunately, the bar did not have Wi-Fi. It was possible that the internet had not yet arrived in Idomeni. It was that sort of town.

It was still hot when we left, but no longer unbearable, and the sun had shifted enough for the buildings to cast short shadows in the square. We headed north out of town, following a narrow road that eventually started to curve back on itself. At this point, we consulted Google Maps again, and then struck out over the fields.

It took about an hour to reach the river. It wasn't very far on the map, but our route ran through a small woodland, with no obvious paths. Thankfully, there were no soldiers patrolling here; as I'd suspected, the Macedonians had their hands full policing the crowds at the train track, and probably the main roads, too. In the larger scheme of things, the river was not even a minor concern.

The channel itself was about thirty metres across, but the water level seemed quite low, and it was not flowing quickly. I'd hoped it might be completely dry at this time of year, but this was good enough for our purposes. Jesus had assured me that he was able to swim, but I didn't want to test this claim if we could avoid it. With luck, we'd be able to wade all the way across.

We didn't bother removing our clothes; with the day being so hot, they'd dry off quickly, so there didn't seem much point. We loaded our valuables into the waterproof bags and set out straightaway. Jesus let out a small yelp of delight as he stepped into the water, and I could understand why. Flowing out of the distant mountains, the river was gloriously cool, and if I'd had any doubts about the wisdom of our plan, they were quickly diminished. Aside from the occasional rock, the footing was not too difficult, and after sloping sharply from the bank, the channel soon levelled out. The water came not much higher than my waist – or to Mohammed's chest – and by carrying our backpacks overhead, we were able to keep our spare clothes dry as well. The waterproof bags were entirely redundant.

After just a few minutes, we were stepping out on to the far bank – a bank that looked pretty much identical to the one we'd just left, but was, apparently, another new country.

We walked for about ten minutes along the riverbank, encountering no soldiers or police officers. The only people we saw were a couple of Macedonian fishermen, who gave us small frowns as we passed. This was understandable, as it was quite obvious where we had come from. Our clothes were no longer dripping, but they were still damp; there was a high waterline clearly visible on Jesus's shirt, and I was conscious of how my trainers continued to squelch with every footstep. I tried to make the situation less awkward by saying hello in English and responding to the frowns with a cheery smile, as if we were just a regular group of hikers enjoying the countryside. Jesus gave an enthusiastic wave, Mohammed scowled, and the men went back to their fishing.

Soon enough we reached a road leading into town. The town

was called Gevgelija, and it was full of casinos. I'd already noted this detail from Google Maps, but it was just as apparent in the three-dimensional world, and incongruous given the size of the place. Gevgelija was larger than Idomeni, but this was not saying much. You could still walk from one end to the other in less than fifteen minutes. In place of the whitewashed houses on the Greek side of the border, the streets here were lined with shops and small apartment blocks painted in pastel shades of yellow and orange. We passed numerous hotels, too – far more than you'd expect to see in a modestly sized border town. I suppose it must have been a consequence of Gevgelija's thriving gambling industry. In any case, I was thankful that finding a room for the night would not present the same headache it had on Samos. It was now late in the afternoon, and I had no intention of spending another night sleeping on the streets.

The hotel I eventually settled on may have been the worst in Macedonia. When I first set eyes on it, it seemed to me *reassuringly* shabby, with cracked plaster and peeling paintwork that I hoped would translate into an affordable night's rest. The interior was dingy enough to hide any water stains that remained on our clothes, and my trainers had ceased their incriminating squelching some time ago.

The man behind the reception desk was short and overweight, with red cheeks, beady eyes and a strange, thin moustache, as neat as if it had been drawn on in fine-tipped pen. I assumed he was the manager because he was smoking a cigar and tried to charge us twice for our room.

'We only want one room,' I repeated. '*One* room.'

'The room is double room, for two persons,' he told us. 'You are three persons.'

'Do you have any rooms for three people?' I asked.

'No.'

'Then we'll take a double room.'

'It has only two beds.'

'Yes, I understand that. We'll be fine.'

The man gave an exasperated sigh before taking another puff on his cigar. 'If you want extra person you must pay extra charge.'

'Why? It won't cost you any more.'

He shrugged, as if this was quite irrelevant. 'One thousand denars – twenty euro.'

Mohammed, who had been following the exchange closely, began swearing at this point ('He's another Macedonian sister fucker!') and Jesus started cackling. The hotelier folded his arms across his chest and frowned deeply around his cigar. He may not have understood Arabic, but he understood that he was being sworn at in a foreign language, by an adolescent, and nobody likes that.

'Mohammed, quiet,' I said, also reverting to Arabic. 'You are not helping this negotiation.'

'He wants to rip us off!' my brother shouted. 'He expects us just to stand here and take it while he feeds us the shaft!'

'I have the situation under control. Jesus, show him your fingers.'

Jesus did not have to ask which ones. He held his right hand aloft, displaying his stumps.

'We are fugitives from war and terror,' I told the hotel manager. 'This man's fingers were cut off by Al-Qaeda. He has suffered enough and should not have to face additional charges for a hotel room!'

Jesus chose this moment to belch loudly, releasing whisky fumes into the air.

'Ten euro,' the hotel manager said.

'We're leaving!' Mohammed shouted in English. 'There are other hotels!' He turned and stomped toward the door, giving me little choice but to chase after him, at which point the hotel manager began to back-pedal, shouting that there was no need for us to leave. He was cancelling the extra charge as an act of charity.

After a short consultation, we decided to stay.

The room was in keeping with the rest of the hotel. There were twin beds that groaned alarmingly as soon as any weight was placed upon them. The carpet and curtains were worn and dotted with many cigarette burns. Other furnishings included a wardrobe with a collapsed interior, and a lamp that cast almost no light. Weirdly, switching it on seemed to make the room even darker, with shadows creeping from every nook and cranny. But none of this mattered, really. It was somewhere to rest, somewhere better than a park bench or train station, and we'd not had to pay for it twice. With so many miles still ahead of us, I wasn't going to spend a euro more than I had to.

There was some additional bedding in the broken wardrobe, and with this and a couple of frayed cushions, I started to construct an extra bed in the corner of the room. I wasn't going to try to persuade Mohammed that we should attempt to share one of the narrow singles; he would have had a fit at the very suggestion. Anyway, all in all, I considered that I'd probably sleep better on my makeshift mattress on the floor. That it would be *me* sleeping on the floor had been my default assumption, but almost as soon as I'd thrown every spare blanket, pillow and cushion into the corner, Jesus removed his flip-flops and stretched out on the newly built bed.

'I think I will sleep very well here,' he said.

After that, he lay flat on his back for some time, his eyes closed and his hands clasped at his waist. I didn't think he was asleep, because he wasn't snoring. He looked more as if he was . . . meditating or something.

I had my first shower in days. The bathtub was stained yellow and the shower curtain was mouldy and the showerhead had not been affixed high enough to the wall, which meant that I had to hunch down to rinse my hair. But this was a trivial concern, all things considered. The water was hot, and the dust and grime and salt and sweat and sand were evacuated from my body like an exorcised demon. It was a beautiful feeling.

Afterwards, I told Mohammed and Jesus that they should shower too, just in case this hadn't occurred to them, and after that, we changed some currency and went to a nearby shop to buy food and a small bottle of detergent. Back in the hotel bathroom, I washed our clothes in the sink, rung them out over the bathtub, and then hung them wherever I could – on the towel rail, on the shower-curtain rail and on various door handles. More or less on a whim, I also cleaned Jesus's flip-flops, which were smeared with sediment from the river. It only took a couple of minutes before they were as good as new. I patted them dry with toilet paper and then set them down on the bathroom floor, where they gleamed pinkly under the fluorescent light.

Jesus was asleep early, but Mohammed stayed up late playing on the phone. I've no idea *what* he was playing, because when I asked he grunted angrily and told me that he needed to concentrate. But that incident aside, he looked as contented as he ever looked these days. Eventually, he gave what I took to be a reluctant sigh and plugged the phone back into the socket at the far side of the room.

'Do you think they'll ever make a phone that recharges in, like, five minutes?' he asked me.

'Maybe they'll make one that doesn't even need recharging,' I told him. 'It could run off solar power or something. Or maybe they could just beam the electricity in wirelessly.'

Mohammed's eyes brightened at the possibility. 'That would be awesome.'

'Yes, it would.'

He was asleep not long after that. I continued to read the Bible that I'd discovered in my bedside drawer. I wasn't sure what it was doing there, since the hotel's proprietor didn't strike me as the sort of man who'd furnish each room with religious literature. I assumed it must have been left by a previous guest. In any event, I'd never tried to read the Bible before; I was familiar with some of the material, but only from its coverage in the Qur'an and *The God Delusion*.

It was not easy to read. This wasn't because of the language, which was modern English and quite straightforward. The inside cover proclaimed that it was the 'English Standard Version', and, for the most part, it presented less of a challenge than reading the Qur'an in classical Arabic – though I should add that it was also somewhat less poetic. The main problem I faced was that the text was tiny and the light very poor. I had to squint to decipher it.

I read the first part of Genesis, before skipping ahead to the Gospel of St Matthew. I wanted to know what the Bible said about Jesus Christ – the sober, Palestinian Jesus Christ.

It started off slowly, with several pages devoted to who fathered whom across the forty-two generations from Abraham to Joseph. But I persevered through this, and had soon moved on to the early days of Jesus's preaching and the Sermon on the Mount.

Most of his ideas seemed like good ideas, regardless of whether he was the son of God or not. I must have drifted off at some point. I remember reading about him healing many lepers, and the next thing I knew, I was waking up with my face amidst the pages. I'd managed to crease several, so I set about trying to iron them with my hand.

My fingertips stopped abruptly, just below the subtitle for Matthew 8:23.

It was in bold type: **Jesus Calms a Storm**.

I closed the Bible with a sharp slap that caused Mohammed to mumble and turn in his sleep. I placed it on the bedside table and stared at the wall for some minutes, and then picked it up again and read through the offending verses four or five times.

AND WHEN HE GOT INTO THE BOAT, HIS DISCIPLES FOLLOWED HIM. AND BEHOLD, THERE AROSE A GREAT STORM ON THE SEA, SO THAT THE BOAT WAS BEING SWAMPED BY THE WAVES; BUT HE WAS ASLEEP. AND THEY WENT AND WOKE HIM, SAYING, 'SAVE US, LORD; WE ARE PERISHING.' AND HE SAID TO THEM, 'WHY ARE YOU AFRAID, O YOU OF LITTLE FAITH?' THEN HE ROSE AND REBUKED THE WINDS AND THE SEA, AND THERE WAS A GREAT CALM. AND THE MEN MARVELLED, SAYING, 'WHAT SORT OF MAN IS THIS, THAT EVEN WINDS AND SEA OBEY HIM?'

I lay back on my bed, and reality trickled from the room one grain at a time, like sand from an hourglass.

I closed my eyes, but I did not sleep.

The Infinite Ticket Office

The following morning, at breakfast, Jesus told us that he had received instructions in his dreams. Those were his exact words. I had a spoonful of yoghurt and muesli halfway to my mouth, but I no longer knew what to do with it. I glanced at Mohammed, who didn't even bother rolling his eyes. He gave the smallest of shrugs.

I placed the spoon back in my bowl and rested my hands on the table, one on top of the other. 'Okay, Jesus,' I said. 'Go ahead.'

'There are men shouting,' he began, 'but it's only noise. I don't understand any of the words. Everything is in a great confusion. There's smoke and lightning, and a sound like metal ripping. It feels like the end of all things. Like everything else has been leading us to this one moment.'

'Us?' I kept my voice level. Mohammed sighed and shook his head.

Jesus gestured a small circle with his left forefinger. 'Us. The three of us. We're all there at this moment. You, Zain, are afraid that something terrible is about to happen, and you want to get away with all possible haste. But I am not afraid. I can see very clearly that a path has opened up before us. There's something . . . like a cave. It appears in front of us like a huge black mouth, like the gateway to the underworld. But this is the path we must take. That message is very clear to me. My job is to lead you through the smoke and lightning and darkness, until we reach a place of safety.'

There was a long silence, broken eventually by Mohammed rising from his seat. 'I'm going to get some more toast,' he said.

I drank some coffee and wondered what to do with this new information. Jesus's strange apocalyptic dream, as vivid as it was vague. If I'd had a reasonable night's sleep – if it hadn't been for the events of the past forty-eight hours – it might have been easier to deal with.

'Listen, Jesus,' I said after a while. 'Your dream was just a dream. That's all. It doesn't mean anything.'

Jesus shook his head earnestly. 'I have had this dream twice now. That's how I know it contains instructions.'

'It doesn't contain instructions. It's just your brain talking to itself, telling itself stories.'

'Pah! My brain is not capable of such wild inventions.'

'It's a dream. Nothing more.'

'But I have had this dream twice, exactly the same. That seems to me—'

'Jesus, please be quiet. I don't want to talk about your dream anymore. I just want to eat the rest of my breakfast in peace.'

Mohammed returned from the toaster and joined us in our silence. A silence that was not at all peaceful.

I spent the next five minutes staring at my coffee cup, but it did very little good. Even from the corner of my eye, I could tell that Jesus was hurt.

The train station was chaos. There had to be a thousand people out front, and one glance was enough to infer that many of them had been there all night. Some were still curled up on sleeping bags or squashed cardboard boxes, and more were slumped on their bags in the shade of the station building. Affixed to the wall was a lone bin which looked to have erupted in the night, spewing its filthy innards over much of the surrounding area. A trail of plastic bottle caps and apple cores led to an enterprising grocer who had set up his stall at one end of the broad concourse, and every so often he bellowed that he had water and vitamins, water and vitamins. Not far beyond this, a couple of mounted policemen surveyed the scene with dispassionate eyes, and there were two more on foot, located at the entrance to the station. Clearly insufficient for a crowd of this size, but I guessed that the majority were still having to hold the border.

Fortunately, a repetition of yesterday's violence seemed unlikely, at least for now. The faces in that crowd betrayed a large range of negative emotions, from restlessness to numbed boredom, from anxiety to anger, but underlying this was a much stronger sense of weariness. Everyone looked bone tired. Of course, it's possible that I was projecting my own mood in this instance, but only to a small extent. For the time being, we were all too exhausted to riot.

There was an extremely long queue snaking out of the station building, which I had to assume was for the ticket office. It was either that or the toilet; but even by recent standards, a toilet queue of this magnitude seemed improbable. It was long enough that its far end stretched out of view, and I couldn't be sure that it was even moving. Most of the people in the queue had chosen to sit on the ground rather than stand, and some appeared to be sleeping, which was obviously not a good omen.

We walked towards the back of the queue while I attempted to do a rough head count, but then Mohammed started swearing under his breath and I immediately lost both my concentration and my enthusiasm for the pointless project. After that, a little girl ran out in front of me and I almost stepped on her. It was Aida, as in the famous Italian opera.

'Hello, Aida,' I said.

She looked at me, wide-eyed and without recognition – perhaps due to my thickening beard – before darting back to her mother in the queue.

'Hello, Sabeen,' I said.

'Zain, Mohammed! It's good to see you. Hello, Jesus.'

Jesus bowed.

'Have you been here long?' I asked Sabeen.

'No, not long. They let us over the border a couple of hours ago. How about you?'

'We got across yesterday afternoon.'

'We walked through the river,' Jesus added proudly.

Sabeen gave me a questioning look, so I nodded in confirmation. 'The border was closed. We had to find an alternative route and . . . well, here we are.'

Her eyes had grown worried. I'm not sure why, since wading through the river was a far more sensible route into the country than waiting on the whim of the Macedonian armed forces. But I suppose that might not have been evident to someone who had not had the chance to compare the two. In any case, her gaze was sufficiently concerned, and concerning, that Mohammed took half a step backwards and shuffled on his feet. No doubt he suspected that she might try to cuddle us again. She definitely had that air about her.

'Are you okay, Zain?' she said after a moment. 'You look . . . well, you look very tired.'

'Yes. I am tired.' There wasn't much else I could say. I couldn't tell her that I'd been awake all night worrying that I was travelling with a prophet. An actual living prophet. This thought could not be aired in the light of day, among sane company. 'You look tired, too,' I added. 'Everyone looks tired.'

Sabeen ignored this. 'Do you have train tickets yet?' she asked.

'No, not yet. We were just—'

'Listen. Maybe you could stay and talk to me for a bit?' She patted the ground next to her. 'I'd appreciate the company.'

It took me a moment to understand the subtext: she was inviting us to cut the queue! Usually, I'd have regarded this action as morally dubious, but she'd phrased it in such a way that it would have seemed impolite to say no – and equally impolite had anyone else in the queue complained. It was very clever, really, and was obviously going to save us considerable time. Judging by the number of people here, it might be the difference between boarding a train today and boarding one tomorrow.

With much gratitude, I sank to the ground, and neither Mohammed nor Jesus hesitated to follow.

In the couple of hours she'd been there, Sabeen had spoken to a number of people at the station, and was able to give us a better idea of the situation, which was even worse than it appeared. There were only three trains a day from Gevgelija, not very large trains, and every inch of space was fiercely contested. Apparently, the ticket office was happy to sell an infinite number of tickets, but the capacity of the trains was, unsurprisingly, finite. To complicate matters further, there was no queuing system once you passed through the station entrance, so boarding the trains was a complete free-for-all – survival of the fittest. Rumour spoke of platforms crowded with hundreds and hundreds of would-be passengers, of frequent fist-fights, of people scrabbling through carriage windows when the doorways became blocked.

'We'll do whatever we can to help you,' I told Sabeen, glancing at her very young children, though I had grave doubts about our usefulness in this context. I wasn't a fighter, obviously. I was probably the last person you'd want guarding your back in an angry crowd. And as for Jesus and Mohammed, well . . . Jesus was a barely functioning alcoholic, and Mohammed was fourteen; he had a terrible temper, and the devil's own vocabulary, but lacked the muscle mass to back it up.

In truth, I half-expected Sabeen to laugh at my offer. But she didn't. She touched my arm and said a quiet thank you, and nothing more.

My exhaustion receded. It did not go away, but it became something fuzzy at the back of my mind, no longer threatening to floor me. I suppose it's possible that I had reached a kind of plateau, a maximum level of tiredness after which no more could be accrued. A tolerance of sorts. The only peculiarity that remained was that niggle of unreality that I'd started experiencing in the night. The movements I perceived around me – people crossing the concourse, traffic on the road beyond – seemed a little too slow, or else too fast, as if time were not quite marching to its expected beat. Colours seemed too intense, and the day too bright.

The sun blazed higher and higher, and the shade from the railway building retreated, taking Jesus with it. He sat against the dark face of the wall and occasionally drank, drawing critical glances from those around him, even though he was not being disruptive. He was just keeping to himself.

Mohammed left us shortly afterwards. He was drawn away by a couple of boys his own age who were passing a football back and forth between them, across ten clear metres at the centre of the concourse. The line between them became a small triangle, and before long, Mohammed was impressing the other two with his ability to juggle the ball between his head, chest, knees and feet. I'm sure you're familiar with this exercise. In English, it goes by the extremely literal name of 'keepy-uppy'; this is the only English word I've ever learned from my brother. His Lionel Messi shirt was freshly laundered and resplendent in the bright sunshine, and his performance was drawing more and more gazes as it became ever more elaborate. But if he was aware of his growing audience, it didn't put him off. My brother thrived on that sort of attention, and I knew for a fact that he could manage a hundred keepy-uppies without breaking a sweat. If he wanted to, he could probably keep that football in the air indefinitely.

I have to admit, it was an impressive sight, even for a non-football-fan. Time seemed to slow and stretch its lazy limbs. The ball rose and fell, flashing in the sunlight, and Mohammed moved with an easy, practised grace. At this distance, I couldn't see the hardness I was used to seeing in his eyes, the tension that never quite left. He looked relaxed and happy. He looked so *normal*

– just a fourteen-year-old boy showing off with a football. I removed the phone from my pocket and I took a photo. It came out a little blurry, but it was good enough for my purposes. The moment was captured, held safely in my palm.

'Your brother is very skilled,' Sabeen said, as I returned the phone to my pocket.

'He thinks he's going to be a professional,' I told her. 'He thinks he's going to play for FC Barcelona. Or Manchester United if things don't go so well.'

'Maybe he will.'

'Not before he gets a good education,' I said.

This made her laugh for some reason.

'What about you? Your brother dreams of being a footballer. What are *your* dreams?'

'Nothing so glamourous.' I thought for a moment, though I didn't really need to. 'I'd like a quiet life. The quietest imaginable. I've always wanted to be an academic, like my father. Lots of time to read and learn and think.'

'What about a family? Children?'

'I think it's unlikely.'

'I'm sure you'd make a great father some day.'

I blushed. Usually, I'm adept at deflecting a comment such as this one. Usually, I'd have said something non-committal, or just accepted the compliment graciously. But for some reason, I found that I didn't want to. Not with Sabeen. It's strange, but sometimes talking to the right person at the right time can untangle the tightest of knots.

So I told her. It came out little more than a whisper. The concourse was noisy, filled with the sound of a hundred different conversations, so it would have been impossible for anyone to overhear us. Still, some things you learn not to shout about. When the potential fallout is a three-year prison sentence, being circumspect becomes second nature.

Her eyes were full of understanding, but her cheeks were flushed; I thought she was probably embarrassed at having embarrassed me. Oddly, this went a long way to diminishing my own awkwardness. 'I haven't told many people,' I said. 'Just a couple of close friends at university. Female friends. I have good instincts when it comes to knowing who to trust.'

'Your parents?' Sabeen asked. 'Did you ever talk to them?'

'No. I think my mum probably suspected, but not my dad. It's not the sort of thing that would have even occurred to him. They . . .' I trailed off, shaking my head. Sabeen waited without saying anything. She was stroking Rihanna's hair, very slowly, over and over. 'I wanted to tell them,' I said. 'I *would* have told them. I thought I had more time.'

'What about Mohammed?' Sabeen asked.

'God, no! Mohammed . . . would not understand. He'd be ashamed.'

'He might surprise you.'

'No. He wouldn't. He'd . . . I'm not judging him for it, but he's a fourteen-year-old boy with a normal fourteen-year-old boy's opinions. In a few years it might be different. Living in a more tolerant country might make a difference. But right now . . . right now, we have bigger things to deal with.'

Sabeen looked at me, but said nothing. After a moment, she shuffled a little closer, carefully, so as not to disturb Rihanna. She placed a hand on my arm. 'If you were my son, I'd be very proud of you,' she said.

I started to cry, very quietly, behind my sunglasses. It was just the smallest of trickles, and quickly suppressed, but it still helped. Sabeen kept her hand resting lightly on my arm, and neither of us spoke for a long time. I wanted her to keep her hand there forever.

On the Threshold

It took us the rest of the day to board a train, and two more to reach the Hungarian border, gateway to the European Union. Regarding that journey, there is little to report. It was exhausting and uncomfortable. It was stressful and tedious. We slumped in a series of airless aisles and corridors, unable to stretch our muscles for hours on end. There were queues for everything. Queues for tickets and trains, queues for food, queues for water, queues for electricity and toilets. Queues to get into Serbia and queues for permits for onward travel. It was at the Serbian border that we were again separated from Sabeen and her girls. They were deemed vulnerable persons and given priority crossing. We were not, and had to wait many more hours.

I felt a deep pang of sorrow and regret when Sabeen left us. Because of the overcrowding everywhere, we'd not had another chance to speak privately. Yet I found the simple fact of her presence comforting. I was so used to having to hide a part of myself, fearing the consequences should anyone find out. But

Sabeen knew. She knew, and, in the best possible sense, she did not care. She treated me no differently from before. So when she was no longer there, I felt as if I'd lost something special.

My sadness had another dimension, of course. Our talk at the train station in Gevgelija had stirred something else – the more painful regret that I'd not been able to tell my parents. *They* should have been the ones to comfort me. They should have had the chance to accept me, to tell me that it made no difference to them. That they were proud of who I was.

I hadn't given them that chance, and I didn't know if I would get the opportunity again. It might be too late.

On the back of this realisation came another. Even if the war ended tomorrow, I could no longer go back to Syria. In truth, I'd understood this from the moment we left. I'd known, when I said goodbye to my mother, that I was also saying goodbye to the only home I'd ever had. But it was only now that I was able to admit this to myself.

Four years ago, when there were people demonstrating in the streets, demanding democracy and civil rights – back then, change had seemed possible. There had been a moment of hope for my country; hope for people like me.

There wasn't much hope anymore. People like me were still being imprisoned every week – those who weren't being thrown from rooftops by Islamist militias.

Now that I'd left, there could be no going back.

I grieved, and I had no choice but to keep my grief private. With Sabeen gone, there was no one else to confide in.

Our experience in Serbia was mixed. The Serbians themselves were kind and generous, perhaps because they had also experienced war in the recent past; some of them could remember being refugees, too. They had temporary shelters and reception centres set up at the southern border, and there was a small army of volunteers dispensing water and halal sandwiches. But the problem was not the country's willingness to help. It was the crushing numbers that continued to pour in. We were thousands, all crammed into facilities that were designed to cope with hundreds. Accessing help was a slow process.

There was little to do but wait, and little to occupy my mind. I made a study of Jesus's alcoholism. It was not something I had planned to do, but because of the situation – because of the many hours spent stationary, often corralled in queues – I found my attention drawn to the details I had previously missed.

His drinking was heaviest in the mornings. He tended to start as soon as he woke up, slow down around lunchtime, and then maintain a steady pace for the rest of the day. If he woke in the night, one swallow of whisky sent him straight back to sleep. Yet despite this round-the-clock schedule, he was not perpetually drunk. I found this incredible. Most of the time, he could walk without falling over and speak without slurring his words. The real difficulties only began when he *stopped* drinking. The general moaning and loss of motivation you already know about, but this was liable to worsen very swiftly. Deprived of alcohol for more than a few hours – as happened when we were queuing to get into Serbia – he started to complain of terrible stomach cramps and nausea, dizziness and blurred vision. At first, I was certain he was exaggerating, or that his maladies were mostly in his mind. I suppose many of us are conditioned to think of alcoholism as a psychological illness, or a moral failing. We're too eager to separate minds and behaviour from brains and bodies. So I was quick to dismiss Jesus's grumblings of severe physical torment. I told him he was just hung-over and he'd have to put up with it. Shortly afterwards, he started sweating and shaking; he looked like a man running a ferocious fever. This was harder to dismiss, especially since he had stopped complaining at this point. He just hunched down, head in hands, and trembled. If this was acting, it was worthy of an Academy Award. I bought him more alcohol at the next opportunity.

The episode was instructive, and forced me to re-evaluate Jesus's drinking problem. Before, I had viewed his daily alcohol consumption as a choice, as if there existed at least some possibility of his choosing differently. Now, I saw that alcohol was literally something his body needed in order to keep functioning. How he had got to this state of affairs was of no immediate consequence. The fact was, in his present condition, he could no more cope without alcohol than a diabetic could cope without insulin injections. In a perverse sense, alcohol was Jesus's medicine. Without it, he became immediately and seriously sick.

This, of course, brought back the question of why he had chosen to come to Europe in the first place, apparently with no friends, no resources and no thought of what would happen next. What if Mohammed and I hadn't chanced to meet him on that beach in Samos? I could imagine no scenario that did not end with him in a Greek jail or a Greek mortuary.

Not for the first time, I found myself wondering what my parents would have made of the situation. That they would have been concerned probably goes without saying. My mother's complaints would have been much the same as Mohammed's – that Jesus was both a burden and a liability. He was a drain on our limited funds, a worrying distraction when we needed to be focused on our own well-being. And however unfortunate his circumstances, that did not make him our responsibility.

But here's the thing: whatever advice my mother might have given, it does not mean she would have followed it herself, had our positions been reversed. In truth, I could not imagine her abandoning a vulnerable, friendless and seriously ill old man just because he was an inconvenience. And I could imagine it even less of my father. They would have done the right thing, regardless of the cost.

I do not believe in fate. I think I have made this clear already. But I do believe that random chance can create obligations and responsibilities that should not be ignored. So it was with the Jesus situation. Fortune had bound us together, and for now, my duty was clear. At the very least, I had to deliver Jesus to the safety of Western Europe, where he'd have some hope of accessing the medical help he so obviously needed. After that, we'd be free to part ways.

With this resolved in my mind, I turned my attention to the problem in hand: our incursion into Hungary.

As you already know, the hundred-kilometre-long, four-metre-tall, wire-mesh-and-razor-wire fence had almost been completed. But it was not all in place just yet. My first hope was to locate a gap and exploit it. Unfortunately, information was surprisingly hard to come by, and when I did find up-to-date posts on a forum, the news was not welcome. It turned out that the only sections of uncompleted fence were along rail lines and roads, or otherwise close to the official border crossings and monitored at all times. Sneaking in at these points would be close to impossible. Hungary was the gateway to the

West, and the resources deployed in its defence were considerable. There were drones and dogs and thermal cameras. There was a fleet of off-road vehicles that continually patrolled the countryside.

But people were still getting over the border. For every one who was being caught and turned back, another was slipping through.

Further research led me to target the forested area between the Hungarian border towns of Kelebia and Ásotthalom. This section of Hungary had been fenced off a month ago, but thanks to the local people-smugglers, there were already numerous holes. For a few hundred euros, the smugglers would show you to one of these holes and see you safely across the border. For a few hundred more, you would be met by a four-by-four on the Hungarian side and driven a short distance north. This was a very useful service, since the roads nearby were apparently patrolled by a local right-wing militia, which sought to capture and detain all illegal entrants.

Unfortunately, we did not have several hundred euros to spare, not if our funds were to last through to the UK. And even if we'd had the money, I would have been reluctant to trust another gang of smugglers.

So our best bet was to go it alone. It would be more challenging than getting into Macedonia – I had no doubt about this – yet I remained confident. If we were caught and turned back, we would try again and again.

At this moment, I could not imagine what would go wrong.

We travelled by bus to the city of Subotica in the far north of Serbia. Here, in a hardware store, I purchased two torches, batteries, and a sturdy pair of wire cutters. And if you think the store-owner had any qualms about selling me wire cutters, then you're dead wrong. He had at least two dozen pairs on display, close to the cash register. I'd imagine it was a good time to own a Serbian hardware store.

Subotica had no refugee shelter for us to rest in, and there was no sense in finding a hotel, since we planned to leave in the middle of the night. Instead, we spent some hours in one of the city's parks, waiting in the shade of a large tree until the afternoon had started to cool. We bought food and alcohol and hiked north out of the city. The point on the border where we intended to cross was ten kilometres away, so we walked for around ninety minutes before stopping. The city became suburbs, which in turn became farmland and scrubland. I checked Google Maps every few minutes to make sure we were still on track, but it was not really necessary. The fields of tall, wiry grass were already criss-crossed with the paths trampled by previous feet, and the discarded water bottles were as easy to follow as a trail of breadcrumbs.

A couple of kilometres from the border, the forest rose before us, and it was here that we made a temporary camp. We sat on our sleeping bags and ate what had become a standard evening meal of sandwiches, chocolate, dried fruit and water. After that, I talked through the plan with Jesus and Mohammed once more, since there would be little opportunity to speak later on. We would make for the border a few hours before dawn. If luck was on our side, we would slip across undetected and head straight-away for the town of Kelebia, walking parallel to the main road but staying concealed among the trees for as long as possible. If we timed it correctly, and managed to avoid the border patrols and local police, we would arrive at Kelebia train station while most of the town still slept, and take the first train of the day north to Budapest.

That was assuming the staff at the station would sell us a ticket. I didn't know if they would. I had budgeted a hundred euros for bribery if necessary, but even this might prove insufficient. I was prepared for the possibility of a very long walk.

It grew dark, and for the first time since leaving Syria, I was aware that it was also growing cold. I got into my sleeping bag and zipped it up to my neck and tried very hard to fall asleep. But tired as I was, it was not easy. It is never easy to sleep when you know that you must, especially in an unfamiliar environment. There were strange night-time noises coming from the forest. The creak of branches and the rustle of small animals. There was very little light. If I turned onto my side, I could see the yellowish glow of the city rising from the southern horizon, but everything else was just different shades of darkness. Overhead, there were only one or two bright stars. Most of the sky was obscured by cloud.

I looked one more time at the map on my phone. I had been able to give it a decent charge at the train station that morning, so I didn't need to worry too much about the battery. Our location was marked by a small blue dot, the border by a thin grey line. So thin it might have been a hair that had fallen across the screen. Borders are like that sometimes. Some are self-evident, drawn by nature in the form of a sea or river or mountain range, but many are nothing more than a line on a map, an arbitrary point at which the land has been carved up by competing tribes of human beings for reasons long forgotten. The only way you can be sure you've crossed the line is when the police arrive and arrest you.

*

I was woken in darkness by the phone vibrating against my hip. *Mum!* My only thought, desperate and overwhelming, was of hearing her voice. I scrabbled for my pocket, and in the space of a few seconds, hope rose, surged and died.

The alarm icon flashed pitifully on the screen. The clock showed it was three in the morning.

I closed my eyes and breathed deeply. Several minutes must have passed before I felt capable of anything else.

Finally, I rose, and using the light from the screen, I located the dark mound that was Mohammed. For once, he didn't try to swipe me when I woke him; I don't know if he'd been sleeping very lightly, or not at all, but he showed no sign of tiredness or disorientation. He simply crawled out of his sleeping bag and started packing up his things, without being asked. Jesus was easier to find, because of his snoring, but more difficult to wake. I had to shake him quite vigorously, all the time whispering reminders that we were close to the border and needed to make as little noise as possible from now on. I guided his grasping fingers to his whisky bottle, and after that his eyes flickered open.

'I had the dream again,' he rasped, far too loudly.

I told him to shush. This was the worst possible time to talk about the dream.

'I need to urinate,' he said.

'Do it quietly!' I warned.

'I will need you to light the way, my friend.'

So I did. I stood at the edge of the forest and held the torch while Jesus relieved himself against a tree. In the quiet of the night, it sounded like a high-pressure hose discharging, but I supposed I couldn't really rebuke him for this. I doubt it was something he could control.

As always, Jesus was wearing the pink flip-flops, but I persuaded him to swap them for the trainers we had obtained in Greece. This was the first time I had succeeded in doing so. He grumbled a bit as he put them on, still insisting that they pinched; but the alternative was facing the razor-wire fence with exposed feet. Given the options, even Jesus could perceive the wiser course.

A few minutes later, we were making our way very slowly through the forest. The trees were not thick at first, and much of the undergrowth had been trampled, forming another make-shift pathway, but there were still many roots and low branches to avoid. Beyond our torch beams, the ground was as black as oil.

I'd estimate we were walking for an hour before we reached the fence. The trees on either side had been cut down, or perhaps bulldozed. Either way, there were about ten metres of completely cleared space on each side of the fence, as if someone had decided to construct a highway through the middle of the forest. The feeling of exposure, stepping out from the trees and into the open air, was profound and nerve-shredding. But there was no time to waste. The longer we waited, the more chance there was of being discovered.

There were no obvious gaps, so I set to work at once cutting our hole. The first problem was the razor wire. There turned out to be three coils of it at the base of the fence, rising to a metre or so off the ground. Using spare clothing as a glove, I was able to cut all three coils and disentangle them enough to form a narrow access point to the wire mesh beyond. Mohammed and Jesus held the torches and I suffered only minor scratches to my forearms. The main body of the fence was much tougher, and I was working at an awkward angle. It took me quite a lot of twisting and jiggling to make the first cut. Mohammed criticised me throughout the procedure.

'You're not diffusing a bomb!' he hissed. 'Give it some muscle!'

'Mohammed, stop talking,' I whispered. 'I know what I'm doing.'

'You don't look like you know what you're doing.'

'Be silent!'

My technique improved, but my muscles started to cramp. It took many more cuts and many more minutes for me to fashion a crawl space, its diameter barely wider than my shoulders. The loose wire mesh still had to be raised by hand to allow entrance, but I decided that this would have to be sufficient. I didn't have to check the phone to know that time was running away from us. Ideally, we wanted to be at the train station before the sun came up.

I held the wire mesh as high as I could and Mohammed scrambled underneath without difficulty. Jesus made it halfway before getting stuck. I disentangled his snagged clothing and Mohammed pulled on his arms. It wasn't very dignified, but it worked; between us, we managed to manoeuvre him face-down across the border. I passed our bags through, and then Mohammed and Jesus did their best to hold up the wire mesh from the Hungarian side while I wriggled underneath. I suffered more cuts, and my clothing ripped in several places. But I no longer cared. Because now we were so close. We were just a short walk and a train ride away from having made it to the West. Our luck had to hold just a little bit longer.

Jesus patted me on my back, grinning his strange, gappy grin, but Mohammed didn't pause to celebrate. He already had his torch beam aimed at the trees ahead. There was no obvious path through them, but we'd just have to press on regardless. The sooner we got away from the fence, the better.

We crept on, and the forest grew lighter, the surrounding blackness receding like a falling tide. Shadows twitched among the trees, and every small noise, every creak and rustle, sounded to my ears like the tread of stealthy footsteps. Progress was excruciatingly slow. The forest was thick and tangled, and travelling in a straight line was no simple matter. We had to stop every few minutes to check our position on the map and ensure we were still going in the right direction.

We'd probably been walking for half an hour when we came upon a narrow road. It was not much wider than a single car, though there was a verge on either side which would allow vehicles to pull over and pass in both directions. All in all, there couldn't have been more than ten metres of open space to cross. But our side of the road had been fenced off from the trees. This fence was not like the one at the border; it was chain-link, only head-high, and could be easily climbed. It had probably been put in place to deter deer rather than illegal border-crossers. Yet it required some minor coordination on our part.

We watched the road for a few minutes, staying concealed among the trees. No cars passed, and there was no sound but the wind. It was louder here, I suppose because the forest road had created a natural wind tunnel. Signalling Mohammed and Jesus to stay were they were, I crept to the fence and looked down the road in both directions. It was deserted, though I couldn't see all that far in the dim pre-dawn gloom. In one direction, the road ran straight for perhaps fifty metres before fading into the darkness, and in the other, it curved sharply, disappearing even sooner.

I went back to Mohammed and Jesus and told them what we would do. As at the border fence, Mohammed would cross first. I would help Jesus up the fence on this side and Mohammed would help him down on the other. I'd follow immediately and we'd continue our journey through the trees. We'd move swiftly, but without hurrying. The map showed that the forest ran for another kilometre at the most, so we'd be reaching the outskirts of Kelebia with plenty of time to spare. Given that Jesus was not a nimble man, and unlikely to be a proficient climber due to his missing fingers, I did not want to risk injury for the sake of saving a few seconds. Exercising the appropriate degree of caution, I still expected us to be across the road and back among the trees in a matter of minutes.

Mohammed barely waited for me to finish speaking, and he didn't bother to remove his backpack. He jogged to the fence and scrambled over it with the dexterity of a squirrel climbing a tree. He clicked his fingers and motioned for us to follow, like he was pretending to be a commando or something. I suppressed my annoyance and ushered Jesus to the fence. Cupping my hands, I attempted to boost him to the top. It was not a simple operation. He didn't weigh much, but he was extremely wobbly. I had to make many adjustments to counterbalance his unsteady and unpredictable movements. Eventually, we managed to manoeuvre into a position where his good hand gripped the top of the fence and his bad hand rested on my shoulder. The wires rattled as he shifted his weight, and it was at this point that I became aware that something was wrong.

The twin beams of light came first, sweeping the trees along the curve of the road. They swung towards us, becoming suddenly dazzling, and at the same time I was able to discern the sound

139

of an engine, previously lost in the wind. There was very little time to react. Mohammed stood in the middle of the road, shielding his eyes against the direct glare of the headlights. Jesus lost his footing and fell on top of me, and we both tumbled to the ground. I pulled myself to my knees just in time to see my brother running into the forest on the far side of the road.

'Mohammed, stop!'

I shouted as loud as I could, but either he didn't hear or he simply ignored me. The approaching vehicle, a large four-by-four, screeched to a halt and two men leapt from the cab. They both had torches. One was trained on the trees where Mohammed had made his escape, and the other took mere moments to locate us among the fallen branches on the roadside. Something was yelled in a foreign language, and we had only a split second to make our decision.

We turned and ran.

Lost

The sound of pursuit came almost at once – shouting, followed by the clanging of metal as the fence was again scaled. I had no way of knowing if it was one or both of the men, though I thought it more likely that they had split up, that Mohammed was now being chased in the opposite direction. If so, the prospect of being able to find him again, here in the forest, was becoming more remote with every desperate footstep. And yet fear kept me moving. It wasn't the fear of capture in itself. My real fear was that we would be captured while Mohammed escaped. How would we ever find him again? I knew my brother: he would not be easy to catch, and he would never turn himself in voluntarily. So even though I was acting on instinct, I believe in this case my instincts were good. We had to evade capture at all costs.

In English, you have a poetic phrase for the surge of adrenaline that takes over in a moment of crisis. You call it the fight-or-flight response. Yet sometimes neither option is a good one. Sometimes, a third course of action is called for. After a minute or so of charging blindly through the forest, with my heart pounding and my mind in tumult, I somehow came to recognise that this was the worst possible plan. The sound of us crashing through the trees would be as easy to follow as a herd of elephants, and I had no doubt that whatever our head start, it would quickly diminish. Our best hope was to hide, to keep still and silent and rely on the darkness to protect us.

I grabbed hold of Jesus's arm and pulled him into a dense and prickly patch of undergrowth. I put a finger to my lips to signal the need for absolute silence, and he nodded once in confirmation. We crouched low to the ground and peered through a lattice of ferns and low branches, back in the direction of the road.

The crack and thump of our follower's footsteps slowed and then stopped entirely, verifying my conjecture. He – or they – hadn't yet caught sight of us, and instead had been pursuing by ear. If we remained silent, we stood a chance.

After a long, tense interval, the footsteps sounded again, much more softly. Moments later, a single torch beam came into view. It was perhaps fifty metres away, though it was hard to judge the distance reliably. It halted on a thick clump of bushes, then slowly swept the forest, back and forth like some terrible lighthouse. We were far enough away that we were probably safe, but only for now. Our pursuer knew that we were hiding somewhere, and he knew the approximate direction in which we'd been running. He only had to be methodical, and he could take as much time as he needed. If he kept advancing and searching, eventually he'd find us. If he got close enough, I felt certain that the thumping of my heart would give us away.

I had no idea what to do. I turned silently to Jesus, and saw an unfathomable sight. He had sat down, and was carefully removing one of his trainers. He had chosen this moment to tend to his blisters – that was my immediate assumption. But after he'd removed the trainer, he returned to his squatting position, holding it firmly in his good hand. He was gazing intently in the direction of our pursuer. I shook my head as vigorously as I dared, trying to catch Jesus's attention, but he ignored me. He was waiting for the torch beam to sweep to a point where it was again angled away from us. As soon as this happened, he rose like a wraith from his crouch. He drew back his arm and let fly.

Thus was the fate of Jesus's second pair of shoes, which he managed to wear for only a couple of hours.

The lone trainer sped through the air in an improbable arc. It passed within inches of tree trunks and branches, and yet struck none. It landed instead with a thunderous crash in some distant foliage. At once, the torch beam shifted and our pursuer started moving away, in the direction of the decoy. He said something in an unknown language, presumably Hungarian, his voice calm but firm. I didn't need to consult with Jesus beyond the briefest glance. We started to crawl in the opposite direction, moving like snails along the forest floor.

I don't know how long we kept crawling. It seemed like hours, and all that time I didn't dare look back. I felt like Lot's wife. I'm sure you know the story; it's in the Bible as well as the Qur'an, and also in *The God Delusion*. Lot and his family are fleeing their hometown as God rains fire upon the Sodomites. They are warned by the Almighty that they mustn't look back at the destruction, on pain of terrible punishment. In a moment of weakness, Lot's wife breaks this commandment and is turned instantly into a pillar of salt.

I never liked that story, but it stayed with me, for obvious reasons.

In any case, I did not risk looking back. I held myself together and I kept crawling.

After some unknown time, Jesus halted, turned, and then sat with his back against a tree trunk. I joined him. We were both sweating profusely. There was no sign of the torchlight, and no noise from the trees.

We rested, and gradually, my heartbeat slowed.

'Well done, Jesus,' I whispered. 'That was good thinking.'

Jesus's response was to remove his other trainer and set it on the ground next to the tree trunk, where it was destined to remain. 'They were uncomfortable,' he said. 'I am very happy to be rid of them.'

'We need to continue with the plan,' I told him. 'If Mohammed got away, he'll head for the train station. All he needs to do is get through the rest of the forest. Any road or path he comes across will lead him into town.'

Jesus thought about this for a few moments, then said: 'What if he did not get away?'

'We still have to get to the station. If he's not there by the end of the day, then we'll go to the police. Either way, we *will* find him.'

Jesus nodded energetically. 'Of course,' he said. 'It is not even a question in my mind.'

I checked the map while Jesus put on his flip-flops. As soon as he was done, we set off through the trees once more.

*

We walked at the edge of the forest, heading parallel to the road until we reached the end of the fence. It was a significant diversion, but going around the fence now seemed a safer option than going over it. We entered the outskirts of Kelebia just as the sun was rising, and followed the train track into town, staying off the roads as much as possible. There didn't seem to be much traffic at this time, but I didn't want to take any chances. I checked the phone and saw that we still had a clear half-hour before our train was due to depart. We would arrive at the station imminently, and, with luck, Mohammed would already be waiting for us.

We had no luck. Kelebia station was very small, and it took only a minute to establish that Mohammed was not there. There were benches out front and on the platforms, and they were empty except for a couple of early-morning commuters. In the ticket office, the woman working the desk glanced at us with utter indifference. It was a glance that made my heart fall even further, for it told me that had we been in a position to buy tickets, she probably would have allowed it. We were someone else's problem – that is what I read in her expression – and she was as disinterested in hindering us as she was in helping us.

This intuition was immediately confirmed. I asked if she spoke English and she nodded. I described Mohammed for her and asked if she'd seen him. She shook her head. I said nothing more and returned to Jesus.

Waiting out front would have been preferable, but it also seemed more risky. Kelebia was a small town, and I knew from Google Maps that the police station was just down the road. We didn't want to risk being taken into custody – or not until we'd given Mohammed a decent chance to find us. Of course, it also seemed possible that the police would do random checks inside the station, but I didn't know this for sure. It was also possible that all their resources were deployed at the border, and they didn't have time to worry about the handful who made it to town undetected. I could have asked the woman in the ticket office, I suppose, but I had no desire to speak to her again. So, instead, Jesus and I waited on one of the empty benches on the platform.

The train to Budapest arrived and departed, and we were the only people left. My anxiety grew. I no longer knew if I'd made the right decision back in the forest. Perhaps we should have turned ourselves in immediately. Perhaps I could have persuaded the men – the police or border guards; whoever they were – to help us search for my lost brother. If I'd been permitted to call for him, and if he'd been hiding nearby, then surely he would have returned to us?

Jesus must have sensed the growing desperation in my thoughts. He had been drinking steadily since we sat down, and now, for the first time, he offered me the bottle. I did not know what to make of this. I suppose it was a kind gesture, all things considered. Jesus did not part with his alcohol easily. After a moment's hesitation, I took the bottle and drank. The cheap whisky burnt my throat, all the way down to my stomach, and on a morning where everything was hideous, this alone felt good.

I wondered if this was how it began for someone like Jesus. A simple anaesthetic when no other was available. Perhaps Jesus was thinking on a similar line. As I raised the bottle again, he took hold of it at the base and gently shook his head. I didn't bother to argue. I handed the bottle back.

'We will find your brother soon,' Jesus said. 'I know this for a fact.'

'You can't *know* something like that,' I told him.

'There is my dream,' Jesus said. 'All three of us are in the dream. This can only come to pass if we find him again.'

I didn't reply. I watched a plastic bag being blown along the train track. The morning sky was vast and blue and empty, and the silence stretched and stretched.

'Jesus, I'm very sorry,' I said eventually. 'I know you believe there's some kind of message in your dream. I don't believe it, and I don't want to hear about it again. If you want to talk, then I have questions I'd like you to answer. Lots of questions.'

'What questions?' Jesus looked suddenly wary.

'You could start by telling me what you're doing here.'

'I don't understand this question. I came with you, through the forest and—'

'What are you doing in Europe, Jesus? What's your plan? Do you even have one?'

He took another long drink, looking away. 'I think you are upset at the moment. It might not be the best time to talk about these things.'

'Jesus. There isn't going to be a better time. We've been travelling together for more than a week and I still know nothing about you.'

'There is nothing important to know.'

'You owe me an explanation. A rational explanation. Nothing about dreams, nothing about God sending you.'

He tried to raise the bottle to his lips again, but this time I caught his arm and prevented it. Anger flashed in his eyes, but I had no intention of letting go. After a moment, he lowered his arm.

I tried again: 'Jesus. Tell me why you came to Europe. Tell me how you even got here. How did you pay the smugglers? You don't have any money!'

He didn't reply directly. Instead, he reached down and opened up his dirty rucksack, which was sitting at his feet. From this he pulled a rolled-up pair of socks. He inverted them, and as they came apart, a tight roll of banknotes fell into his lap. At the time, it was impossible to guess how much was there, but he told me later. It was a little under fifteen hundred euros. Not a fortune, but that was not the point, obviously.

He handed the roll of notes to me without meeting my eyes. 'I am sorry, my friend. I have been dishonest with you.'

There was nothing I could say at that moment. Jesus had chosen to betray my trust. He had been exploiting me from the start. I suppose I shouldn't have been surprised, but this did not make it hurt any less.

'It is not a good excuse,' he continued, 'but it was not my intention to deceive you. Not at first. You assumed I had no money, and you started paying for everything, and, well . . . My plan was to pay you back, before we parted. I thought there would be an opportunity to put the money in your bag while you slept.'

I kept staring numbly at the roll of notes he'd placed in my hands. I didn't know if he intended me to keep them, if this was his attempt at penance. More likely it was another attempt to manipulate me. He wanted me to believe the gesture was sincere and immediately hand the money back. I didn't. For now, I kept hold of it.

'Where did you get this money?' I asked. 'Did you steal it?'

'No. There are many things I have to be ashamed of, but this is not one of them. The money is mine.'

'You stole alcohol. There was no reason for you to do that.'

'No. No reason. Just an opportunity. It is not something I can try to justify.'

'You need to tell me everything.' I said. 'Start with Iraq. Why did you leave? What made you come to Europe?'

Jesus was silent for a long time.

I suppose whatever he said would have come as a surprise. It was always going to be something hard to imagine.

'I have a daughter,' Jesus said. 'She lives in Germany.'

Jesus's Daughter

I will give you the abridged version. In reality, Jesus spoke for well over an hour, and his story hopped back and forth like an agitated frog. The chronology was not always obvious, and neither was his underlying logic. Added to this, there were some large gaps in his memory – astonishingly large; if he was to be believed, there was one that spanned an entire decade. I had to interrupt often, to seek clarification or just to drag him back from some strange and irrelevant digression. But after significant toil, I was able to piece together the following account.

The man who called himself Jesus was born in a suburb of Baghdad in the early 1950s. He was not able to narrow it down any further, and was similarly vague when it came to many of the details of his early life. I will note, at the outset, that he did not tell me his real name at any point, and this was not something I was interested in pressing. All things considered, it seemed a minor detail.

Jesus was the third of three children. His brother was killed at some point during the late 1960s, in the first Iraqi–Kurdish war. His sister died in 2014 of a disease that Jesus was unable to recollect. By this time, he had not spoken to her for decades, and had, in fact, forgotten that he had a sister. He re-learned of her existence at the same time as he learned of her death, via a lawyer's letter some months after the event. The letter revealed that his sister had married into a wealthy family, outlived her husband, and died with no surviving children. But I'll get to that shortly. Jesus's story will be more comprehensible if I tell it in a linear fashion.

Jesus's formal education came to an end at the age of twelve. He worked for several years as a cigarette vendor on the streets of Baghdad. He earned a pittance, and was sometimes paid in cigarettes rather than cash – though he maintained this was not a big problem. As a form of currency, cigarettes were more stable than the Iraqi dinar.

At some point in his late teens, Jesus was conscripted into the army. He hated it. He deserted. He was arrested and imprisoned – possibly for months, possibly for several years. His recollection of that time was extremely vague, and further complicated by subsequent periods he spent behind bars. According to Jesus, all prisons are essentially the same, and he couldn't say for sure what happened where or when or why.

Regardless: upon being released that first time, he was not required to complete his military service. Apparently, the army had concluded that Jesus was not fit to serve. He was dishonourably discharged and sent home, and he picked up his life pretty much where he'd left it. He worked in various jobs in the informal economy. He mentioned being a brick-layer at one point, and a fruit-picker at another, but again, he wasn't sure where or when. Sometimes, he had nightmares about being back in the army.

He got married, and this was another event shrouded in mystery. He gave the impression that he had very little say in the matter. His wife had been his dead brother's fiancée, and it seemed that she was simply passed over to Jesus upon his sibling's demise. Jesus's only other statement on the matter was that his wife did not like him very much.

Despite this, the marriage lasted for at least a decade. Jesus's only child, a daughter, was born a year after the wedding, and he immediately found himself even more out of his depth. He nevertheless maintained that he was able to fulfil the most basic requirements of him as a husband and father – at least until the alcohol took over. He worked very long hours, and often worked away from home. This turned out to be the optimum set-up for both Jesus and his wife. He moved around the country, going from job to job and sending money home to support the family.

He couldn't pinpoint the moment when his drinking became a problem; or more accurately he could not remember a time when he had not drunk to excess. He supposed at some point it must have started to have a more decisive impact on his life – he must have stopped sending money home or struggled to find work – but there was no special incident he could recollect. All he could do was look further down the timeline and try to join the dots.

His wife left him, taking their daughter with her, and if he had any other significant relationships, these likewise disintegrated. He had been estranged from his parents for many years, and eventually lost contact with his sister too. He had acquaintances he made through work, and numerous drinking buddies, but nobody he could classify as a long-term friend.

The next significant chapter of his life he recalled was a time spent working on an illegal fishing boat. Apart from his first job as a cigarette vendor, it was the only work he recollected with any fondness. He and two other men would sail out from Al-Faw, a port town a hundred kilometres southeast of Basra. In case you're unfamiliar with the geography of Iraq, Al-Faw is pretty much the only port in Iraq. The entire Iraqi coastline amounts to a twenty-kilometre strip wedged between Iran and Kuwait. As a consequence, Iraq's territorial waters are almost non-existent, and much of its fishing occurs illegally in the seas of its hostile neighbours. According to Jesus, this business was relatively lucrative, somewhat enjoyable and extremely risky. He spent a significant portion of his time as a fisherman not actually fishing, but confined in Iranian jails, where he was frequently beaten.

The news of his estranged wife's death reached him at the end of this period. He received a letter from his daughter, and was understandably shocked. He had not spoken to her since she was a child, and had assumed that he would never hear from her again. The letter was short and to the point. Jesus's wife had died of a tumour. His daughter was leaving Iraq, permanently. The letter was her way of saying goodbye, and an attempt to lay the past to rest. She hoped that he had managed to sort his life out.

That was everything, but inexplicably, Jesus found himself crying. There was nothing in the letter that hinted at affection, and certainly nothing to suggest that any response was required or wanted. There was no return address. And yet his daughter *had* gone to the trouble of tracking him down. That couldn't have been a straightforward matter. Most likely, it had cost her both time and money.

Jesus returned to his old neighbourhood in Baghdad with the hope that he might be able to see his daughter again. He only wanted to see her once, before she left forever. He thought that would be enough. Eventually, he managed to locate one of his wife's relatives – a cousin who still lived in the area – but by then, his daughter had already left the country. She had been planning to go to Europe; and for the next decade, that was the only information Jesus had.

In 2003, the Americans and the British invaded, again. Jesus regarded this turn of events with absolute indifference. He doubted that it would impact his own existence to any significant degree. Sadly, he was wrong.

The history of the second Gulf War is well known. The Americans and the British invaded. Saddam Hussein was overthrown, captured and eventually hanged. The Iraqi state was dismantled but no one had any idea how to put it back together. There was a power vacuum that was quickly filled by various sectarian militias. The Iranians supplied weapons to the Shiites and the Saudis supplied the Sunnis. Iraq descended into civil war, many people died, and the Americans and British were left scratching their heads.

By 2006, Jesus was living in a part of Baghdad that was more or less under the control of Islamic extremists, including Al-Qaeda. As you probably know, Al-Qaeda hates many things, including alcohol and cigarettes. They started blowing up off-licenses and murdering anyone who sold immoral substances. People who were users of immoral substances were treated less severely. In the first instance, they were merely beaten. But repeat offenders fared much worse.

Jesus was a repeat offender.

One day, he was caught smoking on the street, and you pretty much know what happened next. The Al-Qaeda militia men dispensed justice on the spot. Two held him down and another took out a knife and amputated his right index and middle fingers – the fingers commonly used to hold a cigarette.

He was found some time later by a passer-by, unconscious and bleeding to death. The passer-by took him to a doctor who dressed the wound, gave him antibiotics, and probably saved his life.

In the years that followed, Jesus lived an existence that was vague and meaningless even by his own standards. He could no longer work and was reliant on charity and food stamps for his survival. He was living in a concrete shack that had been built upon land settled by squatters in the aftermath of the 2003 invasion. This was the context in which he received the letter from his forgotten sister's lawyer.

To recap: she had died with no immediate family. Jesus was her last remaining relative, and as such, had just inherited a significant portion of her estate.

He had no idea how the lawyer had managed to find him. Nor did he know what to do with his newfound wealth. Unsurprisingly, Jesus had never had any money before, and now that he did, he found himself deeply apprehensive.

The problem may not be obvious to you. It was not obvious to me, until he explained it.

Jesus was not used to making any important decisions. He lived day-to-day, simply meeting his most basic physical needs and with no prospect of his situation changing, either for better or worse. He collected his food stamps, and he traded some of them for alcohol and tobacco. He ate and he slept. Sometimes he played chess with his squatter neighbours. He was a terrible player, but did not let this deter him.

In short, he never had to consider anything beyond his immediate circumstances. The past and the future stretched away from him in opposite directions, and he was equally powerless with regard to both.

But now, for the first time in many years, he was forced to reflect upon his circumstances. He was forced to consider what would come next.

The conclusion he reached was bleak. Now that he had money, the most likely scenario was that he would drink himself to death.

He was not suicidal – I should make that clear. It wasn't that he planned to kill himself through over-consumption of alcohol. He just assumed it was inevitable. Unless he could dream up an alternative future, his sister may as well have bequeathed him a loaded gun.

Jesus decided to use his money to find his daughter. He had no expectation that this plan would end well, but it was the only plan he had. It was the only alternative future that meant something to him.

He again tracked down his ex-wife's cousin, and used a small deception to secure her help. He told her that he had inherited a small fortune which he could find no use for. He was planning to send this money to his daughter. All he needed was an address to give to his lawyer.

Jesus showed me the address at this point. It was for an

156

apartment building in Berlin. It had been copied in careful, handwritten German and had a phonetic transcription in Arabic on the other side of the paper. Jesus said that he had memorised the pronunciation before he left Iraq. That had been pretty much his only preparation for the trip. He paid smugglers to get him from Iraq to Iran to Turkey, and from Turkey to Greece.

The rest, you already know.

After Jesus finished his story, I no longer felt angry. His story was too wretched to leave me feeling anything other than a deep and weary sadness.

We sat in silence for a while, then I handed back his roll of banknotes. 'You can go to Germany now,' I told him. 'If you get on the next train, you'll be in Budapest this afternoon. You can probably catch a direct train to Berlin from there.'

Jesus wouldn't look at me. He was staring at the train tracks. 'What about your brother?' he asked, very quietly.

'I don't think he's coming,' I said. 'It gets less likely the longer we're here.'

'You should not give up.'

'I'm not giving up. I'll stay here until the afternoon. After that I'll go to the police station. It's the best chance I have.'

'I would still like to come with you, if you'll let me. I want to help you find him.'

'You can't help.'

Jesus still wasn't looking at me, but his face had fallen. He looked as forlorn as I had ever seen him.

'I'm not saying it to be cruel,' I said. 'I'm just being realistic. I need to find my brother and it will be easier if you're not with me.'

157

'You think I would be a burden for you?'

'Yes. That's what I think. It's not your fault, but it's the way things are.'

'Oh.'

'Seriously, Jesus. Think about the situation. I mean, really think about it. How are you planning to help me? What can you possibly do?'

Jesus did think. He thought for so long that I assumed the conversation had ended. I took his silence as a vindication of my point.

Then he said: 'I can make sure that you're not alone. I can try to be your friend. That's the only thing I can do. You will have to decide if it's enough.'

I did not know what to say to this. I gazed for a long time down the still empty platform. 'If we go to the police, I don't know what will happen,' I told him. 'I suppose we'll be arrested. From what I've read, we could be deported, or held indefinitely.'

'These are all things that have happened to me before, as you know.'

'You might not get to see your daughter for a long time.'

'It's already been a long time. Many, many years. A few more weeks will not change anything.'

'You're sure?'

'I have grown fond of your brother. I would not wish to abandon him now.'

Jesus looked at me now, for the first time since he'd finished his story. His expression was the one I'd grown used to over the past week. That strange, simple innocence.

'Okay,' I said finally. 'It's enough.'

Seizure

Mohammed did not show up at the station. Time trickled by, and the probability of his rejoining us went from poor to almost non-existent. Nevertheless, we waited all morning and for most of the afternoon. Jesus drank a little, but we didn't really speak anymore. Two more trains arrived and departed for Budapest. The platform filled and emptied. These were perhaps the most depressing hours I have ever spent. I suppose I've been in worse situations – objectively speaking – when I was physically in danger, or on the day they took my father. But forced inactivity, the absolute impotence of waiting and praying, is its own special type of hell. By the end of the afternoon, I was almost glad that the ordeal was over, and now we could turn ourselves over to the authorities.

At the police station, there was a receptionist who spoke reasonable English, so I was able to explain the situation in full: we were illegal entrants to the country and we were looking for another illegal entrant, my younger brother, who had either been captured by persons unknown or was lost in the woods. But once

I'd finished my account, no one seemed to know what to do with us. Apparently, it was not usual for illegal border-crossers to turn up at the police station and ask to make a missing-person report.

The receptionist made a phone call and gestured that we should take a seat in the waiting area. Some time later, a policeman took us into an interview room and talked to us. His English was not so great, so it took a while. But eventually, he was able to convey the bare bones of what was going to happen next.

We were to be transported to the nearest detention centre for illegal immigrants, which was about thirty kilometres away. From there, we'd either be deported or processed as asylum seekers, depending on the information we gave.

I asked again about Mohammed, and the policeman told me this was not his problem. If my brother had been found in the woods, then he would already be at the detention centre. I could make further enquiries there.

The conversation was immediately terminated and we were taken to a cell and locked in. I tried to point out that there was no need for this treatment, since we had come to the police voluntarily and had no intention of trying to flee, but my argument fell upon deaf ears. For the next couple of hours, Jesus and I were incarcerated in a tiny room containing only one narrow bed and a toilet.

Jesus, of course, had been locked away many times before, and probably in conditions far worse than this. He seemed unperturbed, and even told me that if I wanted to get some sleep, he'd be quite happy sitting on the floor or toilet. I told him I didn't think there was much chance of me sleeping. I was worried about Mohammed. I was worried about the detention centre, and the possibility that the officials there would be as unhelpful as the policeman. I was worried – correctly – that things were about to get even worse.

When we got to the detention centre it was dark. A policeman escorted us through a checkpoint and into what I can only describe as a holding pen. It was a small square constructed of interlocking metal fencing panels, about two metres high. It looked as if it had been improvised in haste. Actually, this was the impression I got from the facilities at large. There was some sort of warehouse or depot that had been repurposed as a jail for illegal border-crossers. Surrounding this was a maze of military tents – the type that can sleep ten soldiers and are tall enough to stand up in. I quickly lost count of how many there were. There was row upon row, separated in several places by more metal fencing. I soon found out that this whole area was 'overflow accommodation'. The Hungarians had already managed to fill their warehouse.

The tent we were eventually shown to was already home to six other border criminals: a Yemeni family, and two Zambian men with whom I was able to converse in English. The whole camp was a frustrated melting pot of the desperate and displaced. I described Mohammed for everyone in the tent, on the off-chance, but no one had seen him. Yet, at this early stage, I still had some hope. One of the Zambians, who had been here a while, thought there might be separate accommodation inside the warehouse where they kept unaccompanied children and pregnant women. There was a chance that Mohammed was here, and being looked after somewhat better than Jesus and I were.

We went outside the tent so that Jesus could drink without offending anyone, and this was when things went from bad to catastrophic. We were sitting on the ground just around the corner, facing out towards the perimeter fence. There were a couple of guards talking beyond the fence, but I paid them little attention. I suppose I had grown complacent. The Hungarians had essentially been ignoring us since we arrived; they didn't even look at us most of the time, and any communication was restricted to simple instructions.

I was only half-interested when I heard one of the fencing panels being unlocked, but when I glanced over, a moment later, I saw that both guards were heading our way. One of them pointed at Jesus's alcohol and mimed that we weren't allowed to drink. Jesus immediately tensed up, clutching his whisky to his chest, and I stood and raised my hands, palms flat, in an attempt to defuse the situation. Stern words were spoken in Hungarian, and I explained, in calm English, that Jesus was not drinking for recreation; he had a severe alcohol dependency, and if he didn't drink, he would become ill.

'No drink!' one of the guards replied. At the same time, the other one crouched down and reached for the whisky bottle.

Jesus reacted predictably; he attempted to slap the man around the face, and any hope of saving the situation vanished in an instant.

I can't really call what happened next a fight. The guards were strong and competent and armed with batons. We were . . . well, we were us. An ageing, malnourished alcoholic and a scared Syrian literature student. I suppose I could have shouted for back-up from the Zambians, but I doubt the outcome would have been better. With the mood in the camp, it could have descended into a full-scale riot.

The guard evaded Jesus's slap and hauled him to his feet. Jesus clawed at him again, and the other guard stepped in with his baton, so I grabbed his arm before he could strike, and was immediately jabbed in the stomach. I went to the ground, the breath knocked out of me, and the two guards swiftly overpowered Jesus. One held him down while the other went through our bags.

'Please!' I wheezed. 'There's no need for this.'

They ignored me, and the rest of Jesus's alcohol was taken from his filthy backpack. There were two large unopened bottles in there; we'd thought it sensible to stock up before going to the police station.

'This is theft!' I cried. 'You are taking our belongings!'

Jesus screamed a series of Arabic insults, and at this point, the Zambians did come running from the tent. Unfortunately, it was too late for them to do anything more than help us back to our feet. The guards were backing away, one carrying the alcohol and the other waving a can of pepper spray back and forth while he shouted in Hungarian.

And that was the end of it. Jesus's alcohol was gone, and his enforced detoxification began.

We passed a difficult night inside the tent. I explained the situation at length, first to the Zambians, then to the Yemeni family, but I don't think any of them believed me when I said that Jesus was likely to become very ill in the next few hours. The Yemeni father was very unhappy upon learning that his family had been assigned accommodation with an alcoholic, which I suppose was understandable. His children – a son and a daughter – could not have been older than ten or eleven, and in an ideal world they would not have had to share living space with Jesus. But as I have said before, the world is far from ideal. This is a truth we can all agree on.

Inside the tent there were two rows of army beds – narrow metal frames covered with thin mattress pads. After some negotiation with the Africans, we moved Jesus to one of the far-corner beds, to minimise potential disturbances. He was extremely anxious. I did my best to reassure him, telling him that I'd try to get his alcohol back as soon as I could, but my words had little effect. We both knew I was clutching at straws.

He deteriorated through the night, following the pattern of symptoms that was now familiar to me, but which must have come as a shock to everyone else trying to sleep in that tent. Jesus did manage to doze – we both did – but this was interspersed with long periods of muttering and moaning, and a hacking cough that soon transformed into an interminable succession of dry heaves. This was followed by complaints of stomach cramps, in the early hours of the morning, at which point I managed to persuade him to come with me to find one of the guards. I thought that if they could see the state Jesus was in, we might have some small chance of getting the help he so obviously needed.

I was wrong. I found a guard who spoke some English at the main gate to our compound, and managed to establish that there were medical facilities in the building I'd seen earlier, but that was as far as I got. I was told that we would get a chance to talk to a doctor when we were processed the following day. Before then, the medical staff would only treat emergencies – and however much distress Jesus was displaying, he clearly wasn't an emergency.

*

By daylight, he was in terrible shape, sweating and trembling but otherwise catatonic. And he still wasn't considered an emergency. Another pair of guards came around, distributing sandwiches and water for breakfast, but their assessment was that Jesus was in no imminent danger. He'd be able to see a doctor later in the day, but there was no possibility of anyone coming over to see him in the tent. The medical staff were overworked as it was.

I told them that unless they were volunteering to *carry* Jesus over to the medical facilities, it was unlikely that he'd be going anywhere. The longer they left him, the less likely it became. The only response I got was a shrug, as if this was not their problem.

A few hours later, I was faced with a dilemma. We were called through to the warehouse building to be registered, but as I'd foreseen, there was no hope of getting Jesus to move. I did not think I should leave him, but at the same time, I knew that this was my best chance of speaking with someone in authority. It was my best chance of talking to a doctor, and it was my best chance of making enquiries about Mohammed.

With much reluctance, I left Jesus in the tent, but only after persuading the Zambians to keep a close eye on him.

Outside the warehouse, I joined the queue of new arrivals waiting to be registered. It was long, and thanks to my procrastination, I was near the back. It took me an hour just to get inside the building, and another twenty minutes to reach the registration desk. Here, a man took my name and fingerprints, and checked my passport and asked if I wished to apply for asylum in the European Union. I told him I did, but certainly not in Hungary. I was going to the UK. He sniffed at this news, then told me that asylum didn't work like that. I was obliged to stay in the first safe country I reached. I responded that Hungary did not feel like a safe country to me, and immediately regretted speaking. I should have smiled and kept my mouth shut.

I said that I'd like to see a doctor, and the registration man asked what was wrong with me. So I explained the Jesus situation, and hit the same brick wall I'd been hitting for the last twelve hours. No one took his alcohol withdrawal seriously. Or perhaps it was just that they had no sympathy for his plight. I probably should have lied, and said that he had some infectious disease, but I was wary of what might happen if the lie was discovered. I didn't think it would help Jesus if I gave the medical staff any reason to doubt my honesty.

Once it became clear that I wasn't going to be allowed to see a doctor on Jesus's behalf, I switched track and explained about my missing brother. I had to do so in great haste, before the already irritated registration man could shoo me away.

'We became separated in the forest,' I said. 'I was told that he may have been brought here too. He is fourteen years old and his name is Mohammed.'

'There are lots of Mohammeds here,' the man said. 'Half the boys in here are called Mohammed.'

I nodded, with infinite patience. 'Yes. It is a popular name on account of the prophet. This Mohammed will be wearing an FC Barcelona football shirt with the name Messi printed on the back. He has a bad temper and swears often.'

'I haven't seen him.'

'I was told there is an area where unaccompanied children are kept. May I check for myself?'

After some arguing, this request was granted. I think it was because it was the easiest way to get rid of me. A guard led me through a central aisle formed from more metal fencing. The accommodation in the warehouse was every bit as crowded as the tents – perhaps even more so. The space had been cordoned into separate sections, and everywhere I looked, there were beds and mattresses pressed up against each other. It was mostly families, and in many cases, there were several small children occupying a single bed.

The section for persons deemed vulnerable was at the far end of the warehouse, and when we reached it my heart immediately sank. There were at least a dozen teenagers there, none of whom was Mohammed.

I left the warehouse, and went back to the tent.

The Zambians were worried about Jesus. They thought he was going to be sick, and from the noises coming from him, I agreed it was a distinct possibility. But after half an hour or so, his dry-retching ceased. He was awake and lucid long enough for me to get him to one of the chemical toilets so that he could relieve himself, but this was the only activity he could manage. He was so shaky on his feet that I struggled to keep him upright, and I knew that anything as ambitious as hauling him to the warehouse, or even to the perimeter fence, was out of the question. I settled him back on his metal bed and he lay there moaning for a very long time.

In the late afternoon, help finally arrived, but it wasn't from the guards or any of the other prison staff. One of the Africans managed to find a doctor who was being held in one of the neighbouring tents. He was Egyptian, about forty years old, and immediately took the situation seriously. He asked me questions about when Jesus had last had a drink, how much he usually drank, and how long he'd been an abuser of alcohol, and I answered as best I could. He took Jesus's pulse at his wrist and laid his hand on his forehead and tried to talk to him for a minute or so, with no success.

'This man needs proper medical supervision,' he concluded, with a small shake of his head.

'I know! I've been telling the guards this for the last twelve hours.'

'He should be in a hospital.'

'I know! Will you help me talk to the guards again? They'll listen to you. You're a doctor!'

'I'm not a doctor in here,' the doctor said. 'I'm just another illegal immigrant, the same as you.' He shook his head again, then sighed. 'Come on. Let's get this over with.'

We went to the main gate of the compound, where two of the guards I'd spoken to earlier were on duty. They did not look pleased to see me again.

'This man is a doctor,' I said, pointing to the doctor. 'He has examined my friend and agrees that this situation is certainly an emergency.'

I guess I was quite emotional, and possibly shouting. The doctor held up his palms in a placating gesture before turning to the guards.

'His friend requires urgent attention,' he said. 'His condition is serious and will get worse.'

One of the guards shook his head and waved us away. The other sneered. 'This is man with hangover, yes?'

'No. He is withdrawing from long-term alcohol use. It's a dangerous thing to do without medical supervision.'

'You're doctor?'

'You don't have to believe me. Get someone else to come and examine him. They'll tell you the same things.'

The guard spat. 'You're doctor. You take care him.'

I started to speak again, but the doctor took me by the shoulder and led me away. 'You're wasting your time,' he said. 'You need to get back to your friend. Make sure he drinks some water. Get some rest. There's nothing else you can do right now.'

'Will you come too?' I asked.

The doctor rubbed his temples, exhaling at length. 'Listen. I have a family. I have two daughters who are scared. I have to look after them. Do you understand?'

'Yes, but—'

'Come and get me later, when things get really bad. I'll do what I can then.'

'Things are already really bad!'

He gave a short laugh, devoid of humour. 'No they're not. Not yet.'

There was nothing to be done. I lay in the tent and dozed when I could, and my sleep was filled with terrible nightmares. I dreamed that I was back on the beach in Samos, and was slapping Mohammed's unresponsive face again and again. My phone rang and I saw it was my mother, so I threw it in the sea. I didn't have the words to tell her what had happened.

Jesus sobbed and shivered in his sleep, and when he seemed at his worst I sat in the darkness and held his limp hand. At one point he awoke and was able to speak. This must have been around midnight, and I was conscious that our tent was half empty. The Yemeni family had found somewhere else to go. I thought it possible that they had dragged their beds outside and were sleeping under the stars. It was probably preferable to being with Jesus and his suffering.

'I think I am going to die now,' Jesus said at one point, his voice a wheezy whisper.

'You're not going to die,' I told him. 'You shouldn't think like that.'

'I want to die,' Jesus said.

And there was nothing I could reply, so I just held his hand again and waited.

'I'm sorry that I lied to you, my friend.'

'You don't need to worry about that now,' I said. 'Just try to sleep.'

'It's not fair to ask . . . When I die, will you go to my daughter for me?'

'You're not going to die.'

'Could you tell her that I tried to make things better?'

'You'll be able to tell her yourself.'

He was quiet for a long time, then said: 'I hope there's no God. I fear his judgment.'

'Me too,' I said. 'Me too.'

That was the last time he was able to talk coherently. He shouted out at several points, later on, but he didn't respond when I addressed him, and seemed to be unaware of his surroundings. There were times when he mumbled whole sentences, and other times when he just sobbed. When I put my hand on his forehead, it was like touching the door of an oven. He must have felt like he was on fire.

It was almost daylight when the seizures started. I didn't know what was happening, and I was terrified. I was woken by the sound of the metal bed frame shaking like there was an earth-quake. The Zambians were both up in an instant, and the three of us crouched at Jesus's bedside as his limbs jerked uncontrol-lably. His eyes were wide open and there were these awful wet choking sounds coming from the back of his throat. I didn't know what to do. I tried to hold him still, leaning my weight into his shoulders, while one of the Zambians ran to get the doctor.

He arrived a couple of minutes later, just as the convulsions were subsiding, and immediately took charge. He asked us to clear a path through the tent so that we could carry Jesus outside.

'Where are we taking him?' I asked.

'We're taking him to the guards,' the doctor told me, his voice cold and quiet. 'We're going to let them see for themselves.'

Jesus didn't weigh much but he was difficult to manoeuvre. I held him under his arms, my hands locked at his chest, and the Africans each took a leg. Then, following the doctor's instructions, we carried him through the compound to the main gate, where two guards were again stationed. Jesus moaned as we lowered him to the ground, and before either of the guards could react, the doctor began to shout, jabbing at the air with an accusing finger.

'You two! This man is critically ill! He is suffering from acute alcohol withdrawal and unless you want his death on your hands you will help us take him to the medical facilities *this instant*!'

There was a moment of silence, then Jesus started having another seizure, thrashing as if possessed. The gates were opened immediately.

The medical facilities were in a corner of the warehouse that had been screened off from the rest of the accommodation.

There was a lone, bored-looking doctor reading a newspaper, but he sprang from his chair as we carried Jesus in. After a brief consultation with the other doctor – the Egyptian – he examined Jesus and gave him an injection that stopped the convulsions. Everyone else was ushered back to the tents, but I was allowed to stay so that I could answer questions about Jesus's alcoholism.

The Hungarian doctor was very angry that I hadn't brought Jesus to him earlier. I could not find the energy to respond. Instead, I lay on the floor and went to sleep.

A few hours later, an ambulance arrived and took Jesus to the nearest hospital. When I asked if I could go with him, I was told *Of course not.*

I was on my own.

The Fear

I was on my own, and I'd never felt it more. For a while, I thought I was going to go insane. A little more than a week ago, I'd carried my brother out of the sea and taken my first shaky steps on the European continent. Now, Mohammed was lost. Mohammed was lost and Jesus was gone and I was alone in a Hungarian detention camp, with no idea when I'd be set free. Or *if* I'd be set free. It might sound irrational, but this was my greatest fear for some time. What if the Hungarians didn't release me? No one knew I was here. There was no one to rescue me or demand my release. It would be as if I had simply dropped off the face of the earth.

The Zambians tried to reassure me. They told me that I was lucky to be Syrian. The Syrians were never held for very long. Everyone knew that my country had torn itself apart, that I had no home to return to. Most likely, I'd be put on the next free bus and sent north to Germany.

The Zambians were not so lucky. They had already been in the detention camp for a week, and expected that they would be deported eventually. They were what Westerners termed 'economic migrants'. This meant that they were fleeing poverty, rather than war or persecution, and for some reason this motive was frowned upon.

I was not reassured. Apart from Jesus, I had not seen a single person leave the camp. It seemed to me that the only way you left was in an ambulance. And in any case, what cause did any of us have to trust the Hungarians? They were not an enlightened people; they treated poverty as if it were a crime!

I retired to my metal bed in the darkness of the tent, and in the darkness, my fears multiplied. Where was Mohammed? Was he still wandering the forests of southern Hungary, lost and penniless? And what about Jesus? If he survived, he was going to wake up alone and scared in a Hungarian hospital. Would they be able to find an Arabic translator for him? How else would they be able to communicate with him? He didn't speak Hungarian, and he only spoke five words of English!

I suppose I must have slept, but in truth there wasn't much to distinguish sleeping from waking. In both states, my mind was occupied with the same dark thoughts. I kept seeing Mum's face, hearing her voice. *You have to take care of Mohammed. There's no one else who can.* It all felt like part of the same nightmare, a nightmare from which there was no hope of escaping.

Eventually, I left the tent and paced from one end of my prison to the other. There wasn't anything to see. There were five other tents in this fenced-off area. There were the chemical toilets. That was about it. Beyond the far fence, in another section of the compound, the story was identical. Same tents and toilets. Same gloomy faces.

I walked back the way I'd come until I reached the main gate.

The guards who'd been on duty the previous day were there again. They had their backs to me, so I rattled the chain on the gate to get their attention.

'My friend was rushed into hospital last night,' I told them. 'He almost died. I thought you'd like to know.'

Nothing.

I turned and walked away.

The Hungarians would not help me when I tried to make further enquires about Mohammed, and neither would they tell me anything about Jesus – where he'd been taken to or how he was doing. I was beating my head against a brick wall. In the end, I decided to find the Egyptian doctor instead, to ask about the likely prognosis.

I found him in his tent, sitting on a bed with one of his daughters, but he came outside to talk to me. He said there were numerous risks associated with sudden alcohol withdrawal, including stroke and heart attack, but now that Jesus was in hospital, he'd be properly monitored and medicated, so the chances of such complications were reduced. When I asked how long Jesus would have to stay in hospital, the doctor told me it would be ten to fourteen days, at least. That was the minimum time it took for the physical effects of alcohol dependency to pass. After that, Jesus would no longer be in any immediate danger.

I had no idea how Jesus would cope in a foreign hospital for a fortnight. Just thinking about it made me shiver. But if he *was* kept in that long, then at least there was the possibility of my being released in the interim. Most of the people I'd spoken to had corroborated the Zambians' story: several busloads of detainees were released every few days – they had to be, or the camp would be swiftly overrun. The problem was the same as in every other country: too many invaders and not enough space to contain them. A man from Damascus I spoke with assured me that despite the Hungarians' bluster, they had no means of forcing us to stay in the country while our asylum claims were processed. Once we were freed, our journeys would simply continue, and this camp would be nothing more than a bad memory.

Of course, I had no intention of continuing *my* journey, not without Mohammed, but the prospect of release did give me some hope. Finding Jesus was just a matter of determining which hospital he'd been taken to, and there had to be some way of tracking down Mohammed. There *had* to be.

After I'd thanked the Egyptian doctor, I walked back to one of the interior fences, as far away from the unhelpful guards as possible. Here I slumped and stared for a while at the blank screen of my phone. There was nothing to see but my own reflection. The phone had died at some point during the morning, and there was nowhere to charge it. I don't know if this sounds like a catastrophe to you, not being able to charge your phone, but it was for me. Another catastrophe. It meant that my last tie to the outside world had been cut. It meant that if Mohammed was in a position to contact me, he'd no longer be able to.

Once more, there was nothing to be done. I put the phone away and took *The God Delusion* from my backpack and read through the chapter entitled WHY THERE ALMOST CERTAINLY IS NO GOD. This was a chapter in which I had learned to take great comfort. I suppose I was the same as Jesus – Iraqi Jesus – in this respect. Neither of us liked the idea that the unpleasantness of death would be followed by the even greater unpleasantness of divine judgment. We were both terrible sinners, according to the Qur'an.

You probably know already what the Qur'an says about Atheists. It says that they're going straight to the hottest part of hell, where their skin will be cooked, regrown, and then cooked again for eternity. *The God Delusion* was the book that reassured me this was *almost certainly* not the case. I first read it when I was fourteen, online and in secret, in its unofficial Arabic translation. Unfortunately, there is no official Arabic translation, because no one will publish it. Even in liberal Arab-speaking countries, the taboo against atheism – against apostasy – is considerable.

And so I never told anyone about my loss of faith, not even my parents. The subject was far too problematic when I was fourteen, and I worried it would lead on to other problematic subjects. I wasn't ready. I thought it was all part of the same difficult conversation I'd be able to have with them one day, in the nebulous future. Of course, I did wonder, later on, whether my parents were genuine believers. Nominally, our family was Sunni. My mother owned a copy of the Qur'an in classical Arabic. She didn't wear the hijab, but she did observe Ramadan every year. My father was exempt from fasting because he was a diabetic, and he didn't attend Friday prayers because he was always too busy with work. Or that's what he said. I don't recall him *ever* setting foot in the mosque.

My parents were progressive and intellectual, so I'm certain that their reading of the Qur'an must have been quite liberal. They would not have read it literally. The problem I had was that a non-literal reading served me no better. Even taken as a wild allegory, it's difficult to find a positive message in the story of Sodom and Gomorrah.

I was still reading, reading and thinking, when another of the guards entered the compound. He was distributing water and sandwiches from a wheelbarrow, and he wore on his face one of those disposable medical masks – presumably, because of all the horrible diseases he might catch from us. I ignored him, even when he came over and placed a wrapped sandwich at my feet. I was sick of eating sandwiches. I continued reading *The God Delusion*, enunciating every word in my head, in my best British accent. More precisely, the accent I was using in my head was an imitation of Professor Richard Dawkins' accent. If you don't know what he sounds like, you can go on YouTube and hear for yourself; there are lots of clips of him taking part in debates and reading from his books. You might be surprised. Even though he's the world's most famous Atheist, he sounds as I'd imagine an English vicar might sound, soft-spoken and kindly.

This was the voice I was hearing in my head when I became aware of the ruckus behind me. It was coming from the next section of prison, just beyond the fence.

'You expect us to eat this filth? We don't even know if it's halal! It might contain pig or dog or whatever else you think is meat in this backward shithole you call a country!'

The new voice made me smile in spite of myself. It reminded me of Mohammed. Except Mohammed was lost in the woods. Also, he couldn't have cared less whether his food was halal or not.

'Seriously, what *is* this shit?'

It was all in Arabic, so obviously the speaker didn't expect an answer. He was probably trying to stoke up the other prisoners – and from the sound of it, he was succeeding. There was an immediate outbreak of angry jeers. It was becoming harder and harder to read.

'We're not animals!' the voice declared. 'We demand real food! Hey! I'm talking to *you*, you goat-molesting son-of-a-whore!'

For a moment, I didn't dare believe it. Just because it sounded like Mohammed, it didn't mean it was Mohammed. Surely it was the lack of sleep, the stress and exhaustion playing tricks with my mind?

I scrambled to my feet, turning as I did.

'Mohammed? Mohammed!'

And there he was: his Lionel Messi top crumpled and dirty, his jaw jutting out like he planned to start a fight with the entire Hungarian army. Whatever fresh string of expletives he'd been about to unleash died on his lips, and for a moment it was impossible to tell which of us was in the most shock.

I dropped *The God Delusion* and climbed the fence. I didn't pause to consider the wisdom of this, but even if I had, I don't think it would have made any difference. The interior fences were only a couple of metres high, and unlike the perimeter fence, they were not defended by guards with batons and pepper spray. They were only there, I assume, to section us off into manageable groups.

Mohammed stood with his mouth open, the wheelbarrow-sandwich-man shouted in Hungarian, and I pretty much threw myself over the top of the fence. I landed poorly, and when I leapt back to my feet, my right ankle shrieked in protest, forcing me to limp and stagger the rest of the way. My brother's expression shifted from surprise to embarrassment to alarm. It's possible he thought I was about to attack him; this is certainly what the guards thought. Four of them came running as I grabbed Mohammed around his shoulders and squeezed him to my chest in a fierce bear hug. Unfortunately, my injured ankle was unable to support this additional weight, and we both ended up on the ground, with the four Hungarian guards on top of us. I'd imagine it looked like a typical scene from the British sport of rugby, where one man picks up the ball and all the other men immediately jump on him. As you probably know, the Americans later adapted this sport as American football, and made all the players wear armour, which was an obvious improvement.

Mohammed and I had no armour. We were first crushed into the mud and then dragged apart by our Hungarian assailants.

'He's my brother, you unbelievable pricks!' Mohammed shouted in Arabic.

'This is my brother!' I screamed in English, and somehow I managed to wriggle loose from the two men who were trying to restrain me. I backed away, crouching low like a cornered animal. 'He's my brother, and if you want to keep us apart then you should be ready to beat me unconscious! That's the only way it's going to happen!'

This melodrama had no effect. Moving as one, the Hungarian guards lunged forward and each grabbed one of my arms.

Who knows what might have happened next? I struggled and thrashed, but was unable to get any leverage on my damaged ankle. Mohammed shouted for help in Arabic, appealing to the mob he'd been attempting to stir to revolt over the non-halal sandwiches.

The woman who came to our aid was old enough to be our

grandmother. She wore the hijab, and she was short and wrinkled and looked like a strong breeze would knock her to the floor.

I stopped struggling against the guards, and Mohammed stopped shouting. The grandmother walked over and simply rested a hand on my shoulder. 'Come on,' she said in Arabic. 'Let's go.'

'She says you should let us go,' I loosely translated, for the benefit of the guards.

They looked uncertain. The old woman tugged gently on my arm, and said: 'Tell them you're not going to cause any more trouble. You're going to come with me and talk quietly with your brother and that will be the end of it.'

I translated this word for word.

The guards looked at each other, speaking in Hungarian. After a moment, one of them shrugged and released my arm with a jerk, and then the other did likewise.

The old woman didn't give them a chance to change their minds. She led me over to Mohammed, patted my arm, and then just walked away as if nothing had occurred, heading back towards one of the many identical tents.

'You just got rescued by an old lady,' Mohammed sniggered. 'Those Hungarians were about to kick your ass.'

'Shut up, Mohammed,' I said.

We sat on the ground and we talked. Mohammed's story was relatively straightforward, and he told it with minimal fuss and minimal effort. I would have expected nothing less from my little brother.

After we were separated at the road, he ran as fast as he could into the forest. Someone was chasing him, and he figured the best way to lose him was to keep changing direction, and to place as much vegetation between them as possible. This proved to be an effective strategy. After a while, Mohammed was certain he had lost his pursuer. The unintended consequence was that he had also lost himself. He had no idea where he was in relation to the road or the border or Kelebia.

He kept walking, and eventually he cleared the forest and was able to take stock. From the position of the sunrise, he deduced that he had mostly been heading north, when he needed to go west. So he turned, putting the sun at his back, and started walking again. The problem, of course, was that he still had only a vague notion of his starting point.

He walked for a long time – probably several hours across uniformly flat farmland. When he saw farm workers or buildings he avoided them. When he found a road, he walked parallel to it, but far enough away so that he could hide from passing traffic. He grew hot and hungry and tired. He had half a bottle of water and a bag of nuts in his bag, but that was all.

Eventually he found a road sign that informed him he had been following the road in the wrong direction. He'd walked for what felt like hours in the wrong direction, and Kelebia was now many kilometres to the south.

At this point he was extremely frustrated. He found a thicket, unrolled his sleeping bag, and had a long sleep.

The rest was more of the same, but in the opposite direction and having exhausted his most basic supplies. He walked. He ate some unripe corn from a field and drank some unsanitary water from a trough that was presumably meant for farm animals. When night fell, he slept in a deserted and ramshackle barn. By the morning he was extremely hungry and thirsty, and no longer confident in his ability to survive in the wild. He knocked on the door of a farmhouse and asked for some water.

A Hungarian woman, who spoke almost no English, made him breakfast, which he ate at her kitchen table. At the same time, she must have called the police, because they arrived not long afterwards. Mohammed was driven to a police station in a village whose name he could not recall, and from there his fate was the same as mine and Jesus's. After most of the day in police custody, he was brought to the detention camp, where he told the guards, over and over, that he was eighteen years old and must be housed with the 'men'. His reasoning was that this was where I would be, assuming that I had also been captured – which was obviously a sensible assumption to make.

Once he'd finished talking, I told him about Jesus. Not everything, just the broad brushstrokes of what I'd found out at the station, and what had happened afterwards.

'You can't die of *not* drinking!' Mohammed scoffed.

'Mohammed, I assure you, you can. I have received medical information that corroborates this fact.'

'Have you looked on Wikipedia?'

'I spoke to a doctor.'

'You should look on Wikipedia, just to be sure.'

'I'm afraid the phone battery is dead.'

Mohammed looked very aggrieved at this news. After a moment, he sighed and shook his head. 'Well . . . at least he's in hospital now. It's the best place for him. It's always been the best place.'

I stayed silent.

'He'll get well eventually and . . . I don't know. I guess he'll get to Germany sooner or later.'

'Mohammed, it's not that simple. I still have his backpack. It contains all his money. It contains his daughter's address, in Berlin.'

'Shit.' My brother looked like he wanted to kick something.

'At the very least, I have to deliver these things to him. And, anyway . . . he's on his own. He's probably scared and confused.'

'He's always been confused.'

'He won't be able to communicate. He doesn't speak any English.'

'He knows a few words.'

'Those words don't count. They're not going to get him very far.'

My brother stared at his feet, scowling. 'How can he possibly have a daughter?' he muttered. 'The idea of him being anyone's dad is just . . . Well, it's nuts, that's all. Completely nuts.'

I waited a few moments, then said: 'Mohammed, I'm not sure how much this will mean to you, but you should know that Jesus didn't have to stay in Hungary. He could have left me at the station. I told him to go.'

'He should have gone.'

'He wanted to help me find you. He would not leave you behind.'

'Shit.' Mohammed continued to scowl. He picked up a small stone and threw it at the fence. 'Okay, fine. You win. We should go to the hospital, give him his things and make sure he's okay. Except we can't, can we? Because we're stuck in here.'

'It won't be forever.'

'Do you even know where they took him?'

'No. Not yet. But I know where I can find out.' I drew my

knees up towards my chest and gave my injured ankle an experimental poke. 'You know, this ankle is bruised pretty badly. I should probably have the medics examine it . . .'

After an elaborate apology for climbing the fence, I managed to persuade the guards that Mohammed should accompany me back to my section of the camp. He was only fourteen, after all, and my tent did have a recently vacated bed. We were escorted back, and I left him in the care of the Zambians while I went to retrieve Richard Dawkins from the bottom of the fence. But when I got there, he was gone. A sharp whistle drew my attention, and I turned to see the Egyptian doctor approaching. He had the book in his hands; it was still wrapped neatly in its *Great Expectations* jacket.

'I think this must be yours,' the doctor said.

'Yes. Thank you.'

I held out my hand, but he didn't return the book yet. He drummed his fingers against the cover. 'Charles Dickens . . . Your English must be very good.'

I felt my face reddening. 'Yes. It was what I studied. In Syria.'

'Ah, I see. Well, I only read a little English, but Mr Dickens . . . seems interesting.'

'He is one of the greatest English writers,' I confirmed.

'He knows a surprising amount about evolutionary biology.'

'Yes.' My face must have been the colour of the setting sun. 'He was very ahead of his time.'

The doctor gave the faintest of smiles. 'Is your foot okay? Would you like me to take a look at it?'

'Thank you, but no. I'm going to try to see the Hungarian doctor later on. I want to ask him some questions.'

185

The Egyptian nodded once, then handed me my book. 'Enjoy your reading.'

'Thank you. I will.'

He turned and left, and I limped back to my tent, wondering if I'd just been speaking to a fellow apostate.

I waited until late in the night, guessing that this would maximise my chances of seeing the same emergency doctor – the one who had examined Jesus. I left Mohammed dozing on the bed and limped over to the guards at the perimeter fence. The same guards as the previous night. They both frowned deeply upon seeing me.

'Hello,' I said.

'You want see doctor?' one of them guessed.

'It's my ankle.'

'It can wait morning?'

'The pain is very bad. I think I may have broken something.'

The guard expelled a weary sigh, then started to open the gate.

At the warehouse, I was relieved to see it was the same doctor on duty. He took about thirty seconds to examine my ankle, then shook his head. 'It's a bruise,' he said. 'You rest it, it gets better.'

'Have you heard anything about my friend Jesus?' I asked.

'No.'

'Do you know which hospital he's in?'

'Szeged Hospital. It's closest.'

'Could you write it down for me? Please?'

The doctor looked at me for a moment, then took a pen from his coat.

*

'Okay, so now we know where he is,' Mohammed said the following morning. 'Now, what's the plan for getting out of here?'

'We sit tight,' I told him. 'Wait for them to let us go.'

'That's not a plan!' my brother complained. 'That's just bending over and taking it!'

'Do you have a better plan?'

'Of course I do! These Hungarian dick-riders expect us just to wait in our cages, like scared little mice. That's their weakness. They're not expecting us to try to escape.'

'Mohammed—'

'We wait until they're not looking. We climb the fence, and we run into the trees. We'll be gone before they even know what's happening.'

'Mohammed, you're an idiot. It's like you've learned nothing over the last couple of days.'

Mohammed gave me a look that said: *Damn right I haven't!* 'These fences are nothing. You proved that yesterday.'

'Yes. And my reward was a busted ankle and a near-beating.' I gestured at my foot. 'How do you expect me to run on *this*?'

'We don't have to do it now. In a couple of days—'

'No, Mohammed. Your plan is ridiculous. In a couple of days we'll probably be out of here anyway. They don't keep us here indefinitely. I have this on good authority.'

'Fine!' Mohammed spat. 'We'll see if you're right. We'll wait a couple of days. If they haven't released us by then, we'll revisit the fence option . . .'

I stopped listening at this point. I just closed my eyes and shook my head, and eventually he ran out of steam.

My brother *was* an idiot, and he was still infuriating. But it was good to have him back.

187

A Medical Miracle

In the end, my plan prevailed. The Hungarians kept us for three more days and then packed us onto a bus bound for the train station in Szeged. From there, we were supposed to travel to Budapest, and then on to another refugee facility in the north. But I didn't speak to a single passenger on our bus who intended to follow this protocol. As soon as they arrived in Budapest they were going to join the thousands already in the capital, waiting to board trains heading west. The Hungarians could not stop this, and ultimately, they did not want to. It was the same as in Greece; they told us we were legally required to stay, and turned a blind eye when we left. As soon as we were over the border, we became someone else's problem.

Of course, this raised the question of why they bothered to imprison us in the first place. It's a question I don't know the answer to. The best theory I heard was that it was all for show: our treatment was a message to others seeking to violate Hungary's borders, a deterrent of sorts.

Fortunately, not everyone in Hungary hated us. At Szeged station, we found volunteers who were handing out food, water and advice. One of them was able to show me where the hospital was on the map on her phone, and I spent a couple of minutes memorising the route. The hospital was only five minutes away on foot – maybe ten, given that my ankle was still slightly tender – so this was not a difficult task.

There is not much to say about the hospital in Szeged. It was almost identical to the hospital in Latakia, which is the only other hospital I am familiar with, except all the signs were in Hungarian. I suppose hospitals follow pretty much the same template wherever you go: wipe-clean and functional, with a strong smell of detergent.

At the entrance, there was a security guard who spoke no English, but after much gesturing, he took us through to the reception, where they did speak English. I explained that we were looking for our friend, an alcoholic Iraqi, whom we had reason to believe had been brought in five days ago, in the middle of the night. The receptionist made several phone calls, and was clearly amazed when our story was corroborated. She told us there was a doctor who wanted to speak to us as soon as possible.

This turned out to be almost an hour later, but the time was not wasted. Mohammed took a nap in the waiting area, and I recharged the phone.

The doctor was a small balding man with thin glasses and hairy hands. I noticed the hands because he greeted us with a gracious handshake, which I was not expecting. He introduced himself as Dr Polgár, neurologist. Fortunately, I knew what this meant because I had watched many episodes of the American medical drama *House*.

'Is there something wrong with Jesus's brain?' I asked. 'Is he okay?'

'He's no longer in any immediate danger,' Dr Polgár assured me. 'But . . . well, we should talk somewhere private. I also have many questions for you.'

He led us through a maze of corridors until we reached a small consultation room. On the way, he told us that the hospital had been given almost no information about Jesus or his background. They had been waiting to see if they could get an Arabic translator in so that they could at least communicate with him, but so far they had run up against a brick wall. This was part of the reason he was so pleased that Mohammed and I had turned up. Prior to this, the only data they had received about their mystery patient, after a phone call to the detention camp, was that he was an illegal border-crosser, Syrian, and went by the name of Jesus.

'He's not Syrian,' I corrected. 'My brother and I are Syrians. Jesus is an Iraqi.'

Dr Polgár frowned at this discrepancy. 'What's your relationship to this man?'

'We met him in Greece. We're travelling companions. Friends . . .' I glanced at Mohammed. 'It's complicated.'

'Does he have relatives?' Dr Polgár asked. 'Anyone we can contact?'

'He has a daughter in Germany, but they haven't spoken for some time.'

'Some time?'

'Twenty years or so. Jesus was a little vague on the details.'

'I'm not surprised. He's . . .' Dr Polgár trailed off. 'Well, that can wait. It will be better if we can talk through these matters properly, without any distractions.'

Once we were seated in the consultation room, Dr Polgár did not beat around the bush. 'Your friend had a stroke,' he said. 'He's lucky to be alive.'

I let this sink in. After a moment of silence, I translated the doctor's words for Mohammed, who frowned and rubbed his temples.

'Is he all right now?' my brother asked. 'I mean . . . how long will he be in hospital?'

I translated this for Dr Polgár.

'I don't know,' the doctor said. 'Physically, he seems as well as can be expected. But he was unconscious for almost three days. He's still under heavy sedation, and we've had no way to assess his cognition. We only have the scans to go on . . .'

At this point, Dr Polgár placed two large black-and-white photographs on his desk and gestured that we should take a look. They were images of brains, one unmarked and the other heavily annotated. 'The image on the left is the brain of a typical sixty-year-old,' he said. 'We had to estimate your friend's age, but it will do for now, as a basis for comparison.'

'He thinks he's about sixty to sixty-five,' I said. 'He wasn't able to narrow it down any further.'

Dr Polgár nodded, apparently unsurprised. 'The image on the right is the scan we took of your friend's brain. Some of the differences are obvious, some are more subtle.'

I looked at the two images. Jesus's brain appeared somewhat smaller. It was not the most striking thing about the two pictures, but it was the first I mentioned to Dr Polgár.

'A shrinking of the grey matter,' he told me. 'This is long-term damage, not uncommon in alcoholics.'

'What about the . . . holes?'

I didn't know how else to describe this feature. There were two of them – darker patches, like symmetrical inkblots amidst the shades of grey. They were the size of a thumbprint on the A4 printouts, and shaped like teardrops.

'They're holes,' Dr Polgár confirmed. 'Exactly as they appear to be. These are areas that have wasted away entirely, probably over many years. Again, some brain damage is not uncommon in long-term alcoholism, but . . .' Dr Polgár trailed off, shaking his head. 'Let me be frank,' he said, after a long hesitation. 'I've been a neurologist for over twenty years, and I've never seen anything like this. The extent of the damage is beyond belief. Your friend . . . well, I don't know what to tell you. You say he has memory problems?'

'Some memory problems, yes.'

'Anything else you've noticed? Strange behaviour?'

I glanced at Mohammed, whose face was like a stone. 'He's a little strange,' I confirmed. 'But . . . well, his behaviour's consistently strange. It's just the way he is.'

Dr Polgár jabbed an accusing finger in the direction of the scans. 'Based on these images, it's incredible that your friend has *any* memory. He should be in a permanent state of amnesia. That he can function at all is . . . well, it's a medical miracle. I don't know how else to describe it.'

I gulped uneasily. Mohammed's face was still impassive. I didn't know how much of the exchange he'd been able to follow since I'd stopped translating; Dr Polgár's English was fluent, far better than my brother's, and we'd been speaking quite rapidly. But I was certain he'd have understood some of it, and he couldn't have missed the uneasy atmosphere in the room.

'This damage,' I said after a moment, 'the holes – they're nothing to do with the stroke?'

Dr Polgár shook his head. 'No. This is long-term damage. It probably spans decades. The damage from the stroke is almost trivial by comparison. He burst a blood vessel in his visual cortex.'

'What does that mean? Can he still see okay?'

'We think so. There *are* potential complications, but we'll have to do a full assessment. You and your brother can help with this. I'll need you to ask questions.'

I nodded. 'When? Can we see him now?'

'It would be better later on. We have to keep him sedated because of his ongoing withdrawal from alcohol. He's likely to sleep for the next few hours. But if you come back this afternoon, he'll probably be lucid enough to talk. Do you boys have some-where to stay?'

'No, not yet. We've come straight from the train station.'

Dr Polgár spent a couple of minutes tapping on his keyboard, then scribbled down the address of a nearby hostel.

'One more thing,' Dr Polgár said before we left. 'Your friend's fingers. What happened?'

'Al-Qaeda cut them off,' I said.

Dr Polgár just shook his head, silently, with his eyes closed. There was nothing to say.

The hostel was ten minutes' walk from the hospital. Our room had narrow twin beds, a desk, a lamp, and nothing else, but compared to the detention camp, it was heaven. There was a bathroom just down the corridor and I spent a good half hour just standing under the shower, rinsing five days' worth of grime from my body. I tried not to think about Jesus and his irregular brain. I concentrated only on the sensation of the hot water running over my face and down my back, of tight muscles slowly relaxing.

We were back at the hospital by four o'clock, and Dr Polgár met us in the waiting area and took us up to the room where Jesus was being treated. On the way, he gave us the latest information concerning Jesus's condition. Not that there was much to say. He had been awake for the last hour. He had eaten a small amount of food and seemed alert, if somewhat agitated. Beyond that, Dr Polgár could not tell us what to expect. Jesus's withdrawal symptoms were not as severe as they had been, but he might appear confused or anxious. And there was still no saying how he would react to seeing me and Mohammed; it was possible that he wouldn't react at all. He might not even recognise us.

Jesus was in a room with three other patients – old white men. Two of them glanced over when we entered, but Jesus did not. He was in the nearest bed on the left side of the room. He looked gaunt. He was wearing a hospital gown that hung limply from his bony shoulders, and there were deep dark hollows under his eyes. Dr Polgár had said he was alert, and I suppose he was, in some sense, but the term was a little misleading. He was propped up in his bed, which was tilted forward, and he seemed to be staring with a strange intensity at a fixed point on the ceiling. I don't know how to describe his expression. On edge, I suppose, but that hardly does it justice. He looked as if he expected the ceiling to fall down on him any moment.

On the bedside table, neatly placed, were the Greek lady's pink flip-flops.

Mohammed and I stood at the near side of the bed while Dr Polgár drew a curtain across to give us some privacy. Still, Jesus did not react.

'Hello, Jesus,' I said. 'It's Zain. And Mohammed.'

His eyes widened, but his expression did not change. It was impossible to tell, at this point, if he recognised my voice or was simply responding to the use of Arabic.

Slowly, he turned his head. 'You are the boys from my dream,' he said.

Mohammed groaned.

'He knows who we are,' I told Dr Polgár.

Jesus stretched out his hand. It was the mutilated one; a small tube had been inserted into one of his protruding veins, with surgical tape holding it in place. He grasped my wrist. 'Can you get me something to drink?' he pleaded.

'I'm sorry, Jesus. I can't. Not anymore.'

A moment passed, then he started to cry. I didn't know what to do. I just stood there as he continued to hold my wrist, and waited for the tears to subside.

Eventually, Jesus calmed down. I was able to establish that he did recognise me and Mohammed from real life, as well as his dreams. He remembered certain events from the past fortnight, but his memories were vague and confused, or else they were inaccurate, or missing entirely. He knew that he had first met us on a beach in Greece, but insisted that he had not merely found us, but had pulled our unconscious bodies from the sea. He would brook no argument on this fact, and I soon gave up trying to persuade him that his recollection was false.

Regarding other incidents, his memory was equally fanciful.

He said that he remembered nothing of coming to Hungary, but he did recall walking through a long dark tunnel; this, he thought, was his most recent memory.

'We crawled though a hole in a fence,' I told him. 'It was a tunnel, of sorts. Maybe that's what you're thinking of?'

'No, there was no crawling,' Jesus insisted. 'We walked, the three of us, in single file, for a very long time. Hours and hours on end.'

'We walked through a forest,' I told him. 'It was very dark, and we couldn't see the sky. That could be it.'

'There was terrible danger,' Jesus said. 'We had to stay on the *exact* path. Our lives depended on it!'

I translated most of this for Dr Polgár, who suggested I should change the subject. He could see that Jesus was becoming agitated again.

'Perhaps we should keep things as simple as possible,' Dr Polgár said. 'Could you ask him what year it is?'

Jesus thought about this for a very long time, staring at the ceiling once more. 'It's 1999,' he said.

I translated this for Dr Polgár, who immediately started writing some notes on the clipboard he was carrying.

I coughed gently. 'It's 2015, Jesus. 2015.'

I expected more of a reaction to this, but Jesus just nodded thoughtfully. 'The future.'

'Ask him about his vision,' Dr Polgár suggested. 'Can he see everything clearly? Are there any obvious problems?'

'I see many things . . .' Jesus responded.

Unsure what to do with this rather cryptic statement, I simply translated it, word for word.

'He needs to be more specific,' Dr Polgár said.

'That's how he always talks,' Mohammed noted, in English.

'What do you see, Jesus?' I asked. 'What do you see right now?'

'I see the ceiling,' Jesus responded. 'I see a strange room. I see a strange man dressed in white.'

'That's Dr Polgár,' I said. 'I told you about him. He's been looking after you.'

'I see darkness and light,' Jesus said. 'I see a woman's face. She's very beautiful.'

I reported all this to Dr Polgár, who immediately frowned. 'Can you ask him to elaborate? Is this what he imagines, or what he actually *sees*?'

Unfortunately, Jesus was unable to cope with this distinction.

'The woman's face,' I said. 'Do you see this in the same way you see the ceiling and Dr Polgár? Or is it different? Is it more like . . . when you close your eyes and picture someone?'

'It doesn't matter if I have my eyes opened or closed,' Jesus said. 'I see the same things.'

'It's possible he's hallucinating,' Dr Polgár said. 'It would not be surprising, given the stroke damage. Does he recognise the woman's face? Is it someone he knows?'

'She's very beautiful,' Jesus repeated.

'Maybe it's your daughter?' I suggested.

Jesus's eyes widened. He gripped the side rails on his bed with both hands. 'I have a daughter?'

'Yes. You're . . . That's why you came to Europe. She lives in Germany.'

Jesus's expression hadn't changed.

'He doesn't know about his daughter,' I said to Dr Polgár, who started scribbling furiously on his clipboard.

197

And after that, Jesus would not say anything at all. He was back to staring at the ceiling. Occasionally, he shook his head, but that was the full extent of his communication. Dr Polgár said it might be better if we left.

'We're stuck here, aren't we?' Mohammed asked, as we walked back to the hostel some time later.

'What do you mean?' I said.

'I mean we're stuck in Hungary, at least for now. You saw him. He's a mess. We can't just leave him here.'

I thought about this for a long time. I didn't know what had finally caused my brother to change his perspective, but it felt like a significant step.

'Mohammed, you've grown,' I said.

'Shut up,' Mohammed said.

Convalescence

We stayed in Szeged for another week, and we visited Jesus every day – often twice a day, for many hours at a time. Because of Jesus's rather unusual circumstances, Dr Polgár left instructions at reception that we were to be allowed access even outside of standard visiting hours. He thought that us talking to Jesus would help with his rehabilitation; and, of course, it made things far easier for the hospital staff. In the first couple of days, they were able to run a number of tests to assess his physical and mental condition. An extensive vision test revealed excellent eyesight for a man of his age, and his motor skills seemed likewise unimpeded. He was weak on his feet for a while, but Dr Polgár said this was probably because of the medication and the extended period in bed. He encouraged us to walk Jesus up and down the corridors a few times every day, and soon enough, Jesus was able to undertake this task unaided. Physically, he seemed to have escaped his stroke with minimal damage.

His sedatives were tapered and then stopped entirely. This would have been approximately a week after his enforced detoxification from alcohol began, by which time, Dr Polgár assured us, he was no longer physically dependent. Jesus would still suffer cravings for many months and possibly years to come, but his body could now function without alcohol. By the time he was discharged, we would not have to worry about any more seizures or strokes. The biggest challenge would be keeping him dry.

'What about his memory?' I asked. 'Will it come back?'

Dr Polgár squinted at me through his thin glasses, his forehead wrinkled in thought. Eventually, he gave a small shrug. 'I can't even make an educated guess,' he said. 'I've told you: his brain is a complete anomaly. All you can do is keep talking to him. See what happens.'

So I kept talking to him. There were some days when he hardly said a word, and just stared at that same spot on the ceiling, as if it held some profound mystery that no one else could see. But there were also periods when he was far more communicative, and wanted to go over everything that had happened since we met him in Greece. In general, his memory was still very hazy, yet there were some incidents that he recalled with minimal prompting. And however much he had distorted or embellished these incidents, they still retained some basis in reality.

'I remember a ferocious storm,' he told me. 'With waves high above our heads.'

'Yes,' I said, somewhat uneasily. 'That happened.'

'You were scared, but there was no need to be. It was very beautiful.'

'Yes, I suppose it was. In a way.'

Jesus thought for a few moments, focusing on his spot on the ceiling. 'It was good to be outside,' he said. 'With so much sky and open space. I have spent a lot of time in prison.'

'You spent some time in prison,' I confirmed. 'And we were

held at a police station in Hungary, then at the detention camp.'

'I was in prison for about a year, I think. They spoke a foreign language, but treated me kindly.'

I gave a slow nod. From what Jesus had told me, he'd never been treated well in prison, but if that was what he now believed, I did not want to upset him.

'What else do you remember?' I asked.

'I remember walking through the desert,' Jesus said. 'We walked for many hours – me and you and little Mohammed. The sun was like a furnace.'

'I'm not little!' Mohammed protested.

'Mohammed, be quiet,' I said. 'Jesus, we didn't walk through any deserts. We walked through the mountains, in Greece. Maybe that's what you're thinking of?'

'No, it was a desert,' Jesus insisted. 'There was no water and my feet were burning. The light was intense. Then a messenger came. She gifted me some shoes.'

He glanced across at the pink flip-flops, which were again perched on the bedside table. I decided not to pursue the point.

'What else?' I asked. 'Do you remember the train station where we waited for Mohammed? Do you remember talking to me about your life in Iraq?'

Jesus shook his head.

'What about coming to Hungary? The forest, the fences?'

He thought about this for a very long time. 'I remember a tunnel. It was dark, and very dangerous.'

I glanced at Mohammed, who rolled his eyes.

Jesus was silent for some time, then he shuddered, turning to me with a mournful face. 'Can you get me something to drink?' he asked.

I poured him a cup of water from the jug on his table and handed it across. He held it, but did not drink. He did not say another word.

Despite my frustration at being stuck in Hungary, Szeged was not an unpleasant city in which to spend a week. It was an old city, with broad squares filled with statues and monuments. A large river ran through its centre, and from its bridges you could see the spires of churches stretching to the sky. There were parks and gardens, and streets lined with tall trees. The city wasn't especially big – it was somewhat smaller than Latakia – but after our time in the detention camp, it felt huge.

For a week, we lived as frugally as possible. Fortunately, Szeged was not an expensive city. Everything we needed was within walking distance, and you could buy cheap but tasty food in the local cafés and restaurants. Most of the time, we stuck to our diet of fruit, chocolate and supermarket sandwiches, but a hot meal every once in a while wasn't going to bankrupt us. Nevertheless, I was always aware of how much we were spending, down to the last forint, and I was determined to save as much as possible for the journey ahead. So most evenings we stayed in our tiny hostel room and rested, and after the previous week, even this felt like a strange luxury. We had privacy and a toilet and washing facilities. We had unlimited electricity, which in itself was enough to keep Mohammed happy; it meant he could go on the phone as often as he wanted. I got back into the habit of showering every day, and I finally got around to shaving my beard off. I looked clean and respectable. No one could mistake me for a threat to their national security.

Regarding the local people: most were not unfriendly. Most did not pay us very much attention. We only had one unpleasant experience, which came one evening as we were walking back to the hostel. A group of boys, probably not much older than Mohammed, began to shout at us from across the street. Most of it was in Hungarian, but at one point one of them shouted in English that we should 'Go home.' It was a ridiculous thing to say, obviously, but Mohammed was fuming, nevertheless. I took hold of his arm.

'Ignore them, Mohammed.'

'Arseholes!' He spat the word in English, probably not loud enough for them to hear, but not far short.

'Mohammed, you are not to start anything! It's the last thing we need right now.'

'I'm not starting anything. They are!'

'Don't let them get to you. That's what they want.'

'What do they think, we're here for fun?'

'They're just ignorant. Keep walking.'

'I'd *love* to go home,' he shouted in English. 'If I could, I'd fucking go home tomorrow!'

This was met with another barrage of insults. A couple of the boys strutted up to the kerb on the far side of the street, their chests puffed out. I gripped Mohammed's arm more firmly. There were five of them in total. If we weren't careful, we were going to end up in the hospital with Jesus.

'Come on,' I said. 'Just keep walking.'

Mohammed shook his arm loose and rounded on me. 'You know, just once it would be really fucking great if you stuck up for yourself! If you stuck up for *us*.'

I tried to keep my voice low and soothing. 'Mohammed, looking after you is my number-one priority. That's why we're just going to walk away.'

'You're my brother! You're supposed to have my back!'

'Mohammed, it's okay. You'll calm down as soon as we're away from them. It's going to be okay.'

'How, Zain? How is it going to be fucking okay? You said we'd be safe in Europe! Look around you. Most of them wouldn't piss on us if we were on fire! Most of them would be queuing up to throw on the petrol!'

There was no calming him down. I was used to my brother's temper, of course, but this was something new. His voice was desperate, right on the edge of hysteria. I grabbed his arm again and pulled him down the street, as forcefully as I could without hurting him. The angry jeers followed, but soon we were out of earshot. Mohammed freed his arm with a sharp jerk, then quickened his pace so he did not have to walk with me. I let him go. There was no hope of talking to him when he was like this.

When we got back to the hostel, he immediately locked himself in the bathroom. I gave him five minutes, which became ten minutes, then went to knock on the door.

'Mohammed, please come out and talk to me.'

This was met with silence. I hoped very much that it *was* still Mohammed in there. It was a communal bathroom, after all, shared between all the rooms on the corridor. I quelled a brief surge of panic. Of course it was Mohammed. He wouldn't leave without telling me, whatever state he was in.

I tried again. 'Mohammed, I'm sorry. Take all the time you need. When you're ready, I'll be in the room.'

I had to wait another five minutes or so. I sat on one of the twin beds and tried to figure out what I was going to say to him.

What I *could* say to him. I felt like an idiot. I was so used to him being brave – ridiculously brave most of the time. It was easy to forget that he was only fourteen.

When he came back, it was obvious that he'd been crying, but I didn't know how he'd respond if I brought it up. I wondered how Dad would handle a situation like this. Better than I could, that was for sure.

Mohammed sat on the other bed and looked at me, somewhat reluctantly.

'I'm sorry I lost it,' he said.

'It's not important. I mean, you don't have to apologise. It isn't—'

'I tried to phone Mum last night.' He blurted it out very quickly, as if fearful that he might change his mind. 'It was while you were in the shower. I just . . . well, I had to know.'

My stomach dropped, and I found myself without any words. A long, awful silence passed, then I acted on pure instinct. I sat beside him on the bed and put my arm around his shoulder.

'Mohammed, I'm so sorry. I should have—'

'They've taken her too, haven't they? Otherwise she'd have called. There's no other reason . . .'

My throat felt tight and dry, but I forced myself to speak. 'Yes. They've probably taken her too. But . . .'

I couldn't bring myself to finish. I wanted to say that she would not be mistreated. She had done nothing wrong and they'd have to release her eventually. Dad too.

I wanted to say these things to my brother, but I no longer knew if they were true.

'You should have told me,' Mohammed said quietly. 'I have a right to know what's happening.'

'Of course you do. I was trying to protect you. I'm sorry.'

We sat in silence for a long time after that. We sat in silence, and Mohammed didn't try to move my arm from his shoulder.

'Do you remember when I broke Mum's vase?' he said eventually. 'I was ten, I was juggling the football in the front room, even though she'd told me not to about a million times.'

'Yes, I remember. It used to belong to Grandma. A genuine antique.'

'You told her it was you, that you knocked it over with your school bag.'

'She would have skinned you alive. I figured she'd go a little easier on me.'

'Yeah. That's what I figured too. You never put a foot wrong. Never got in any trouble.'

I shrugged. There wasn't much I could say to this. It was completely true.

'I didn't mean what I said earlier,' Mohammed told me after a moment. 'You *do* have my back. I know that.'

'Of course. Always.'

'But you can't protect me from everything. I'm not a kid.'

'I know. It's just . . . Mum told me to look after you. It's not always easy to know how to do that.'

Mohammed nodded to himself, and some minutes must have passed before either of us said another word.

'Do you still want to stay here?' I asked. 'Because it *is* your decision too. Jesus is out of danger. We don't have to stay in Hungary if you don't want to.'

Mohammed thought for a while, then let out a weary sigh. 'Well, we've come this far with him. We might as well get him to his daughter. Assuming she actually exists. Face it, he's never going to get to Germany on his own.'

'No. Probably not.'

'Well, fuck it. What's a few more days?'

'Thank you, Mohammed. I'm—'

He cut me off, nudging me in the ribs. 'Don't you dare say you're proud of me.'

'I won't say it,' I told him.

A few more moments of quiet.

'I miss them,' Mohammed whispered.

I squeezed his shoulder. 'Me too. I miss them every day.'

It was on our seventh day visiting the hospital that Dr Polgár asked if he could talk to me in private for a few minutes. I left Mohammed with Jesus, and we went through to the same consultation room where Dr Polgár had shown us the scans, one week earlier. This was the first time since then that he'd wanted to talk privately, and I found it a little strange. Worrying, even. But I didn't have long to wonder. Dr Polgár got straight to the point, before the door had even closed behind us.

'We're going to release your friend,' he told me.

I thought about this for a moment. There was something in Dr Polgár's tone that said he wasn't entirely happy with this turn of events.

'Is he well enough?' I asked. 'I mean, his memory is still full of gaps, and his mood . . . well, it's not completely stable. It can change very quickly.'

Dr Polgár regarded me over his steepled fingers. 'It's far from ideal. Some would say it's irresponsible to release a man like him with no further medical support. Ideally, he'd have a schedule of follow-up appointments, an interview with a psychologist, access to addiction counselling, but . . . well, I don't have much choice in the matter.'

At this point, Dr Polgár passed me several sheets of A4 paper that had been stapled together. 'What's this?' I asked.

'It's his hospital bill. You don't need to worry; if he's granted asylum it will disappear. But at the moment he has no legal status. So we have to charge him for healthcare, even if he has no means to pay for it.'

'How much is it?'

'About six hundred thousand forints. Just under two thousand euros.'

I stayed silent.

'There's a lot of pressure on us at the moment,' Dr Polgár continued. 'Political pressure, financial pressure. I've already kept him here longer than I should have. Long enough to give him a chance of recovery, if he can stay sober.'

'I'll keep him sober,' I promised.

'I'm sure you'll try.'

I nodded. I thought that was the end of it, but Dr Polgár stayed in his seat, looking at me very intently. 'I'm afraid there's an additional complication,' he told me. 'Your friend is still technically under detention. Before I discharge him, I have to phone the border police. They'll transport him back to the detention centre so that his asylum claim can be properly processed.'

My heart skipped several beats. If Jesus were taken back into custody, I didn't think it likely that Mohammed and I would be allowed to go with him. And he had no documentation. No passport, nothing. It could be weeks before they let him out. *If* they let him out.

I took a breath, then explained all this to Dr Polgár, as calmly as I could. 'He needs care,' I concluded, 'and he isn't going to get it in a detention centre. Trust me: those are not nice places. It would be far better if he left with us. We can take him to his daughter, in Germany.'

Dr Polgár's expression didn't change, but after a moment, he nodded. 'Yes. I agree with everything you've said. The best thing would be if he goes to Germany. It's the best chance he has for getting the help he needs. Which gives me a dilemma.' He lowered his eyes and gave a small shake of his head. 'My conscience says I should let him leave, but I'm legally required to contact the border police before he's discharged. It could cost me my job if I don't.'

I waited for a moment. 'Where does that leave us?'

Dr Polgár didn't answer for what seemed a very long time. A clock ticked on the wall, but otherwise, the room was completely silent. Finally, he sighed, shaking his head again. 'I can give you until tomorrow afternoon. I won't be making any phone calls until then. Do you understand?'

'Yes,' I said. 'I understand. Thank you.'

Dr Polgár nodded, then pushed a small package across the desk. 'His medication. Acamprosate and thiamine. He needs to take the acamprosate three times a day and the thiamine once.'

I took the package and put it in my pocket. 'Thank you.'

'If I were you, I'd leave during morning visiting hours. There's less chance of anyone noticing. If you run into any trouble with the nurses or security . . . well, I'm afraid you're on your own. I can't help you.'

'You've done enough already. More than enough.'

Dr Polgár gave the smallest of smiles, then extended his hand. 'Good luck getting to Germany.'

That was the last time we spoke. When Mohammed and I

came back to Jesus's ward the following morning, Dr Polgár had made sure he was elsewhere.

We drew the curtain around Jesus's bed and he changed out of his hospital gown and into his travelling clothes. Then we left. I don't think anyone gave us a second glance, but it was difficult to maintain a normal pace as we walked down the corridor. Jesus's flip-flops slapped noisily on the hard floor, and Mohammed cast furtive looks every time we passed a doctor or nurse.

By the time we reached the main entrance, I was sweating, and Mohammed's posture was stiff and awkward. Only Jesus seemed unperturbed. He looked as calm as if he were taking a stroll in the park.

The familiar security guard was on the door. He looked at Jesus for a moment, and Jesus nodded politely; it was a slow and serene nod, almost a bow.

'He's been discharged,' I said, rather pointlessly, since the man spoke no English. He continued to look at Jesus, but made no move to stop us as we left.

Outside, I breathed a deep sigh of relief.

'Well, that was fucking easy,' Mohammed said.

'Mohammed, don't swear.'

Jesus was looking at the sky, his eyes wide. His expression was a strange mix of fear and wonder.

'Jesus?' I asked. 'Are you okay?'

It took him a while, but eventually he nodded. 'What next, my friends?'

'Next . . . Germany. We're going to see your daughter.'

PART 3

Into the West

Neukölln

On a direct train, under optimum circumstances, the journey from Budapest to Berlin should have taken twelve hours. Instead, it took us three days. It was the same story as in Serbia and Macedonia: thousands upon thousands all trying to board the same trains and buses, endless queues, people sleeping wherever they could – often in the open air, on the streets or in the broad concourses in front of the stations. Some had pitched tents on the cold concrete, but most had only sleeping bags, scattered across pavements and plazas like a thousand colourful cocoons.

Everyone we saw was dirty and dishevelled. Everyone was exhausted; you could see it in their eyes, the weeks spent travelling, the many thousands of kilometres. And yet there was a subtle difference now. People seemed less frustrated, less impatient, and once we had crossed the border into Austria, the change was dramatic. There was a palpable sense of relief, of hope, even. This, finally, was the West, and for most, the journey was all but over.

Not so for me and Mohammed; and as for Jesus, who could

say? I don't think any of us had a strong expectation of what would happen next, but an immediate and lasting family reunion seemed an improbable hope. Jesus had not communicated with his daughter for over a decade, and had now lost even his memories of her.

'I'd say it's fifty-fifty she even *exists*,' Mohammed said to me, one evening in Vienna, while Jesus napped on a bench at the train station. 'Seriously, what evidence do we have to go on? That story he told you in Kelebia? The story he no longer remembers?'

'We have her address,' I said. 'We've both seen it.'

'Pah! We have *an* address. An address he keeps folded away in a pair of old socks!'

'The address is real,' I pointed out. 'We know that at least.' I took the phone from my pocket and tapped on Google Maps. The street was saved in my recent history: *Flughafenstraße, Neukölln, Berlin*. It might have looked like gibberish at first glance, but that was just the nature of the German language, with its tricky extra letters and implausibly long words. I tried reading the address aloud to Mohammed and was somewhat stunned when he started correcting my pronunciation.

'Noy-*kerln*,' he told me, as if this were the most obvious thing in the world. 'The O with the little dots has to be pronounced *errrr*. Like in Özil.'

'What's an Özil?'

'He's a German footballer. He used to play for Real Madrid. Now he plays in the Premier League. For Arsenal.'

'Arsenal? *Arse*nal? Are you kidding?'

'Google it, dick-licker!'

I did; and I'd never have believed it, but my brother's extensive knowledge of international football was finally proving useful. Arsenal was a genuine football team, and Neukölln was pronounced precisely as he'd said it would be; I found an audio clip that reproduced it in a synthesised Stephen-Hawking voice.

'Okay, great,' I said. 'So we have a real address in Berlin, and we'll be able to say it to a taxi driver without embarrassing ourselves.' Mohammed gave me a look that said *You're welcome*, which I ignored. 'We have no reason to doubt Jesus's story,' I told him. '*I* remember it, even if he doesn't.'

Mohammed didn't bother replying. The doubtful glance he threw at Jesus was enough to make his feelings clear. And I suppose his doubts were somewhat justified. Jesus's memory had not improved since leaving the hospital; in truth, it appeared to be getting worse. There were times when it seemed he could remember nothing before coming to Europe, as if his life prior to this had ceased to exist. When I pressed him – when I recounted the details he'd given me in Kelebia – his expression was that of a man trying to peer through fog. To complicate matters further, he was still finding it difficult to distinguish his memories from his dreams, and his dreams from reality. He no longer talked about receiving 'instructions' in his sleep, but insisted that he saw the same events playing out every night, in images far more vivid and reliable than anything else he remembered. Sometimes, after he woke, I caught him regarding me and Mohammed with a strange, speculative light in his eyes. It made me feel uneasy.

All in all, it was difficult to say how Jesus had been affected by events in Hungary. Mohammed would have claimed that Jesus's grip on reality had always been tenuous. Certainly, he had always been peculiar, but, if anything, this had become more

215

apparent to me since he'd been released from hospital. Now that he was sober, he was quieter, and a little more distant, but it was an other-worldly sort of distance, as if he were not quite with us. Often, I found him staring at everyday objects – trains, lampposts, bottled water – as if seeing them for the very first time. As if they were some strange puzzle he was determined to crack.

As for his addiction, he had now stopped asking me to buy alcohol for him, and he had not attempted to buy any himself, but I wasn't so naïve as to think that his problem had disappeared. I was still keeping a close eye on him. I saw how his fingers grasped air while he slept, and always upon waking, searched for the bottle that was no longer there.

Three times a day I made sure he took his acamprosate, which was supposed to help control his cravings. The other medication Dr Polgár had given me – the thiamine – turned out to be a vitamin pill. Vitamin B1. When I Googled it, I discovered it was often deficient in alcoholics, and a long-term deficiency was associated with brain damage and memory impairment. At its most severe, thiamine deficiency led to a condition called Korsakoff's psychosis, characterised by chronic amnesia.

As far as I knew, Dr Polgár had never put a name to Jesus's condition; he had never proffered an explicit diagnosis. What I remembered him saying was that Jesus's brain damage was beyond anything he'd ever seen before – that given the extent of it, he should not have been able to function. *A medical miracle.* The phrase Dr Polgár had chosen still made me shiver.

On the train from Vienna to Munich I tried to get a clearer idea of what was going on in Jesus's head. As always, there were no spare seats, so we were standing side-by-side in one of the doorways, while Mohammed sat on the floor with his knees drawn up to his chest. Jesus was staring out of the narrow window in the door. I don't think he'd moved a muscle since we boarded.

'Jesus? Are you okay?' I had to repeat the question a couple of times, at increasing volume, before he responded.

'I am okay, my friend.' He looked at me only briefly before turning back to the window. 'The train, it moves very fast. It's like the whole world is racing by.'

I tried again. 'Jesus, how are you feeling? You've been . . . well, I don't know how you've been since Hungary. Strange, I suppose. Not yourself.'

He looked at me a little longer this time, then nodded carefully. 'The world is a strange place. I have noticed this recently.'

I didn't know what to say to this. It was like we were having two different conversations.

Jesus shot me a broad, gappy grin, then said: 'I feel old, my friend. I feel like someone's put me in an old man's body.'

'Well, a lot has happened in the last two weeks,' I told him. 'You must be tired.'

'Yes, I am tired.' His grin faded, and for a moment he looked as sombre as I'd ever seen him. 'My dreams,' he said, 'sometimes they trouble me.' He shook his head, as if changing his mind about something. 'No, this is not for you to worry about. What will be, will be.'

He turned back to the window, to the world that was racing by.

So that was that. I still had no real idea how Jesus was feeling. I wasn't sure *he* knew how he was feeling; his mood seemed to change at an alarming pace. But, whatever the case, I decided that I should not push him any further, not right now.

All that was left was to go to the address in Berlin. If Jesus's daughter did exist, then seeing her might stir his memory. It surely had to provoke *some* response?

It was the best chance we had.

We found another hostel in Neukölln, only ten minutes' walk, or two stops on the *U-Bahn*, from Flughafenstraße. As always, money was a concern, so I asked for the cheapest room they had available. This turned out to be an eight-bed dormitory, which we would share with three young Dutchmen and two backpackers from New Zealand. The Dutchmen were in Berlin to attend a musical festival. The New Zealanders were 'just travelling the world'. They stood with their eyes wide and their mouths hanging open as I explained that we were on our way to the UK to seek asylum, but were in Berlin to visit Jesus's estranged daughter, who probably lived in the area.

The beds in the dormitory were bunk beds. After some deliberation, we decided it would be best if Mohammed took the bunk above Jesus and I would sleep under one of the Dutchmen. I hoped that Jesus's snoring would not keep everyone awake, but there was nothing that could be done about it. Anyway, it was a problem for later.

We had decided that the early evening would be the best time to visit the address on Flughafenstraße. That would give us enough time to clean ourselves up and have something to eat. We all agreed that it would be better to arrive looking presentable, and not as if we'd spent the last three days sleeping at train stations.

Unfortunately, making Jesus look presentable was no simple task. His beard had always been unkempt, but over the past few weeks it had grown extremely wild, and his eyebrows were not much better. He had lost weight in hospital, and the clothes that had been donated to him hung limply from his scrawny frame. And, of course, there was nothing to be done about his footwear. The pink flip-flops were all he had, and I doubt he would have parted with them anyway; he still believed they had been 'gifted' to him by a lady in the desert. But at least they fitted him. They were the only item of clothing that did.

Despite Jesus's somewhat strange appearance, no one paid us any attention as we walked from the hostel to Flughafenstraße. For the first time since coming to Europe, it might not have been obvious that we were refugees. The shops and restaurants that lined the streets told of the large number of Middle Easterners who had already settled in Neukölln. Scattered among the German and American chain stores were Turkish kebab houses and Lebanese falafel shops, and, at one point, a grocery store flying a Palestinian flag. Some of the signs were in Arabic as well as German. If it hadn't been for the cold wind and the distinctive European architecture, there were stretches where I could have imagined I was back home.

Flughafenstraße was a long, mostly residential street running west towards a large park. Small shops and cafés sat below large apartment blocks. There were German cars parked at the road-side and bicycles chained to trees and lamp-posts. As far as I could judge, it was a perfectly average neighbourhood. There was quite a lot of graffiti on the buildings, but I didn't think this signified anything in particular. From what I'd seen, there was graffiti all over Berlin; it seemed it was a city people wanted to write on.

It took us five more minutes to reach the address. It was an apartment block the same as all the others we'd seen – five storeys high with pale-grey walls and tall windows that glared red in the evening sun. We stood for some time just looking at it from the opposite side of the street. Jesus flinched as a car passed in front of us, his eyes darting around like a startled animal's. It was the first sign he'd shown that he was nervous, but I suppose he had every reason to be. I was nervous too, on his behalf. Only Mohammed seemed unaffected; if anything, he looked fed up, and maybe a little bored. Weirdly, this did much to reassure me. After his meltdown in Szeged, my brother was back to his old self: a surly teenage rock. You could put him in almost any situation, no matter how bizarre or unfamiliar or awkward, and he'd face it with the same weary cynicism.

I placed my hand on Jesus's shoulder and gave him a gentle nudge. 'Okay. Let's get this over with.'

The apartment block had an intercom system. This was not ideal, as explaining why we were there would have been difficult enough face-to-face, and, inevitably, it would fall to me to do the explaining. But there was no point in hesitating. I buzzed the apartment number, and we waited.

Nothing.

I tried again, holding the button down for a little longer.

Jesus shuffled awkwardly, and I swear I could hear my own heart pumping. The situation was completely crazy, of course. I didn't have any clear plan of what I was going to say. I didn't even have a name I could ask for, since Jesus had never told me what his daughter was called. He'd never told me what *he* was really called.

Time stretched and stretched. Mohammed slouched against the wall.

'Maybe it was not destined to be,' Jesus said quietly, sounding almost relieved.

'I could try a neighbour,' I suggested. 'Maybe someone will let us in. Or they might be able to tell us who lives there.'

'Maybe no one lives there,' Mohammed said, very unhelpfully.

'Shut up, Mohammed. Jesus has travelled thousands of kilometres to be here. We're not giving up.'

I pressed again. There was no sound to indicate that the intercom was even working. Mohammed started to say something, probably something sarcastic, but his commentary was cut short when the intercom crackled to life.

'Hello?'

A man's voice. English, but spoken in what I thought was a German accent. Surprise, confusion and disappointment fought a brief battle in my head. Then I launched forth before the voice could go away. 'Hello? We're looking for a woman whom we believe lives here. Hello?'

The line had gone dead.

I looked at Mohammed and Jesus. 'I'm not sure what just happened,' I confessed.

Mohammed rolled his eyes. 'Some German man lives there! Here in Germany. Who'd have thought?'

'Why would a German answer his intercom in English? That makes no sense.'

'It makes as much sense as his long-lost daughter living here!' Mohammed jutted his jaw towards Jesus, who also looked confused – even more so than usual.

A sudden thought came to me. I took out the phone and accessed an online German dictionary. The word for hello was the same as in English, or near enough. Hallo, with an 'a'. I explained the mix-up to Mohammed and Jesus, then pressed the intercom buzzer again, but this time no one answered.

'He probably thinks I'm a nuisance caller,' I said.

'You *are* a nuisance caller,' Mohammed told me. 'You're pestering some random German man for no good reason.'

'We don't know that he's a German. We just know that he answered the intercom in German.'

'Well, he's not Jesus's daughter. That's for sure.'

'I think we need to try again. We can give it ten minutes or so.'

Mohammed glowered.

'What do you think, Jesus?' I asked.

Jesus shrugged. 'We've come this far. I think we can wait ten more minutes.'

So we did. Or we waited almost ten minutes. At that point, a German man arrived on the doorstep. I assumed he was German. He eyed us with great suspicion as he took out his key and unlocked the door. This was only reasonable, since we were loitering there for no obvious reason. Regardless, it was time to take a gamble.

'Excuse me?' I addressed him in English. 'We are trying to visit family in this building, but no one is answering the intercom. May we come in and knock on their door? It will only take a minute.'

I had no idea if he'd understood me or not. The suspicion remained in his eyes. But then, after a short hesitation, he shrugged and pushed the door open, gesturing for us to step through.

'Thank you.'

There was a corridor inside, with a stairwell leading off it, and

I headed straight up as if I knew exactly where I was going, which of course I didn't. It took quite a lot of wandering before we found the correct apartment. But once there, I didn't hesitate; no time for delays or second thoughts. I knocked on the door.

The man who answered looked to be around forty years old, and he was not German. He was Middle Eastern, with dark eyes and a neatly trimmed beard and moustache. A good-looking guy.

I still had no plan, so I just started talking, in Arabic. '*As-salāmu alaikum*. My name is Zain. This is Jesus and Mohammed.'

Jesus gave a small bow. Mohammed nodded, looking just as irritated as ever. The man in the doorway glanced at each of us in turn, clearly at a loss.

'Are you from the mosque?' he asked after a moment. 'We already have a Qur'an . . .'

'We're not religious persons,' I clarified. 'We're . . . well, it's a little complicated. Mohammed and I have come here from Syria. Jesus is from Iraq.' The man's eyes flicked back to Jesus – just for a moment, but it was enough to give me some hope. I hadn't been able to pinpoint his accent, but Iraqi was my first guess. 'We're looking for his daughter,' I said. 'She left Baghdad about twenty years ago and came to Germany. We were given this apartment as her last known address.'

There was no mistaking it this time. The man stared at Jesus in wide-eyed silence. 'I think you'd better come in,' he said.

Reunion

We sat in the apartment and sipped coffee, me and Jesus and Mohammed, squashed together on a small sofa in a small living area. The man we'd met at the door sat opposite on a wooden dining chair, his hands clasped tightly in his lap. Jesus's son-in-law. His name was Jehad – a problematic name to carry in the West, but not uncommon in the Islamic world, especially among older generations. The other occupants of the room were a young boy called Ya'qub – Jesus's grandson – and a Persian cat called Nura. Despite a somewhat lingering glance at Mohammed's Lionel Messi shirt, Ya'qub had accepted that we were 'friends of Mummy' without protest, and was now sitting on a cushion on the floor, watching German cartoons. Nura had settled almost at once on Jesus's knee – a fact that astounded Jehad, who claimed the cat never took to strangers. But she'd obviously discerned some quality in Jesus that set her at ease. I hoped this was a good omen.

Jesus's daughter Leila was not yet home. Jehad told us that she worked in a care home for the elderly. He drove a taxi, and they often had to alternate their shifts. But we could expect her soon. He'd tried to phone her, to give her some chance to prepare, but the call had gone straight to voicemail. He suspected she was on the *U-Bahn* and could not get a signal.

So that left the five of us, six if you included the cat, all crammed into that small sitting room. The conversation was never going to be straightforward, but there was plenty of ground we needed to cover. That Ya'qub was within earshot was no great problem; he was absorbed in his cartoons, and couldn't have been more than five years old – young enough that our conversation was beyond him. In truth, it was beyond all of us. We just had to struggle through as best we could.

I tried to tell our story as succinctly as possible. I explained how we'd met on the beach in Greece, after Mohammed and I had swum across from Turkey. Jesus interjected that he'd rescued us, pulling our near-drowned bodies from the water. Mohammed scowled and rolled his eyes at me, but I decided to let the detail go uncontested. Instead, I hopped us across the various borders, relating only the essentials – the information Jesus had given me at the train station in Hungary, his subsequent illness and hospitalisation. Jehad didn't interrupt once, but his expression grew more and more dumbstruck; by the time I'd moved on to Jesus's significant and growing amnesia, he had the look of a man who'd been involved in a serious traffic accident – that stunned alertness that comes after the moment of impact.

After I'd finished, he poured more coffee and gestured that we should help ourselves to some food. On the low table before us was quite an elaborate platter of fruit – sliced apple and melon and dried dates. Next to this was a tray of small cakes and pastries. Because when all else fails, Arabic hospitality will endure.

I made sure I took one of everything, and a subtle prod in Mohammed's side was sufficient warning for him to do likewise. We'd both eaten already, of course – personally, I was stuffed to bursting – but manners were manners.

'That's . . . quite a story,' Jehad said eventually.

I nodded. It was all I could manage right then, with a mouth full of melon.

He turned to Jesus. 'Your life back in Iraq . . . you really don't remember a thing?'

'Correct,' Jesus confirmed. 'I remember nothing before coming to Europe. It's as if I have been reborn.'

It sounded unbelievable. I realised that, and was about to leap in with the further information Dr Polgár had given me, regarding Jesus's irregular brain scan. But Jehad just nodded in mute acceptance. I guess it was all he could do. He wasn't going to call his father-in-law a liar, not upon their first meeting.

'We hope that seeing his daughter, seeing Leila, might bring something back,' I said.

'I suppose that's possible,' Jehad said, with a doubtful shake of his head.

'All things are possible,' Jesus said, scratching the cat behind her ears. He seemed much calmer now. Maybe petting the cat was helping him. Or maybe it was hearing our story told again, or the fact that we'd been in the apartment for some time and no disaster had befallen us. Every so often, he'd glance over at Ya'qub, his eyes widening, but otherwise, he looked serene. As if he'd just come out of a deep and satisfying trance.

Jehad cleared his throat. 'Um . . . Jesus . . . should I call you Jesus? Is that what you'd prefer?'

'It is my name,' Jesus said.

'You used to be called Mahmoud. That *was* your name.'

Jesus raised his eyebrows a fraction. 'I do not remember this name.'

'He's always been Jesus to us,' I said. 'That's the only name he ever gave.'

'Jesus is a good name,' Jesus said. 'It is the name I prefer.'

'Okay. Well . . . Jesus.' Jehad cleared his throat again, then took a small sip of coffee. 'Jesus. I don't know if I've done the right thing, bringing you in here. I mean, I think Leila will want to see you, but it's going to be a shock for her. A huge shock.'

Jesus nodded. 'I am prepared for this.'

'Yes, but . . . well, the way she's spoken of you . . .'

'I'm prepared for that too. I believe I have been a terrible father.'

'Not terrible, necessarily. Just absent.'

'I'm afraid I don't remember.'

'Leila assumed you were dead. She thought you must have died years ago. With your . . . problems, it seemed a certainty.'

'I am not dead,' Jesus said. 'I am here in Germany.'

I decided it was time to intervene. 'We don't want to be an imposition,' I said. 'If Leila doesn't want to see him, if she needs some time, then we'll leave immediately.'

Jehad thought about this, then gave a small shake of his head. 'There's no good way to go about this. I just wish I had time to think.'

'We could come back,' I suggested. 'If you think you need to talk to her first.'

Jehad barked a short, humourless laugh. 'What can I possibly tell her?'

'I've no idea,' I admitted.

227

'I should at least try to call her again,' Jehad said. 'It might help to—'

He was cut off by the sound of the door opening. The apartment's front door. Nura sprang from Jesus's lap. Ya'qub leapt to his feet.

'It's Mummy!' he announced. 'Mummy, your friends are here to see you!'

In Arabic, Leila means night. It's a name that's associated with a particular type of dark beauty – lustrous black hair and bronzed skin and mahogany eyes. Often, it's a name given to a girl who happened to be born at night. And sometimes, it's just a pretty name, one the parents found pleasing to the ear. Arabic names are like that: they can mean many things or nothing at all.

In the case of Jesus's daughter, I suspect she must have been an unusually beautiful child. Either that, or someone had had a prophecy. Jesus's wife, I suppose. From the scant autobiography Jesus had given me in Kelebia, I doubt that he played any significant role in choosing his daughter's name.

The woman who stood in the doorway was beautiful, and when I tell you this, you know I am giving you an objective fact. In all honesty, it was astonishing that any part of her had come from Jesus. Her hair was jet black, falling to her shoulders in gentle curls – hair as black and thick as Jesus's was white and wiry. Though I guess Jesus's hair might have been just as black in his previous life; his eyebrows suggested as much. She was not wearing a hijab, but I didn't know what to make of this, if anything. Almost every Muslim woman I'd seen on the streets of Neukölln wore the headscarf, but I was just as used to not seeing it. Back in Syria, it was far from ubiquitous – especially in cities – and not wearing it said nothing about the state of your faith. The assumption was that it was still present and strong.

The eyes with which she regarded us were large and dark, slightly tilted and ever-so confused. This was not a surprise. The surprise was how quickly she managed to regain her composure. Her gaze lingered on the three of us for mere moments, and she gave as much attention to me and Mohammed as she did to Jesus. She picked up Ya'qub, holding him tight to her chest.

'It's a little late to be watching cartoons, young man.' This was said with a pointed glance at her husband, mock exasperation.

'I was allowed because your friends are here,' Ya'qub explained. 'We waited for you.'

Her response was another confused smile, followed by a stern, querying look at Jehad.

That was when I understood. I'd been so focused on how Jesus might react upon seeing his daughter. Would he recognise her? Was there some deep-buried memory waiting to resurface? It hadn't occurred to me that she might not recognise him, or not immediately. But why would she? It had been two decades since she'd last seen him, and she'd never expected to see him again. She'd assumed he was dead.

Jehad had started to tell her that she should sit down; he'd pour her a coffee and explain everything. But at the same time, Jesus started to rise. Her eyes shifted to him as he made another of his strange formal bows. I think it was a good thing Jehad *hadn't* poured her a coffee, because she would certainly have dropped it at this point. She gasped and took a step back, squeezing Ya'qub even more tightly against her.

Jehad must have decided the opportunity for a gentle build-up had passed. 'They turned up half an hour ago,' he said. 'He claims he's your father.'

'I've been told this is the case,' Jesus stated.

'It's a little complicated,' I added. 'Jesus has lost his memory.'

'*Jesus*?' Leila said, her voice barely more than a whisper.

'I am Jesus,' Jesus clarified. 'I used to be Mahmoud, but this is something I no longer recollect. I stopped drinking and it has left me with many problems. Every day is a struggle.'

Jesus sat down again.

Leila began to cry.

So I told our story again. Leila sat and listened quietly, holding her son in her lap. When I'd finished, she said she was going to put him to bed. Nothing else. She had stopped crying, and her face gave no hint of what she was feeling.

'I'm not tired!' Ya'qub protested. 'I want to stay up with your friends!'

'I'll stay with you until you're asleep,' she told him.

'Are you not sad anymore?'

'Say goodnight, Ya'qub.'

After she'd left the room, Jehad went to make more coffee. It was too late to be drinking coffee, but never mind. There was not much else we could do.

Nura climbed into Jesus's lap again and purred noisily as he stroked her under the chin. He looked thoughtful, but otherwise at ease. As calm and compliant as the cat. As for Mohammed, who knew? My guess was that he was probably eager to leave, but his face gave nothing away. He'd hardly had to say two words since coming to the apartment. He was just an unwilling spectator to someone else's soap opera.

When Jehad came back, I asked him if Leila was going to be okay.

'Yes, she'll be okay. She just needs some time.'

'Is she angry?'

'Maybe. It's a lot to take in. I'm sure you understand.'

'Yes, of course.'

We all sipped our fresh coffee, and the silence stretched. Leila was taking a long time to put Ya'qub to bed. But, then, she had said she'd stay with him until he fell asleep. I had no idea how long it might take for a five-year-old boy, over-stimulated on cartoons, to settle down.

When Leila returned, she was not interested in small talk. She sat on the dining chair next to Jehad's and regarded Jesus and the cat for at least a minute.

'What happened to your fingers?' she asked.

Jesus looked wonderingly at his stumps, as if seeing them for the very first time.

'Al-Qaeda cut them off,' I said.

I suppose Leila had become immune to further shocks, because she just nodded her head a couple of times, as if this were a perfectly normal explanation.

'I don't remember it,' Jesus said, after a moment.

'Have you really stopped drinking?'

'Yes. I have not had alcohol for a very long time.'

'Two weeks,' I said. 'It's been two weeks.'

'A long time,' Jesus repeated.

'You can't stay here,' Leila said. 'You know that, don't you?'

Jesus nodded. 'I did not expect to stay here.'

'We have a room in a hostel,' I said. 'It's not far away.'

Leila turned to look at me. Her dark eyes might as well have been frosted glass, revealing nothing. 'How long are you staying in Berlin?'

'I don't know. A couple of days, maybe. We want to get to the UK as soon as we can.'

She thought about this for some time.

'Er, Jesus. Do you have a number we can contact you on?' Jehad asked. He was looking at his newly discovered father-in-law with a degree of scepticism. Justified scepticism. Jesus had little more than the shirt on his back.

I scribbled my mobile number on the back of a receipt and handed it over.

'Would it be better if we left now?' I asked.

Jehad looked at Leila, who gave the smallest of nods. 'Yes, I think it would,' he said. 'I'm sorry but . . .'

'There's no need to apologise. We understand.'

'Let me show you out.'

'Thank you.'

Leila didn't move a muscle. She was staring at the bare floor-boards, and didn't even glance up as her husband ushered us back to the hallway. He waited with a strained smile while we put our shoes on. Only Jesus seemed immune to the awkward-ness of the moment. He slipped into his pink flip-flops with enviable ease.

'Well, that went as expected,' Mohammed said later, as we walked back down Flughafenstraße towards the hostel. It was now completely dark outside. The air had grown chilly, and none of us had jackets. We were still dressed as if this was the Mediterranean. I thought we'd better rectify this before we left Germany.

'You didn't think she'd even exist,' I told Mohammed. 'Or have you forgotten that already?'

He ignored this.

Jesus was walking a few steps ahead of us, lost once again in his own strange world.

'He's coming with us, isn't he? All the way to the UK.'

'We don't know that yet,' I said. 'Things didn't go *that* badly.'

'She hardly welcomed him with open arms.'

'No. But did you ever think she would? She needs some time to think. That's entirely understandable.'

'He's coming with us,' Mohammed repeated, sounding resigned. 'It's inevitable.'

I shrugged, and we walked on in silence for a minute or so.

'Jesus's daughter is *hot*,' Mohammed whispered.

'Mohammed!' I hissed. 'You can't talk that way about her. She's his daughter! She's old enough to be . . .' I didn't finish this thought, for obvious reasons. 'She's probably three times your age.'

'Yeah, she's old,' Mohammed conceded. 'But still . . . How on earth did he manage to produce something like *that*?'

'Boys like you are the reason the burka was invented,' I told him.

My brother snorted at this. 'Are you telling me you didn't notice? Okay, maybe you didn't. It's *you*, after all.'

I didn't respond to this. It was typical Mohammed. The irony was, he didn't really believe it. If he genuinely suspected what he was insinuating, he'd refuse to walk on the same street as me.

Jesus was still a couple of steps ahead, his hair shining wildly in the angled light from a street lamp. I quickened my pace to catch up with him.

233

'Jesus? How are you feeling? Are you okay?'

'I am well, my friend. It is a fine night.'

'Yes. It's a fine night,' I agreed.

He nodded, but said nothing. He wasn't going to talk unless I asked him direct questions.

'Um, Jesus? Back in the hospital, in Hungary, you mentioned an image, sort of a . . . vision. A beautiful woman's face. Was that Leila? Could it have been her?'

'A vision? I don't remember this vision.'

'Did you recognise her at all? Did she look familiar?'

'She did not.'

'Oh. Okay.'

We walked on, not talking. Jesus's flip-flops slapped against the pavement.

'I think the cat liked me,' he said, after several minutes had passed.

I put my hand on his shoulder. 'Yes, Jesus. The cat liked you very much.'

He nodded to himself, as if this had been the whole point of the evening.

So much for getting some answers, I thought. Right now, Jesus seemed more of a mystery than ever before.

On Tempelhofer Feld

Jehad phoned the next morning at ten o'clock to ask if we wanted to come for a walk.

'A walk?'

'It's a nice day.'

It *was* a nice day, far warmer than the previous.

'Where did you have in mind?' I asked.

'There's a park nearby. Tempelhofer Feld.'

'I think I've seen it,' I told him. 'On Google Maps.'

Tempelhofer Feld was the site of a former airport, which had been shut down in 2008. Prior to this, northwest Neukölln had been one of the cheapest areas of Berlin. Anyone who could afford *not* to live next door to an airport did precisely that, and streets such as Flughafenstraße – literally 'Airport Street', Jehad told me – were left to those of the lowest socio-economic status: the working class, the unemployed, and the immigrants.

But this had all changed seven years ago, when the last planes departed. Shortly afterwards, the people of Berlin held a referendum and voted to leave the land undeveloped, as the city's newest and largest public park. And almost overnight, the worst streets in the area became some of the most desirable in Berlin.

In response came a second swarm of immigrants – wealthy white immigrants, from other parts of the city, from Northern Europe and the United States. They were mostly young. They were artists and creatives, entrepreneurs and small-business owners looking to relocate.

As the money flooded in, the area was rapidly transformed. Junk shops became antique shops. Run-down grocery stores became organic bakeries. The property developers followed soon after, refurbishing ancient tenements as luxury condos, and rents began to soar. The previous inhabitants were increasingly priced out of the market, and many had to move to the new 'worst streets in Berlin'. Eventually, the government had to enforce legislation to protect the rents of long-term inhabitants. This, Jehad said, was the only reason he and Leila had been able to stay in their building. If they were newcomers to the area, they'd struggle to afford the rent on the tiniest studio apartment.

Jehad told us this as we walked slowly along one of the two old runways, which still traversed the full width of the park. I found it all interesting enough, even if Mohammed didn't, but I suppose it was just talk to pass the time. The real conversation was happening a few paces ahead of us, where Jesus and Leila spoke to each other. Or I hoped they were still speaking. The park was windy enough to render any exchange inaudible from just a few metres away.

Ya'qub had been sent to nursery for the day, to give Leila some time alone with her father. He usually went in just a couple of times a week, when both his parents had to work. But this was an exceptional circumstance, obviously. It was as exceptional a circumstance as you could imagine.

I was nervous, again, on Jesus's behalf. More than this, I suppose I felt weirdly protective of him. It was ludicrous. He was sixty-something years old, but I was certain he needed a chaperone to supervise his walk in the park. I found myself worrying, again and again, about his capacity to have a normal conversation with another human being. Not that the conversation with his daughter was going to be normal, not by any standard. I guessed a large part of it would just be Leila filling him in on the unflattering details of his early life, all the things he'd forgotten. Beyond that, who could guess what they'd find to talk about? It would be a difficult conversation – that was the only thing I could be sure of. It would be difficult, but it needed to happen.

Leila looked calmer this morning. That was one good thing. And it wasn't the blank, shocked calm that had come over her by the end of the previous evening. She looked tired and a little wary, but that was all, and to be expected. As for Jesus, once again it was impossible to tell what he was thinking or feeling. He did turn around occasionally, as if to make sure that we were still following, but his eyes were masked by his 1980s wraparound sunglasses.

It was a bright, bright morning, with barely a cloud in the sky, and on Tempelhofer Feld it seemed like the death throes of summer, a final protest against the changing of the seasons. The grass at the edge of the runway was long and wiry, and had turned a yellowish brown. When Jehad had said that the Berliners had decided to leave the area undeveloped, he had not been exaggerating. It was a vast open space, probably a couple of kilometres end-to-end, like a huge impact crater carved out of the surrounding offices and apartment blocks. Away from its edges, it was almost treeless. Tangled grasses and wildflowers grew among the now-defunct landing lights and distance markers, and where smaller pathways joined the runway, the tarmac had started to crack, and had been colonised by lichen and other small plant life. The place felt apocalyptic, like the decaying remnant of some lost civilisation. Except none of the locals seemed to have noticed. They zipped past on bicycles and rollerblades and ate ice creams and flew kites on the grass. I suppose when you're used to a place, all of its strangeness disappears.

We walked on down the runway, and Jehad continued to tell us the history of the site. The terminal, visible in the distance, had been built by the Nazis in the 1930s.

'You know about the Nazis?' Jehad asked.

'Yes, we know about the Nazis,' I confirmed. Mohammed gave a non-committal grunt. I was almost certain he knew about the Nazis – as the bad guys in *Indiana Jones*, if nothing else.

'Of course you do,' Jehad nodded. 'You're smart boys.'

The Nazis had built the terminal on the site of an existing airfield, and, as was typical of the Nazis, they didn't go small. The terminal curved for almost two kilometres, dominating the skyline. Hitler had envisaged the airport as not merely a transport hub, but as a symbol and statement of German power.

Ten years later, when German power was no more, the Americans took over Tempelhof Airport, using it as their main military base in Berlin. During the early part of the Cold War, Tempelhof had been vital in getting supplies into West Berlin.

'You know about the Wall?' Jehad asked.

'I know there *was* a Wall,' I said. 'But that's pretty much all I know.'

'Right. Well, it was built in the early 1960s and ran right down the edge of Neukölln. But even before that, West Berlin was basically an island, administered by the Americans and French and British, but surrounded on all sides by Soviet territory. Early on, the Russians decided they were going to block all the supply routes into West Berlin. They thought the Americans would be forced to abandon the city in a matter of weeks. Instead, the Americans spent the next year flying everything into Tempelhof – food and fuel for two million people. They had planes landing every couple of minutes. It was one of those insane stand-offs that typified the Cold War.'

'You know a lot of history,' I said.

Jehad shrugged modestly. 'A hobby of mine.'

'Seriously. You could be a tour guide.'

He laughed at this. 'No, I don't think so. I'm just a taxi driver.'

We'd probably been walking for a quarter of an hour at this point. I guessed we'd covered half the runway by now, but it was so long, and the terrain was so uniform, it gave the illusion that we'd hardly moved. We could have been walking on a treadmill. The only sign of progress was the incremental rising of the terminal, which stretched featureless across the horizon.

Jehad must have caught the direction of my gaze, because he gestured expansively at the building, his arm making a broad sweep of its length. 'I heard the Germans have a new plan for Tempelhof,' he told me. 'It was approved in parliament very recently. They want to use it as a temporary home for refugees. They think it can house several thousand of your countrymen.'

'I wonder what the Nazis would think of that.'

'I don't imagine they'd appreciate the irony.'

I thought about this for a while. 'Is that why Germany's so eager to help us? Because of its history?'

Jehad shrugged. 'Maybe it's part of it. I mean, it's a hell of a history to overcome. But . . . well, there are probably many reasons. I'm sure altruism is part of it. But it's an economic decision, too. Germany needs migrants to keep the economy growing, and lots of the Syrians coming in are like you. They're young and educated. There are doctors and scientists and engineers. In some ways, Germany's being extremely pragmatic.'

'Most Syrians worship the German President,' I said. 'They think she's our country's saviour.'

'They call her Mama Merkel,' Mohammed put in.

Jehad nodded a couple of times. 'Yes, I'd heard that. I doubt it will be so simple, though, whatever Mama Merkel intends. Germany's like every other country on the planet, with thousands of conflicting interests and opinions.' He paused for a moment, still gazing at the terminal building. 'If I told you that every Syrian is honest or every Iraqi is generous you'd laugh in my face. Well, it's the same in Germany. It's the same everywhere. You get kindness and cruelty, tolerance and prejudice. There are plenty of Germans who don't share Mrs Merkel's vision for their country. All they see are more Arab invaders.'

I nodded slowly. 'That's how they treated us in Hungary. As invaders. But people think it will be different here, with so many being welcomed in.'

Jehad shrugged again. 'Well, maybe it will be different. Who knows? Maybe it will be different in the UK, too.' The tone of his voice made it clear how likely he thought this was. 'But too often people think in terms of "us" and "them". They see outsiders coming to their country, living in little foreign enclaves in the city, bringing with them their own languages and culture, unwilling to adapt to German life. That's what they see, and it becomes almost a self-fulfilling prophecy.' Jehad shook his head for a moment, before continuing. 'Let me ask you this. What do you think would happen if you took a few thousand Germans and put them all together in Baghdad, or Damascus, or any place that wasn't their own? They don't speak Arabic, the culture is alien to them, and many of the locals view them with suspicion. Do you think they'd simply lose their German identity and integrate?'

'Probably not,' I said; Mohammed snorted.

'Exactly. They'd band together for strength and support. They'd speak German and drink German beer. Eventually, they'd build churches and community centres. And it's the same for any nation or culture under the sun. In a foreign environment, people gravitate to anything familiar, especially when they feel insecure or threatened. It's not particular to any one race or religion. It's just human nature.'

I nodded without comment. I couldn't tell Jehad any of the many reasons I thought things would be different for me: that I was already an apostate, and a closet homosexual to boot. That I had more cause to feel threatened in Latakia than I did in Berlin. Instead, I asked about Ya'qub. 'He was born here,' I said. 'Won't things be different for him?'

'Yes.' Jehad's eyes definitely softened at this point. 'We hope so, anyway. He's five years old and he already speaks German better than I ever will. When he writes his name in the Roman alphabet, he spells it the Germanic way – Jakob, with a J. We wanted him to have a name that works in German as well as

Arabic.' His eyes shifted to Leila for a while. Then he shrugged and looked at me and Mohammed once more. 'The truth is, Leila and I will never be German citizens. It doesn't matter if we stay another thirty years. We'll always be Iraqis living in Germany. It's how we're seen and it's how we see ourselves. But we hope things will be different for Ya'qub. We want him to be able to make a life for himself here, without any constraints.'

Jehad smiled, and there was a small silence.

'May I ask you a question?' I said. 'About Leila?'

'Of course.'

'She doesn't wear the hijab. That seems . . . unusual in Neukölln.'

'It is.'

'And from what you said, most people who come here tend to become more religious, more protective of their identity.'

Jehad shrugged again. 'She used to wear it. She stopped soon after she started work.'

'Why? Was it to fit in with the Germans or did she . . .'

I couldn't actually ask if she'd lost her faith. It would be too impolite. Fortunately, Jehad started speaking as soon as I'd trailed off.

'It was to make her life easier. She works with the elderly and some of them . . . Well, I probably don't need to tell you. People tend to get more set in their ways as they get older, less tolerant of change. She's had to put up with a certain amount of abuse. Some of the residents want to pretend Germany is still an all-white, all-Christian nation. With some of them, it's not even their fault. They have Alzheimer's. They have trouble controlling their behaviour.'

'Oh.'

There was another silence, longer this time. Luckily, Mohammed was on hand to say something wildly inappropriate.

'At least she'll be well equipped to deal with Jesus,' he said.

From a hundred metres away, you couldn't tell that the terminal had ceased to function. The windows were like rows of white teeth, gleaming in the sunshine. The long curve of the building gave the impression that we were standing at the bottom of an amphitheatre. Tourists took photographs. Joggers and cyclists and rollerbladers continued to criss-cross the scene. But as a backdrop, Tempelhof Airport terminal looked like a building frozen in time, squat and still and silent.

We had been standing there no more than a couple of minutes when Jesus returned from his private conference with Leila.

'She'd like to talk to you now,' he told me.

'To me?'

'Yes.'

'You've finished?'

'Yes, we've finished.' Jesus spoke his words matter-of-factly. No indication of how the conversation had gone. As for Leila, her body language also gave nothing away. She stood with her arms folded, no more than ten metres away. Just waiting.

There was nothing else to do. I took Jesus's place at her side and we continued our walk – parallel to the terminal and then back down the second runway. But after a minute or so, I hardly noticed our surroundings. Our conversation was the kind that holds all your attention, leaving no room for anything else.

'He thinks he's going with you,' Leila said. 'To the UK.'

'Yes. That's what we assumed, too.'

She didn't say anything for a moment. She looked at me with

her dark, serious eyes. 'Except he doesn't just think, does he? He *knows*.'

'What did he tell you?'

'Lots of things. Things that don't make any sense.'

'He told you about the dream?'

'Yes. As far as I could work out, he thinks he's going to guide you to the UK. He thinks you won't get there without him. Am I right?'

'Yes. That's pretty much it.'

'It's ridiculous. He's never been anywhere near the UK. To my knowledge, he's never even left Iraq, or not before now.'

I didn't correct her. She didn't need to know about the several months he'd spent in Iran and Kuwait. Anyway, being in jail didn't really count. 'He doesn't expect to guide us in a conventional sense,' I told her. 'He thinks there's something he's going to do for us. Or I think that's what he thinks. Sometimes, it's hard to know with Jesus.'

'Jesus.' Leila shook her head. 'I'm not going to get used to that.'

'I don't think I can start calling him Mahmoud. He's Jesus to us.'

Leila was silent for a little while. 'There's something very strange about him, isn't there? You sense it when you talk to him.'

'He's always been a little . . . odd,' I said, picking my words carefully. 'He was odd when we first met him, and the last month hasn't done anything to change that.'

'He talks like he's half somewhere else. It's as if he's . . . He's like an empty vessel. That's the impression I get. Does that make sense to you?'

'I think so, yes. It's something that happened after Hungary. I don't know if it's because of his memories or the alcohol withdrawal. Or maybe it's something else entirely.' I thought for a few moments, trying to put complicated ideas into words. 'I suppose, before Hungary, he used to have a motivation to get him through the hours. He had drink to worry about. It wasn't a *good* motivation, but still, it kept him going. And I think that's what's missing now. Sometimes when I look at him . . . Well, sometimes I look at him and I just get this overwhelming sadness.'

Leila thought about this. 'Is that why you helped him? Out of pity?'

'Is pity such a bad reason?' I shrugged. 'He thinks he's going to guide us to the UK. It doesn't matter how ridiculous the idea is. It gives him a purpose. It could be the thing that gets him through the coming weeks.'

Leila regarded me for a very long time without saying anything. 'You're a little bit odd yourself, do you know that? Not a typical nineteen-year-old boy.'

I didn't respond to this. I'd spent most of my adolescence trying to project the sense that I was *entirely* typical, so being told that I'd failed did not fill me with joy.

'You don't have to take him with you. You know that, don't you? He can get the help he needs in Germany, one way or another.'

'I think we do have to,' I told her.

'What about your brother? What does he think?'

'Mohammed agrees. More or less.'

'More or less?'

'Believe me, that's as good as it gets with Mohammed. He

tends to disagree with everything as a matter of principle. If you tell him the sky's blue, he'll say it's not.'

Leila smiled at this. It was a very brief smile, but for that moment, it lit up her face.

'You might find it hard to believe,' I told her, 'but Jesus *has* been a good friend to us. To both of us. He has helped us.'

'I *do* find it hard to believe,' Leila said. 'I can't imagine him being of much help to anyone.'

'He helped me evade a border guard. He threw his shoes to create a diversion.'

Leila didn't respond to this. What could she say?

'And he refused to leave us,' I continued. 'He refused to leave Hungary until he knew my brother was safe. It would have been far easier for him to walk away.'

Leila continued to look at me for a moment, then shrugged. 'It's not that I doubt your word, but still . . . I think you're probably trying to paint him in the best possible light. I'm sure the instances where he's been anything other than a burden have been few and far between.'

I said nothing. Mohammed would have agreed with her every word.

The silence stretched for some time, then she said: 'I don't know my father. You need to understand that. He was barely there when I was growing up. He drank. He stayed away from home. Mother always said staying away was the best thing he could do for us.'

'He isn't a bad man,' I told her. 'He's had a difficult life, too.'

'Yes, I'm sure he has. But it doesn't change anything between us. We're virtual strangers. And now he doesn't even have his memories. I'm as unknown to him as he is to me.'

'You could think of it as a fresh start.'

She thought about this for a while. 'I'm not sure I want a fresh start. I'm not sure what good it would do either one of us. Can you understand that?'

'Yes. I think so.'

'I made my peace with not having a father a long time ago. And when I look at him now . . . Well, there's regret, I suppose, but that's all. I feel nothing else towards him. Maybe that sounds terrible, but there it is.'

'It doesn't sound terrible,' I told her.

'In a sense it doesn't even matter. He can't stay with us.'

'He didn't expect to.'

'Yes, I know. But that's not what I'm trying to say. There are other complications right now.' She sighed deeply, brushing back a strand of hair that had fallen across her face. 'I'm pregnant,' she told me. 'Three months, as of yesterday. His timing couldn't be much worse.'

'Oh . . .' I couldn't find anything else to say. I didn't know if congratulations would be appropriate, given the circumstances. 'Did you tell him?'

'Yes. I told him.'

'How did he react?'

'He didn't react. The same as with everything else. Not that it matters, one way or the other. You understand why I'm not in a position to help? There's no room for him in my life right now.'

'Yes, of course. I understand.'

'A year from now, who knows? I might feel differently. But at the moment . . . well, I need time, that's all. I need time to think. A couple of days was never going to be enough.'

'No.'

We fell silent again. I hadn't looked around once since I'd started talking to Leila, but I had to assume Jesus was still following with Mohammed and Jehad, oblivious to what was being said.

'You're determined to go to the UK?' Leila asked.

'Yes.'

'You realise it won't be easy? They have tight border controls.'

'So did Hungary.'

'Hungary isn't surrounded by water. The English Channel is thirty kilometres at its narrowest point. You're not going to swim *that.*'

'Yes. I know.'

'Of course you do. I just had to be sure.' She paused for a moment, then said, 'Can I ask why? Why the UK? It would be far simpler for you to stay in Germany. It's Germany that's offering unconditional asylum.'

'The UK has always been our dream,' I said. 'I speak the language fluently. It's what I was studying in university. And Mohammed's English is pretty good too. We'll have better chances in the UK. It's our best chance of a future.'

'You don't think you'll ever go back to Syria?'

'No. We're not going back. *I'm* not going back. Mohammed will have to make his own decision, when he's old enough.'

Leila nodded a couple of times, but her lips were drawn together in a tight pout. 'Can I ask you one more thing?'

'Yes, of course.'

'It's . . . well, you don't have to answer. I'll understand if you don't want to.' She hesitated a moment. 'Your parents. Are they . . . What happened to them?'

The question no one ever asked. I was shocked to find myself responding. I was shocked that I was able to lay out the facts so calmly. As if talking about someone else's family.

'My father was arrested,' I told her. 'Two weeks before we left Syria. He's a university lecturer. He was accused of helping some young men to avoid military conscription. Falsifying documents, aiding the creation of bogus student exemptions. We didn't know anything about it until the day he was taken. My mother didn't either.'

Leila nodded slowly. 'You say he was accused. Did he do it?'

'I never got to ask him. But yes. I'm sure he did. He's that kind of man. You wouldn't think it if you didn't know him well. He's mild-mannered. He's like a lot of academics, I suppose. Thoughtful and quiet, a little reserved. Not the sort of man you'd expect to be so brave. But . . . well, he has this incredible resolve, especially when it comes to matters of principle.'

Leila rested her hand on my arm as we continued to walk.

'My mother didn't think it was safe for us to stay after that. She was worried that *I'd* be conscripted, just to teach my father a lesson. I don't know if any direct threats were made, but . . . well, she wasn't going to take the risk. She emptied her savings account. It wasn't a huge amount, but she thought it would be enough to get me and Mohammed to Europe.'

'She didn't think of coming with you?'

'I'm certain she wanted to. But she wasn't going to leave without my dad.'

I had to take a deep breath, to steady my voice, before continuing.

'You have to understand: when people are arrested in Syria, they just vanish. There wasn't much of a legal process before the war, but it's gone completely now. We weren't told where my father was being taken. If he has a hearing, it will be behind closed doors. A sham.

'My mum thought she might be able to petition for his release. She had some chance of success. She's a school teacher, with a good standing in the community, and there are limits to what the government can get away with. They need to retain some middle-class support, or they won't survive in the long run. Or that's what my mother believed. She thought she'd be safe enough staying in Syria. If she could secure my father's release, then afterwards they'd be able to flee the country. Sell our apartment, follow me and Mohammed to Europe. That was her plan.'

Leila didn't say anything, but she squeezed my arm very tightly.

'She used to phone us every day. Usually twice a day. But just before we left Turkey, the phone calls stopped. I have to assume she was arrested too. Someone probably decided she was causing too much trouble. There's no other reason . . .'

I trailed off, and Leila stayed silent.

'I didn't want to leave her,' I said.

'Of course you didn't.'

'She said I had to take care of Mohammed. It was the most important thing I could do for her.'

'It was. I'm sure it gave her a huge amount of comfort, knowing her boys were going to be safe.'

I didn't say anything for a while. Leila continued to squeeze my arm. Cyclists continued to zip past.

'They might release her eventually. I have to believe that.'

'I'm so sorry, Zain. Your problems are so much bigger than mine. And you've been completely selfless.' I hadn't looked at her the whole time I'd been talking about my parents, and I didn't look now. But I knew she was crying, it was plain in her voice. 'You didn't do the wrong thing, bringing my father here. I need you to know that. It was a wonderful, generous thing to do, regardless of what comes of it.'

I nodded mutely.

'I wish there was something I could do to help you.'

'Just listening has helped. I've not been able to talk about it before. Not properly.'

'You have no obligation to my father. You shouldn't make your life any more difficult than it already is.'

'Thank you. I know what you're trying to do, but . . . He's coming with us. We *want* him with us.'

'You're sure?'

'Yes.'

Leila gave another deep sigh. 'Okay. I don't know what else I can say to you.'

'There's nothing else you need to say.'

She held my arm and we kept on walking, down the runway and towards the distant park gates. 'Hold on to your dreams,' Leila said. 'You deserve them.'

The Jungle

I asked Jesus if he wanted to stay in Berlin another night to rest, but he told me no. He wanted to get me and Mohammed to the UK as soon as possible. That was how he put it, and I found his phrasing oddly comforting. Some things had changed about him, but his belief in his 'purpose' had not. He may have been delusional, but he never questioned that we *would* make it to the UK; nor did he doubt that he had some crucial role yet to play.

So we checked out of the hostel that afternoon, almost as soon as we'd got back from Tempelhofer Feld. Our detour in Germany had been short, and nothing concrete had come of it, and yet, for some reason, it did not feel like a waste of time to me. I suppose my overriding feeling was satisfaction that we had at least tried. We hadn't abandoned Jesus in Hungary; we had done everything we could to reunite him with his family. And with that knowledge in mind, I felt happy devoting all my energy to the final challenge we would face.

*

We travelled on an overnight bus from Berlin to Brussels, then caught a morning connection to Calais. It was the only stage of our journey that was easy. It was so easy it felt wrong, like time had sped up, or distance had shrunk. I checked the phone, as we rumbled down an anonymous motorway in northern France, and found that we'd come almost a thousand kilometres since the previous evening. A thousand kilometres, gone in less than a day!

The bus arrived at the port mid-afternoon, under a heavy, overcast sky. It dropped us off at the ferry terminal, just before border control, which of course we could not cross. Instead, we turned back the way we'd come and walked along the side of the road, past several hundred metres of backed-up traffic. Unfortunately, the port had been designed to make pedestrian access as difficult as possible. There was no pavement, just a narrow strip of sandy dirt and grass, slightly raised from the road and bordered by a colossal fence topped with razor wire. The fence ran on both sides of the road as far as the eye could see. It forced us to walk in single file, almost within touching distance of the stationary traffic. Every so often, a lorry horn would blare or an angry driver would wave us back from the road, as if there were some place else we could go.

'They think we want to get on their trucks!' Jesus shouted.

'We *do* want to get on their trucks,' Mohammed shouted back.

'Not yet,' I said. 'We're just walking.'

Jesus waved enthusiastically as another lorry blasted its horn at us. Mohammed glared up at the cab and gave the sign of the five fathers. You may not know this sign, but you should Google it when you have a moment. It's used to tell someone that their mother is promiscuous.

'Ignore them,' I told Mohammed. 'You too, Jesus.'

'I don't like France,' Mohammed said. 'It's dismal.'

'We won't be here long,' I told him. 'England is just across the sea.'

'Why is the sea so grey?' Jesus asked. 'I do not think the sea is meant to be this colour.'

They were both right. Beyond the fence, the sand dunes stretched forlornly to the water's edge. The sand was a strange colour – not golden, like it was on the beaches of northern Latakia, but a kind of washed-out brown, like uncooked batter. On the opposite side of the road was a grim industrial landscape. Factories, chimneys, long concrete yards.

'Just keep walking,' I said. 'It will be better once we can get off the road.'

'When will that be?' Mohammed asked.

'I don't know. This fence isn't on Google Earth. It must be recent.'

'It looks like it goes on forever.'

'It can't go on forever. Just keep walking.'

So we kept walking, Mohammed followed by Jesus followed by me. After a kilometre or so, the road curved inland, but the fence continued, and our path remained narrow and precarious. The traffic started to move, and before long, the lorries were thundering by, blasting us with dust and diesel fumes as they passed. I could see the camp now – the migrant settlement that everyone called 'The Jungle'. It was sprawled across the dunes and scrubland beyond the fence, hundreds of tents squatting against a distant treeline. That was where we needed to be, and for now, there was no obvious way in.

A little further on, we came to a lay-by where two police vans were parked. Four policemen watched intently as we approached. They were wearing big boots and military caps.

'Ask them how we get in,' Mohammed suggested.

I didn't have time. One of them immediately removed his baton from his belt and started waving us down the road.

'Do you speak English?' I called.

'Get off ze road!' the policeman shouted back.

Mohammed swore in Arabic. 'What does he think we're trying to do?'

'He thinks we want to break into these trucks,' Jesus yelled.

'We're not trying to board these vehicles,' I told the policeman. 'We've become accidentally trapped here because of the fence.'

This went some way to defusing the situation. The policeman I'd been talking to said something in French and the others fell about laughing.

'I don't think they believe you,' Mohammed said.

'How do we get inside the camp?' I asked the policeman. 'Could you show me?'.

He pointed down the road, then started waving his baton again, with a sort of lazy aggression, as if swatting away a fly. He said a French word several times.

'I think he is telling us to shoo,' Jesus translated.

Another five minutes of walking brought us to a slip road, and here the fence ended. There were plastic bollards and more policemen – at least a dozen this time, and in full riot gear – but they didn't stop us or try to talk to us; they just watched impassively as we made our way towards The Jungle.

There was a main entrance point, of sorts, located at the bottom of the slip road next to an underpass. There were small vans and cars parked here, and volunteers were unloading supplies from their boots. A group of dark-skinned men sat smoking on a broken pallet. There was a line of chemical toilets that seemed to have leaked their contents into the road. The smell was appalling.

'Well, this is nice,' Mohammed said.

'Shut up, Mohammed.'

'I think we should find a hotel. What's French for hotel? Google it.'

'We're not going to a hotel. We can't afford it.'

'Jesus can.'

'We'll be able to get information here. That's far more important. Anyway, we won't be staying long.'

Mohammed threw up his hands, then turned to Jesus for support. But Jesus wasn't paying any attention. He was staring at two men who were pushing a shopping trolley loaded with firewood, apparently mesmerised.

A woman with hair the colour of straw was picking up litter with a stick. Having established that she spoke English, I told her that we were two Syrians and an Iraqi, recently arrived from the Middle East, via Berlin. She was very polite. She asked me to wait while she spoke to a colleague, who was then able to direct us to another colleague who directed us to an information point. Unfortunately, no one was there giving out information. I later found out that no one was actually running the camp, or not in the usual sense. There was no one in charge, no chain of command, and no one acting in any official capacity. Just an army of volunteers doing their best to manage the chaos.

In a shack constructed of chipboard and tarpaulin we found an Afghan selling groceries. He spoke excellent Arabic and told us that we should head to the 'welcome caravan', where they'd be able to provide us with useful information. We'd find it if we kept walking south on the main road through the camp. The caravan was impossible to miss, because it was pink.

So we headed south. The main road was essentially a car-wide strip of mud running through an endless sea of temporary shelters. These were not just tents; there were also dozens of jerry-rigged huts. The sturdiest were built from nailed planks, and had roofs of corrugated metal; others looked to have been cobbled together from whatever materials happened to be lying around: cardboard and broken pallets, driftwood frames covered with plastic sheeting that flapped in the wind. Many of the larger structures had signs painted in multiple languages, advertising food and energy drinks and cigarettes for sale. There were cafés selling hot meals for a few euros. There was even a church – a huge construction covered in snow-white tarpaulin, with a tower rising several metres and topped by a wooden cross. Within moments of arriving, it was clear that The Jungle was less a camp than it was a shanty town, with a full range of services and its own spontaneous economy.

As for how many people were living in this town, it was difficult to guess. I heard estimates, later on, ranging from three to six thousand, with hundreds more arriving every week. Whatever the case, it was bustling; that much was immediately evident. People sat at the roadside on an odd assortment of improvised or donated furniture, playing cards and smoking, tapping on their phones and eating from polystyrene trays. From somewhere, loud music was playing, its bass beat strong and insistent.

After a while, I saw that Jesus was attracting a fair number of lingering glances. This was not unusual. People often wanted to stare at Jesus because of his pink flip-flops and wild white hair and black-as-death eyebrows. But it soon occurred to me that there might be another reason so many people were staring. I hadn't noticed at first, but The Jungle was populated almost entirely by young men. Jesus was older than the average person we passed by at least forty years! In this setting, even more than usual, he looked ancient and incongruous, like some itinerant preacher who had stumbled into a youth camp.

The pink caravan was pretty much at the southernmost point of the site. It was painted with flowers and hearts and a peace sign.

'That's the gayest thing I've ever seen,' Mohammed noted.

I ignored this, and tapped on the inside of the open door. The man who answered was small and white. He was wearing the Northern European hat known as a 'beanie'. He spoke English with a French accent and was extremely helpful.

He told us that the camp had self-organised into sections based on nationality. Unfortunately, the Syrian section was to the far north, back the way we'd come. He said it was easy to find because it was right next to the hospital tent, which was run by a charity called Médecins Du Monde. He showed us the spot on a printed-out map.

'You need tents?' he asked. 'We 'ave tents and blankets 'ere.' He gestured to the back of the caravan, which I now saw was crammed full of bagged tents and blanket rolls.

I didn't give Mohammed the chance to tell him we weren't staying. 'Yes, thank you,' I said. 'That's so kind of you.'

We took two tents and three blankets – the man assured us

he had an adequate stock of them – and then we walked north to the other end of the camp.

We would do a lot of walking over the coming days.

The Syrian section of the camp was in a sandy area partially sheltered by dunes and low prickly bushes. There were maybe fifty tents pitched there, and a length of thin rope was serving as a washing line, but this was pretty much the only sign of life. No one was sitting outside. The only reason I knew it was the right section was that someone had written 'Save Syria' on the side of one of the larger tents. The message was in English, painted thick and black. The canvas rippled in the gusty breeze, making the letters quiver angrily, like words shouted into the wind.

We found a space at the edge of the site and started to set up. The ground wasn't flat – it was at the base of a broad grass-covered dune – but it was the best we could find. If we slept with our heads at the highest point, it wouldn't cause too much discomfort.

Unsurprisingly, Jesus was not much help when it came to pitching a tent. He sat to one side with his hands in his lap while Mohammed and I scurried around like worker ants in the sand. There were no instructions to follow, just a faded three-part diagram that had been printed on the side of the bag. Parts one and two were indecipherable, and all part three showed was the finished tent.

'Do you need some help?'

The voice belonged to a man not much older than me, tall and slim and stubbled, with an easy smile that seemed entirely out of place in this environment. He was wearing dark jeans and a grey hooded top with an elaborate blue logo – a star encased by stretching, angular wings. Underneath the logo was text reading US AIR FORCE.

This man was not from the US Air Force. I probably don't need to tell you that. He was a Syrian named Firas, wearing donated clothing. I asked him about the hoodie later on and he told me that he'd found it in one of the boxes that were brought daily into the camp. He'd chosen it so the French police would think twice before fucking with him. Mohammed gave a firm nod of approval when he heard this, but I'm almost certain it was intended as a joke.

Firas assembled both tents with embarrassing ease. He was so adept that there was little for me to do. I just handed him poles as directed, while Mohammed sat on the dunes next to Jesus and nodded occasionally, as if he were the project manager. At the same time, Firas and I exchanged the bare bones of our stories, which turned out to have much in common.

Firas was from Tartus. If you don't know, Tartus is Syria's second-largest port, just down the coast from Latakia. It's an hour's drive between the two cities – or it used to be, before road blocks and checkpoints. So, relatively speaking, Firas lived just down the road from us. He was twenty-one years old. He was an engineering graduate and had left Syria as soon as he'd finished his degree, to avoid military service. He was going to the UK because he had an older brother already there, granted asylum in the city of Birmingham.

'How many Syrians are here?' I asked.

'A hundred, maybe. Most of them are at the Day Centre right now, queuing for food.'

'The Day Centre?'

'It's the only part of the site that's authorised by the French government. There's accommodation there for a couple of hundred women and children. They have showers and clean toilets. We're allowed to use them in the afternoons, but it's hardly worth it. If you want a shower you have to queue all morning for a ticket. And it's basically the same deal with the food. They provide hot meals once a day, but there's never enough for everyone. If you're not there two hours early you don't eat. Or not unless you're a child. Children get prioritised. You'll probably be okay, Mohammed.'

'I'm not a child!' Mohammed protested.

Firas raised his palms and laughed. 'Okay. A minor, then. Either way, you shouldn't complain. You'll be the one being fed. You could probably try your luck, too, Zain. Have a good shave beforehand, tell them you're seventeen.'

'I don't think I'd feel comfortable with such a deception,' I told him.

'Ha! Give it a week or so. Hunger's a great motivator.'

'What about Jesus?' I asked. 'Shall we say he's seventeen, too?'

Jesus grinned maniacally, displaying the many gaps in his teeth. Firas grinned back and gestured at Jesus's feet. 'We might be able to get you some new shoes, at the very least. The volunteers distribute shoes on Tuesdays. There's a huge demand, so it's complete chaos, but I'm sure we could find you something better than *those*.'

'These are my shoes,' Jesus said. 'They have carried me far.'

'Jesus is quite attached to his shoes,' I explained. 'You won't persuade him to change them.'

Firas gave me a look that said this was completely crazy, which of course it was. Mohammed rolled his eyes.

Once both tents were pegged down, Firas inspected them. 'These look in reasonable shape. They shouldn't leak too badly.'

'We won't need them for long,' Mohammed told him. 'We'll be in the UK soon.'

'Yeah, you and everyone else here,' Firas said.

'It can't be that hard. We've already crossed ten borders,' Mohammed rejoined.

'Trust me. No one's camped here for the scenery.'

'How long have you been here?' I asked.

'Too long.' Firas thought for a moment, his eyes fixed on a narrow stream of litter, curling around the dune. 'It's coming up to four months now.'

'Oh.'

'I'm not trying to depress you. Some people *do* make it across much quicker. I've heard of a couple of people who made it through on their very first attempt. And I know people who've been here even longer than I have. Lots of people. But it's mostly a matter of luck. You just have to be in the right place at the right time. And until then, you just keep on trying.'

'How often do you try?'

'Every night.'

'At the port?'

'No. No one bothers much with the port anymore. It's too easy for the police to stop us. They only have to guard the access roads. The fence keeps us from getting to the lorries, unless they're backed up way past the slip road. Of course, if you have money you can pay a smuggler for access to one of the overnight lorry parks, but it doesn't come cheap. The last I heard, they charge a hundred euros just to cut a hole in a fence. And if you want a guaranteed place in a refrigerated truck, prices start at a thousand.'

'You can't trust the smugglers,' Mohammed spat. 'They'll shaft you as soon as look at you.'

Firas nodded. 'It's almost impossible to get through border control. It doesn't matter how well you're hidden. They have sniffer dogs checking every vehicle before they're allowed onto the boats. You'd be better off using your thousand euros for kindling.'

'What about the trains?' I asked. 'Isn't it the same problem there?'

'Some of the problems are the same. They have sniffer dogs and attack dogs, and about five hundred cops and security guards policing the terminal. But it's a huge area, and there are long stretches of the perimeter fence that back onto open fields. It's impossible to stop all of us. Sometimes the police don't even try. They focus on protecting the platforms and loading areas.'

'What about the tunnel entrance? Don't they guard that?'

'Ha! You plan on *walking* to the UK?'

I shrugged. 'If we can't get on the trains or lorries . . .'

'Well, you wouldn't be the first. But I don't think anyone's succeeded. The fence around the entrance is about ten metres high, and they have cameras everywhere. You won't get within five hundred metres of the entrance before they set the dogs on you. You'd be better off trying to jump onto a moving freight train.'

'But people *do* get through?' Mohammed pressed. 'Otherwise there'd be no point trying.'

'Yes. People get through. Maybe a dozen on a good night. Out of a couple of thousand trying. You can do the maths for yourself.' Firas shrugged. 'Come with me tonight, if you want. I don't mind showing you what's what. Who knows? Maybe some of your beginner's luck will rub off.'

Mohammed nodded vigorously, while I shook my head. 'We should get some rest first. I don't think we should be trying anything while we're tired.'

'Fuck, Zain!' Mohammed spat. 'We could be in London tomorrow! We should check it out, at the very least. We need to know what we're up against.'

I looked at Jesus, and was surprised to find him nodding along vigorously. He really was determined to get us to the UK as soon as possible.

'No one ever leaves before dusk,' Firas told me. 'If it's rest you need, I doubt anything will be happening here for the next few hours.'

I frowned, thinking about the five hundred security personnel, not to mention the attack dogs. No one else seemed to be taking these threats seriously.

'Okay, fine,' I said eventually. 'We'll go. But no one is to do anything dangerous. We need to come up with a plan before we go charging in.'

Firas snorted at this, tucking his hands into the pockets of his US Air Force hoodie. 'Charging in is pretty much the *only* good plan. There's no point being cautious. You'll see.'

I looked at Mohammed until he met my eyes. 'No one does anything dangerous,' I repeated.

The Trains

It took us two and a half hours to walk to the Eurotunnel terminal. Firas had warned us that it was a long way, and of course I'd seen on Google Maps that it was the other side of town. But I wasn't prepared for the reality of it. It was twelve long kilometres – twelve kilometres just to get in sight of the trains!

We set off as the sun was sinking behind the petrochemical works. On Firas's advice, we were carrying not much more than the clothes on our backs. In my pockets I had the phone and charger, my wallet, Jesus's medication, and my passport, with the photo of Mum and Dad folded in its pages. But everything else had been left in the tent. There was nothing extraneous to slow us down.

We walked out of The Jungle as part of a group of about twenty other Syrians – all aged between eighteen and thirty, all fleeing violence, or the possibility of violence. I'd already met several of them that afternoon, when they got back from the food queues. There was Ali, who'd found himself without food, water or electricity during the siege of Aleppo. There was Said, who'd lived as a refugee in Lebanon for two years, having seen his family home destroyed early in the war. There was Khaled, fleeing Daesh, and Ismael, a draft dodger. There was Rahim the Deserter, whose family had paid an enormous bribe to get him out of the army and over the border. Everyone's story was a variation on the same theme.

Our group was part of a much larger procession – a pilgrimage, really. By the time we reached the underpass at the main road, the crowd was thick on every side. People were smoking and sipping energy drinks, and some were even wheeling bicycles. It seemed strange at the time, but made perfect sense in retrospect. With a bicycle, you could get to the trains in half an hour, and conserve precious energy for the night ahead. In The Jungle, bicycles were a prized possession.

The overwhelming majority of our congregation were young men, as in the camp, but now there were a greater number of women too. African women in their early twenties, wearing trainers and tracksuit bottoms and hijabs. Older women holding the hands of their children. Occasionally, I'd glimpse an entire family, or a father carrying a child in his arms. But even amidst this new diversity, Jesus still stood out as a lone, white-haired anomaly. He was the oldest person in the vicinity by a couple of decades. Earlier, Firas had taken me to one side to express his concerns about this. Was Jesus capable of walking so far? Could he crawl through a hole in a fence? Could he run, if necessary? These were concerns I shared, obviously, but there was nothing to be done about them. All I could tell Firas was that we'd made it this far with Jesus – all the way from Greece – and there was no way I was going to abandon him now.

Firas had shrugged, as if to say this was my decision, and my funeral.

I suppose it was. But as we exited the camp, I took a mental note of all the people who would face challenges at least equal to ours. The families. A woman who was obviously pregnant. It wasn't any sort of reassurance, but Jesus was not the only person ill-suited to the task at hand. Nor was he the only one ill-equipped. I saw other men in sandals or flip-flops, and several wearing crude leather slippers, constructed from too-small shoes with their backs squashed down or cut away.

Through the underpass we encountered our first group of riot police, about twenty of them. They had formed a line blocking the far slip road, but were not trying to stop anyone who was heading towards the town. I don't suppose they could have stopped us without . . . well, without starting a riot.

'They get more aggressive the closer you get to the trains,' Firas told me. 'Sometimes they blockade the roads leading to the town centre, too. That's a pain because it can add another half hour if we have to take the back roads. But mostly they concentrate on the area around the tracks and terminal. There's not enough of them to guard every route in.'

We walked without break through the industrial suburbs and into the town centre. We passed the Town Hall and proceeded along tidy streets lined with shops and bars and restaurants. There were a number of French people out and about, sipping wine and smoking under wide canopies, but few gave us a second glance. Most seemed absolutely determined to ignore us.

After two hours of walking, Firas called a halt so that he could debrief us. We were standing on the grassy verge at the edge of a small roundabout. Google Maps told me that we were to the southwest of Calais, no more than a kilometre from the train tracks.

The other Syrians did not wait with us; Firas said that large groups tended to run into problems this close to the terminal. Police vans patrolled the roads along the perimeter, and if they saw a crowd forming, they'd immediately call in back-up. Our best plan was to stick as a small unit and stay off the major roads. If we were careful, we should be able to reach the perimeter fence undetected, saving a lot of unnecessary hassle.

Before we set off again, I asked Firas for a moment and took the opportunity to check how Jesus was doing.

'My feet are tired,' he told me.

'It's not much further to the trains,' I said. 'But if you need more of a break, we can take one.'

He shook his head resolutely.

'You're sure?'

'We've been through a lot together, haven't we? Many hardships.'

'Yes, Jesus. We've been through a lot.'

'My feet will not fail me now. I am certain.'

I thought about this for a moment, then nodded. He looked so scrawny in the yellow light at the roadside, so frail; but his eyes were resolute. I put my hand on his shoulder. 'Okay, Jesus. Let's get going.'

The field we walked through was tangled with waist-high grass, and very dark. The sky had clouded over again, so if there was a moon, it was not visible. We had only the glow from the road to guide us, and whatever weak light was reflected back from the low clouds. But Firas never hesitated. He led us in single file through the undergrowth, his movements smooth and confident. He must have made this journey a hundred times in the course of four months. He must have walked over two thousand kilometres, just trying to board a train. It was an astonishing thought, and somewhat demoralising.

We stayed pretty much parallel to the road, and before long I could see smudges of yellow light illuminating the distant fence. Below this ran a long embankment – a blue-black shadow that seemed to detach itself from the surrounding night. As we drew closer, Firas motioned us towards a dark hollow below the fence. It took me a second to register what it was: a small tunnel passing underneath the train tracks. It was about the width of a car and carried a drainage ditch through the embankment. The sides were steeply sloping concrete, but, following Firas's lead, we shuffled through on our bottoms, moving sideway like crabs. There was just enough clearance to manage it. Only Jesus got his feet wet.

On the other side, we found ourselves on a narrow road, lit only by the lights along the railway line. Firas gestured that we should huddle close, then spoke in a terse whisper. 'We're about fifteen minutes from the loading area, where they drive the lorries onto the trains.'

'How do you drive a lorry onto a train?' Mohammed asked.

'The lorries drive onto long flat-bed trailers, which the train pulls. That's not important right now. You'll see for yourself soon enough.' Firas pointed down the road, where a large overpass spanned the train tracks. 'It's a fifteen-minute walk and there's not much cover, but it's far easier to get through the fence here. We'll scout along it until we find a hole. There were several yesterday, but that's not a guarantee. The French patch them up as soon as they find them.'

'We have wire cutters,' Mohammed announced. 'We bought them in Serbia.'

'Perfect,' Firas said. 'You're going to be popular tonight. They're almost impossible to buy in Calais because the locals all hate us. They trade for about fifty euros in the camp.'

'I don't have them *with* me,' I clarified, and Firas and Mohammed gave me identical stares. 'What? I thought we were just here to look. No one said we'd be cutting through fences.'

'You're not going to see anything worthwhile from this side of the fence,' Firas told me. He shook his head, closing his eyes briefly. 'It doesn't matter. There's always a way in. That's the easy part. But next time, bring the wire cutters. It's just common sense.'

My blushes were probably hidden by the darkness. 'Okay, fine,' I told Firas. 'If we can find a way in, we'll go in. But I need to know what to expect. What happens once we're through the fence? What's the plan?'

Firas shook his head again, as if I were being terribly naïve. 'The plan is simple. Keep your eyes open. Look for any opportunity to get aboard a lorry or train. If you see a security guard, hide. If one of them sees you, run. They might not even bother chasing you, depending on how overworked they are.'

This all sounded reasonable. 'What about the police?' I asked.

'Most are stationed outside the fence, as crowd control. But there are usually a hundred or so in the terminal too. Their priority is protecting the passenger trains and loading platforms, but it's a huge area. They can't be everywhere at once. With a bit of luck, you can hide under a vehicle. With even more luck, they won't find you and haul you out of there.'

'Don't they check the trains before they depart?'

'Of course. But they're not infallible, even with the sniffer dogs.' Firas shrugged. 'The only way to avoid the checks entirely is to wait until the trains are already moving. If you're quick, you can jump on as they're leaving the loading area.'

'You're joking?'

'I've seen it done. Time it just right and you can sprint to the trains before they've picked up too much speed.'

I turned to Mohammed and Jesus. 'No one is to attempt this. Are we clear? We stick together and we look for a safe place to hide ourselves.'

Mohammed glared at me, but I ignored him. 'What happens if the police find us?' I asked Firas. 'Will we be taken into custody?'

'Ha! Not a chance. If they arrested every stowaway they found, they'd fill all their cells in an hour. They'll just escort us back to this side of the fence, and later we try again. Think of it as a very frustrating game.'

I was incredulous. 'They'll let us go? Just like that?'

Firas shrugged again. 'If you're unlucky, they'll rough you up a bit. But it's not likely unless you provoke them. If worst comes to worst, don't fight back. They'll just pepper spray you, and then it's basically game over. It stings like fuck for hours.'

'They wouldn't pepper spray Mohammed!' I exclaimed. 'He's a child!'

'I'm not a fucking child!' Mohammed hissed, causing Jesus to chuckle to himself.

'They'll pepper spray anyone,' Firas said. 'Women, children;

anyone who gives them an excuse. Listen. Just don't do anything stupid. If the police catch you, don't put up any resistance. Cut your losses and try again later. Simple.'

'I don't like this,' I said.

'No one *likes* this,' Firas replied. 'Just keep your mind on the bigger picture. It doesn't matter how many times you get caught. You only have to succeed once.'

Mohammed nodded vehemently at this. He was obviously set on going in tonight, with or without me.

'We stick together,' I repeated.

Firas gave me an encouraging pat on the back. 'That's the idea.'

'Anything else we need to know?'

Firas thought for a moment, as another group of men began to emerge from the drainage tunnel. 'Don't try to get on the train roofs,' he said. 'It looks like a good place to hide, but you'll probably get electrocuted.'

'Okay.'

There was nothing else to say.

We crept along the perimeter fence, looking for the holes that Firas had found the previous night. It did not take long. Just down the road, a small crowd had formed. Maybe a dozen people, with more scrambling down from the overpass every minute. The fence had been strategically cut at its base, then wrenched up from the ground, leaving a gap just large enough to crawl through. People were taking it in turns to hold the chain link up so that others could scramble underneath without catching their clothing. It was very orderly; not that surprising, since we were all used to queuing.

Once we were all through, Firas led us across a dozen sets of train tracks to the other side of the line. He crouched in the shadow of a low bush, motioning for us to join him. There was no sign of security yet, but no one who'd made it through the fence was hanging about. People were dispersing across the width of the train line, moving in small groups at a steady jog. 'It's always sensible to scatter as soon as you're in,' Firas whispered. 'They have cameras along the track, and if they see a big group coming, the police will be all over it in minutes.'

Having said this, he pulled his hood up and nodded for us to follow him again.

We walked quickly. There were some metal sheds at the rail-side, but not much else that offered decent cover. I supposed the best option, if security came, would be to lie flat on the ground, as far from any overhead lighting as possible. There was a slight dip at the edge of the rails, and some patchy grass. From a distance, it was possible you'd be missed. As for the cameras . . . well, there was nothing to be done about them. It felt very eerie, knowing that we were probably being observed from a control room somewhere, but I had to trust Firas on this. It made sense that the police would have to prioritise the biggest threats. Still, it was difficult not to feel vulnerable.

If Mohammed and Jesus were similarly nervous, they were giving no sign. Mohammed had on his strong and serious face. Jesus stumbled every so often, his flip-flops making hard work of the loose rocks that had fallen at the rail-side, but, for the time being, he was keeping up admirably, and his eyes shone with the same determination I'd seen earlier.

When a security guard finally arrived, it was as if he'd materialised from thin air. A freight train had been rumbling past on one of the central tracks. It was the first we'd seen, and while it was not moving quickly, it was still fast enough; no sane person would have attempted to board it. I don't know how long it took to pass, but it seemed to go on and on. And as the last carriage disappeared down the line, it revealed the security guard. He was standing on the far side of the track, blocking the path of two of the African women we'd seen breaching the fence ahead of us. He was speaking on a walkie-talkie.

Very slowly, I crouched low to the ground, and Mohammed and Jesus followed my example. I don't know if it was the movement, glimpsed from the corner of his eye, or just a coincidence, but that was the moment the security guard looked over. We were only metres from the nearest light, and could not have been hard to spot.

Firas hadn't bothered to crouch. He was standing with his hands in his pockets, observing the three figures across the tracks as if they were actors in a mildly interesting play. 'Okay. Change of plan,' he said. 'Let's get moving. The whole complex opens up just ahead. If we can get there before back-up arrives, we'll have every chance of hiding.'

'What?' I thrust my jaw in the direction of the security guard. 'He's seen us! He won't just stand there while we keep going.'

Firas actually laughed at this. 'What else can he do? The moment he moves those girls will be gone. Trust me. I bet you a thousand euros he doesn't even twitch.'

This assessment proved correct. We started jogging, my heartbeat quickened, and the security guard simply watched us as we passed, still speaking into his walkie-talkie.

The area around the loading platforms was unfathomably large. We crossed a dozen more sets of train tracks and climbed over a low steel barricade, finding ourselves at the raised edge of a huge grassy bowl. In the distance were brightly lit roads and bridges, carrying a long line of traffic to the trains. We waited in the dark grass just long enough to catch our breath, then proceeded at a trot towards the platforms. We crossed a small yard near some train sheds, and were blasted by lorry horns as we negotiated a long road running parallel to the platforms. After that, there was a final stretch of grass, in which we lay motionless, my heart still pounding like a drum.

The platforms were protected by twin rows of security fencing, and even at the quickest glance, it was clear that this was not the sort of fencing you could get through with wire cutters. You'd struggle with power tools.

'We have to go around it,' Firas whispered. 'It's open at both ends, obviously, so the trains can get in and out.'

'Is it guarded?' Mohammed asked.

'Of course! The whole area's swarming with cops. The good news is they won't be able to see us easily from the platforms, not if we stay a few metres back. All that lighting works against them, means they can't see shit on this side of the fence. We'll be able to hide near one of the openings. Pick our moment and then . . .'

Firas trailed off with a sardonic smile.

'Then what?' I pressed.

'Then there's no point planning,' Firas whispered. 'That's the part when we'll need all our luck . . .'

It took the police about a minute to find us, encircle us, and lead us away from the trains. Or that's how it seemed. One moment we were darting along the tracks, the next we were being escorted back to the perimeter fence. The two policemen who accompanied us were very matter-of-fact about the process. One led and the other followed a couple of paces behind us, neither speaking more than a word or two in French. On Firas's advice, we remained as meek as spring lambs, and no one got pepper sprayed.

During the long, mostly silent walk to the nearest gate, I had time to reflect on what I'd seen. The platforms were impossibly long. That was my first impression. They must have been a kilometre or more – which made sense, given the size of the freight trains. And I guessed there were probably a dozen platforms, based on the number of tracks running into the loading area. This gave me some small cause for hope. At a conservative estimate, the police had ten kilometres of platform to monitor. If we could get there undetected, we *would* have opportunities to board the trains. The problem, of course, was getting around that final fence; and, at the moment, it seemed insurmountable.

'It's not impossible,' Firas told me, once we'd been released outside the compound. 'You have to remember that the police aren't always watching. They get distracted, their attention starts to slip, especially at the end of the night. Sometimes, they have to be elsewhere, if there's trouble at the fence or a mass break-in. The chances come; you just have to be ready for them.'

'So what now?' I asked.

'I already told you. Now we try again.' Firas gave a wide grin. 'Come on, I'll show you some more places that are worth trying.'

Later, we sat in one of the fields to the south of the perimeter fence. There were lots of us there, probably a few hundred scattered across the flat dark land. It had turned much colder, and some people had lit fires, burning whatever dead vegetation could be found, using plastic litter for kindling. Many were eating chocolate bars and drinking the energy drinks they'd brought from the camp. I made a mental note to do likewise next time. My phone showed that it was coming up to two a.m. We were all very tired.

We'd made it back into the Eurotunnel compound twice, but had been caught long before we made it to the platforms. On the latest attempt, we'd been turned back the moment we were through the perimeter fence. Mohammed had been complaining relentlessly for the last hour, saying that we needed to change our strategy; perhaps make a break for the tunnel entrance. Jesus hadn't complained once, but now he was lying flat on his back with his eyes closed. Whether he was sleeping or not, he'd clearly had enough.

'How do you do this every night?' I asked Firas.

'You'll get used to it.'

'But it's so dispiriting!'

'Think of it as a job. Some of it's tedious, some of it's reasonably stimulating. Once your shift's over you get to go home to your bed.'

I nodded glumly. I didn't bother to point out that our beds were sleeping bags in cold, and possibly leaky, tents. I did not have the energy.

Firas drew his knees up to his chest. His hands were tucked into the sleeves of his US Air Force hoodie, so that his arms appeared to end in rounded stumps. 'The important thing,' he said, 'is to remember why you're doing this. Think of what you have to gain. One lucky break and you could be in the UK a couple of hours from now.'

'Do you still think that? After four months of trying?'

Firas shrugged. 'My brother's waiting for me. One day I'll get through, and when I do, I'm not even going to phone him. I'm just going to turn up on his doorstep and surprise him. The look on his face: that's what I always think about. That's what keeps me going.'

Cold and tired as I was, this still made me smile. 'Make sure you give me his address,' I said. 'Maybe one day I'll turn up and surprise *you*.'

'That's the spirit. Think positive.'

We kept trying for another hour, then decided to call it a night. We were dead on our feet, and still had the walk back to the camp to get through. Nevertheless, Firas tried to talk us out of it.

'If you can stick it out, there are always more opportunities later on. The police'll be tired too. Seriously, the hour before dawn is prime time for getting onto the trains.'

Mohammed just shook his head.

'Tomorrow,' I told Firas. 'We'll try again after a full night's sleep.'

'Your loss.' He gave another broad smile. 'If you don't see me in the morning, it means I'm having breakfast in the UK.'

'Here's hoping,' I said.

Half an hour later, as Mohammed, Jesus and I trudged through Calais's deserted streets, it started to rain.

A Game of Chess

This was our life for a month. At night the trains, by day sleep and queues and creeping disillusionment.

September became October and the temperature dropped. We bought gloves from one of the grocery shacks and procured thick tracksuits and nearly waterproof jackets from the donation boxes. Jesus took to wearing socks with his flip-flops.

When it rained it was miserable, and it rained often. The water pooled between the dunes and turned the dirt roads into rutted bogs. It dripped through the seams of our tent and made everything smell of damp and decay. I would not have believed it possible, but for several days the sun vanished entirely, and the sky was like a slate-grey dome that some malevolent giant had placed upon the earth.

'The UK won't be like this, will it?' Mohammed asked one morning, as we lay in our sleeping bags, listening to the static hiss of rain on canvas.

'Of course not,' I told him.

'And we will get there? Eventually?'

'We'll just keep trying until we do.' I tried to project confidence in my voice, a confidence I no longer felt.

Despite the conditions, the camp continued to grow, week by week. At one point, there were probably a hundred new arrivals a day; Firas said it was the fastest expansion he'd seen in four months. Tents sprang up like spring flowers among the dunes, and the riot police charged with protecting the port grew increasingly edgy. One day, without warning, a large group of them entered the camp and forced everyone back fifty metres from the road. The hundred or so tents within this new 'exclusion zone' were then bulldozed, along with whatever meagre possessions were contained inside. When residents tried to protest, they were immediately tear-gassed.

Given this increased hostility, it was reassuring to discover that not everyone in Calais felt the same way. There was a woman living in a house not far from the Day Centre who let us sit on her front lawn and use her Wi-Fi. When she went to the shops, she always smiled at us and asked in English if we needed anything. As if we were simply her new neighbours! There was never any pity in her smile; she just treated us as normal human beings. And let me tell you: sometimes that means as much as anything.

Then there were the locals who came every day to distribute clothes and food and firewood. At weekends, they were often joined by English day-trippers who had filled their car boots with donations. Unfortunately, there was never enough to go around. More precisely, there was a surplus of women's clothing and a deficit of men's. And some of the donations were just plain crazy. The outer edge of the campsite became a dumping ground for high-heeled boots and leather handbags, and decorative underwear that never failed to draw Mohammed's eye. Children's toys were a problem too. Not far from our tent, just off one of the tracks leading to the underpass, was a large brown teddy bear with only one eye. It had one paw raised to the sky and looked as if it was drowning in a sea of ash and partially burnt litter. I felt a deep, deep sadness every time I saw it. Eventually, I dug a small hole and gave the bear a decent burial.

Around this time, I learned from a Sudanese shopkeeper that The Jungle had been set up on the site of a disused landfill, as this, apparently, was the only part of Calais in which our tents were tolerated. That we were literally living in a rubbish dump came as no great surprise, not anymore. We'd travelled close to five thousand kilometres to be here, and the UK was just across the sea, twenty minutes away by train; and yet it seemed further away now than it ever had before.

'I wonder what Mum would think of us being here,' Mohammed said, after I'd told him about our campsite's former purpose. 'I doubt this was the Europe she imagined for us.'

'No. Probably not.'

We sat in silence for a while as the wind gusted among the dunes, swirling sand and dead leaves and carrier bags. Talking about Mum and Dad hadn't got any easier, but at least we *did* talk about them now. We talked about them most days, and once every week, we tried to phone home. Together. There was no real hope of course, not anymore. They would have contacted us, had they been in a position to do so, but still we stuck to this weekly ritual. I suppose, more than anything, it was a way of telling each other that we hadn't given up. Nor would we. Not until we knew for certain.

'I think Mum and Dad would understand,' I said eventually.

'I think they'd . . . well, I think they'd be proud that we're still fighting for our future. Holding on to an ideal, I guess . . .'

I trailed off, conscious of how I must sound. I expected Mohammed to call me out on it any second. Tell me that I was a pompous idiot, and as delusional as Jesus. But he didn't. He nodded. 'That *is* what they'd say.'

Life in the camp was one of stringent routine. Every day was essentially the same, and looked something like this:

We got up late, seldom before noon and often as late as two or three p.m. As far as The Jungle went, this was entirely standard. We were all night owls by necessity. No one rose in the morning unless they wanted to queue for a shower.

There was a water point, surrounded by a permanent marsh, where we washed and brushed our teeth. There was an area behind one of the uninhabited dunes that served as a latrine. Nobody used the actual toilets, because they were basically unusable.

Breakfast was sourced at one of the dozen shops or cafés on site, along with additional food and energy drinks to get us through the coming night. Food was not expensive, but after travelling all the way across Europe, little of Mum's money remained. It was Jesus's inheritance from his dead sister that fed us every day. Without that, we would have been entirely dependent on the Day Centre and the food parcels provided by local charities. Of course, in a sense it was money that Jesus owed us – some of it, anyway – but I was not certain he remembered much on this point. In any case, none of us mentioned it. I thanked Jesus for his generosity, and even Mohammed had the good grace to hold his tongue.

'It's *our* money,' Jesus said, looking pleased as punch. 'It belongs to all of us.'

After breakfast, there was a gap of a couple of hours that could be productively filled with small tasks. On the rare sunny days, I would wash some of our clothes at the water point and drape them to dry across our tents. More often, I would charge the phone. There were several generators around the camp, but the closest to us was run out of the back of a huge truck that had been parked on site by Christian missionaries. Extension sockets sprouted like hydra-heads from every available power point.

In the late afternoon, we went to the Day Centre to queue for our evening meal. This was always some sort of meat – not pig – served with bread or rice in a polystyrene tray. It had taken only one day for Mohammed to come to the conclusion that he was a child after all, at least for the purpose of queuing. He switched to the priority line, and this freed up at least an hour in his evening schedule, which he invariably spent playing football with some of the other adolescents. Although there was not much room for it, sport was hugely popular in the camp. On one occasion, someone managed to organise an Afghanistan-versus-Pakistan cricket match, which was played on the bulldozed ground of the exclusion zone. The riot police watched with interest, but did not try to stop it.

Some evenings, after we'd finally eaten, Jesus and I would watch Mohammed play for a while, but too often it was raining. On these days, we'd go to one of the other communal areas instead. The long-term residents of the camp had set up a wide range of services and amenities. You already know about the many shops and cafés, but this was just the tip of the iceberg. There were two churches – the Protestant and the Ethiopian

Orthodox. There were probably half a dozen mosques – Sunni, Shia and non-denominational. The mosques were not nearly as showy as the Ethiopian Orthodox church; really, they were just large tents with rugs inside. No one had managed to construct minarets. Nevertheless, the call to prayer was still recited five times a day, with the acting mu'adhdhin simply cupping his hands to his mouth and bellowing into the sky.

There was a barber and a bicycle repairman. There was a school where local volunteers taught lessons in French and English. There was even an Eritrean nightclub – a large dark marquee fitted with a disco ball and wireless speakers. I'm not sure it actually opened at night. Most of its business seemed to occur in the afternoons and early evenings. They played their music very loud and sold super-strength lager for €1.50 a can. Needless to say, I kept Jesus and Mohammed well away from there.

Most evenings we sat quietly in the library-bookshop. It was filled with donated books, lovingly organised by language and genre. The man who ran it was a forty-year-old Iraqi Kurd, and a fellow bibliophile. He was also a keen chess player, and would usually play a game or two with Jesus while I read. The fact that he *could* play chess came as a surprise to Jesus. I told him that he'd mentioned it before, in Kelebia, but obviously he had no recollection of this. The strange thing was, he turned out to be quite good, in direct contradiction to what he'd told me earlier.

'You said you were terrible,' I told him. 'You said you never won a game.'

'I don't remember this,' Jesus said. 'But I don't remember learning to play, either. Perhaps I used to play badly and now I play well?'

'How is that even possible?'

Jesus shrugged. 'I cannot answer this question, my friend. But it feels very natural, playing this game. I don't even have to think about it. I look at the board and I know what I must do next.'

The Kurdish bookseller gave a dissatisfied grunt at this news. It was one thing to lose, and another to hear that your opponent was not even trying. That he was making his moves based on nothing more than blind intuition. It was an outrageous claim, really, and I'm not sure the Kurd believed it. But I did. Once, I would have queried it, or, at the very least, I'd have felt unsettled by his explanation. But I suppose I was past being unsettled by Jesus. At some point, I had become immune to the strangeness of the man, and now just accepted him as he was. Mostly, I was pleased he'd rediscovered a hobby.

Something I noticed during those quiet evenings in the book-shop: while Mohammed and I were finding each day in The Jungle increasingly draining, for Jesus, the opposite was true. Over the course of a month, he seemed to grow stronger and stronger. In a sense, it was like he was returning to life. Day by day, his face appeared less gaunt, and the dark hollows under his eyes began to fade. I'm fairly sure he was the only person in the entire camp who was gaining weight rather than losing it. It was as if every scrap he ate went towards putting meat back on his bones, and with that and all the walking – twenty-four kilo-metres every single night – he was soon looking in better shape than ever before. Not in great shape, for sure, but when I thought back to how he'd appeared in his hospital bed in Hungary, the transformation was remarkable.

When I asked him how he was doing, he no longer talked about feeling tired or old. 'It is as if I have been given a second chance,' he said. 'I probably should have died in Hungary. I felt like I was dying. I remember *that.*' He gave a brief, involuntary shudder, but it was soon replaced by his usual gappy grin. 'My life is a gift. It's up to me to use it well.'

I thought he was probably talking about his supposed 'purpose' again, his role in getting us over this last, unconquerable border. So I smiled and nodded and said nothing to contradict him. If it kept him happy and motivated, then where was the harm? And for the most part, he did seem happy. He tolerated the conditions we were living in far better than Mohammed or I did. He never complained about the rain or the cold or the smell of burning litter. He just accepted the situation as it was, patiently awaiting the fulfilment of his destiny. Sometimes, I wondered if it was also a side-effect of his acute amnesia; since he had lost so much of his past, what choice did he have but to live in the now, taking each new day as it came? In any case, I started to think of him as Jesus mark two. Zen Jesus: utterly sedate in the face of our daily hardships.

There was only one thing that was able to disturb his newfound tranquillity. Unsurprisingly, it was alcohol. Since the camp was made up mostly of young men, far from home, frustrated and bored, drinking was not uncommon. Nor was it confined to the Eritrean nightclub. Every so often, we'd see people drinking in doorways, or on the dunes or at the side of the dirt streets, and every time we did, the transformation in Jesus was instant. He became agitated. His expression revealed an awful mix of loathing and longing. There was not much to do at such times but to steer him safely away, to allow him the time he needed to recover.

And recover he did. Sometimes it took ten minutes, and sometimes several hours, but eventually he'd become calm once more.

He started to smile again, or he'd chuckle at Mohammed's latest profanity. Often, I think my brother invented these new and increasingly absurd insults just to provoke this response. He no longer talked about ditching Jesus, and it wasn't *just* because we needed his dead sister's money to buy breakfast. More than this, I think we both appreciated Jesus's ongoing and unshakable belief in our shared endeavour. However unrealistic, however misguided, it was still a comfort, of sorts.

One night we almost made it; or so it seemed at the time. We'd been waiting at the loading-area fence when a dozen other intruders began their own incursion, on the far side of the tracks. While the police were distracted, we managed to slip between two lorry carriers that were being loaded on adjacent platforms. Once aboard, we hid beneath the nearest vehicle – me, Mohammed and Jesus, lying side-by-side with maybe a foot or two of space between our faces and the undercarriage. It was cold and it was uncomfortable, but for a short time, I thought we'd actually done it. I lay rigid as a corpse, not daring to move, barely daring to breathe, and praying – praying! – for the train to start its journey.

It felt like an hour, with every moment dragging its feet. But in reality, I doubt we were there all that long. We were hauled out by two police officers with a sniffer dog, and had the usual silent walk back to the perimeter fence.

That was the closest we came to the UK. Most nights, we were chased away before even getting to the loading area. Sometimes, we worked in small teams, with one group creating a diversion while another sneaked past. More often, we stayed on our own, trying to keep as far away from the police as possible. I saw the effects of their tear gas and pepper spray from a distance, and that was enough to convince me that we did not want to get caught up in any of the larger crowds.

As for Firas, we saw him often – always wearing his US Air Force hoodie, like it was some sort of lucky charm – but after that first night, he preferred to work alone. He thought he'd have a greater chance of success without us, and particularly, without Jesus. It was difficult to disagree, and I certainly didn't resent him for his decision. I liked Firas. I liked him more and more as the weeks passed. He was able to stay upbeat and confident, whatever the circumstances. He didn't seem to care if it had been raining for a week, or if he'd just been ejected from the Eurotunnel compound for the fifth time that night. He always had the same easy smile, the same positivity. It was something I tried to emulate, but with limited success. It was hard to stay positive. For every person who made it to the UK, there were a hundred who did not.

There were fatalities too – at least two or three every single week. People were struck by trains. People fell from moving vehicles. They were electrocuted on the tracks or crushed by cargo. We always heard about these incidents the next day. The French and English newspapers sometimes ran the stories, and word spread quickly through the camp. Sometimes, the police put up information about the deaths, thinking it would be a deterrent for the rest of us. It was not. The truth is, after hearing about the first few deaths, the shock quickly wore off. It became normal. It's terrible, how quickly death can become normal.

A Leap of Faith

The day that changed everything started like any other. We got up at midday. We washed at the swampy water point. We ate breakfast at the Afghan Café. I tried not to think about how little money we had left, and how long it might have to last.

It was mid-afternoon when I noticed Firas was missing. Usually, I'd have seen him by then. It wasn't raining and he didn't tend to stay in his tent if he could avoid it. Under normal circumstances, he'd have been sat around chatting, passing the idle hours before the dinner queues began.

I went to the Christian generator truck to charge the phone, and when I got back, he was still nowhere to be seen. I went to check his tent, in case he was ill. There had been a lot going around recently, so this was a distinct possibility. The previous week, Médecins Du Monde had tested the camp's water supplies, and found every one positive for E. coli.

Having established that he was not in his tent, I picked my way through our Syrian enclave until I found a small group smoking at the roadside.

'Has anyone seen Firas?' I asked. 'He isn't in his tent.'

This was met with the biggest smile I had ever witnessed from Rahim the Deserter. 'Last seen five o'clock this morning,' he told me. 'He'd just jumped onto a train heading for the tunnel.'

It took me a moment to process this information. 'He's gone?' I asked. 'You actually saw him go.'

'With my own eyes.'

I punched the air. I literally punched the air and whooped with joy. The others were laughing at me as I ran off to find Mohammed and Jesus, but I did not care.

'He made it?' Mohammed asked. 'He actually made it?'

I could understand my brother's astonishment. It was almost unbelievable. Five months of trying, and then gone just like that. But in the end, it was exactly as Firas had said. It didn't matter how many times you failed. All it took was one lucky break.

What would he be doing now? If his luck had held a little longer, if he'd evaded the police at the other end too, then he might be on his way to surprise his brother in Birmingham. Maybe he was already there. But, really, the details didn't matter. Even if he was in custody in the UK, it would only be a temporary set-back.

Mohammed's face split in a huge grin. It was probably the first time I'd seen him smile in days. Jesus's reaction was more under-stated – probably because he'd never doubted the way Mohammed and I had. Nevertheless, he looked very satisfied. He nodded quietly to himself, patting my little brother fondly on the shoulder.

He made it. The thought echoed over and over in my head. He finally made it. That there was any other possibility didn't even occur to me.

*

They found Firas's body close to the tunnel entrance. An unidentified male, believed to be Syrian – that was what the police reported, but we all knew it had to be him. He had broken his neck when he fell from the train. He probably died instantly.

Jesus told me that I should come and get some food, but I knew I wouldn't be able to eat. All I wanted, right then, was to be alone, so that I could think.

'He was a kind boy,' Jesus said. 'He didn't deserve to die.'

'No. He didn't.'

I told him to take Mohammed and get their evening meal. I'd meet up with them afterwards.

I walked through the camp with no destination in mind. It was cold. It seemed like it was getting colder every week. But it wasn't raining, at least.

Eventually, I found myself inside the Ethiopian Orthodox Church. I came here sometimes, when I needed somewhere quiet and comfortable to think. I'd spoken to one of the 'clergymen' the first time I visited – a theology student from Addis Ababa – and he'd said it was okay for me to be there, even though I wasn't a Christian. God would not mind.

The Ethiopian Orthodox Church was the most impressive structure in The Jungle, by some margin. Once inside, you could actually forget that you were in a former rubbish dump in northern France. It was rainproof and windproof. It was carpeted with rugs and blankets, and there were cushions to sit on. It even had electric lighting, which ran off a diesel generator out back, though it was not switched on at the moment. There was light streaming through the clear plastic sheeting that formed a section of the roof. This illuminated the makeshift altar, above which pictures of Jesus Christ had been hung. The European version of Jesus Christ, with his glossy hair and miraculously white skin.

Today was the first time I'd seen the church empty. I suppose everyone else was queuing for food. In any case, it suited me perfectly. I sat on a cushion in the corner, pressed up against the white plastic walls, and for the longest time I just took in my surroundings. The space could have easily held a couple of hundred worshippers, and it looked even larger now that it was empty. The outer shell was constructed of timber, but the three supporting columns, spaced evenly through the interior, were slender tree trunks that had been stripped and cut to size. The building was quite an achievement, all things considered. It made me think, not for the first time, about all the dormant potential that surrounded me in the camp. All the technical skills, the education, the industriousness, the creativity.

Firas was going to be a civil engineer. That was what he'd trained for, back in Syria. He could have built schools and bridges and hospitals.

I didn't want to dwell on the details of his death, but it was difficult not to. The image was stuck in my head: his body lying lifeless at the rail-side, his neck snapped like a cheap piece of wood. I hoped he had no time to realise what was happening. I hoped he died still believing that he'd finally made it, that he was on his way to see his brother.

I waited for Mohammed and Jesus back at the tents. Firas had been well known and well liked in the Syrian section of the camp, and the mood was grim. Even so, I could see that everyone was getting ready for the night ahead – for another night at the train tracks. I'd witnessed the same thing before, though not so close up. People lost friends and companions. They lost family. And still they kept going, night after night. Many had seen much worse, in their own countries, and no one had got this far without developing a certain resilience. No one except me.

I was not resilient. I was not strong enough to continue. That's what I'd realised this afternoon.

'I think we should go back to Germany,' I told Mohammed and Jesus when they got back. 'Germany wants us.'

Wants may have been too strong a word, but I was using it relative to the UK's position. The UK did not want us. And neither did France. They'd rather we died than allow us to board a train.

I'd expected some resistance from Mohammed. In a way, I think I'd been hoping for it. But he just shrugged. 'Anywhere we don't have to live in a tent,' he said.

'It will be winter soon,' I told him. 'It would be stupid to stay here much longer. We have to admit it was a mistake and move on.'

'I'm not arguing with you.'

Only Jesus hadn't lost his faith. Jesus, who didn't even have a good reason to be here. Just a delusional belief in dreams and destiny.

'I don't think you should be so hasty,' he said. 'You are too sad to make good decisions at the moment.'

'This *is* a good decision. It's the rational decision.'

He looked at me and then Mohammed, frowning slightly. 'What happened to the boys who swam across the ocean to come to Europe? They would not have given up so easily!'

I didn't respond to this. There was no point.

'Pah! I did not pull you from the sea to have you turn back now, when we're so close.'

'You didn't pull us from the fucking sea!' Mohammed snapped.

'I remember it,' Jesus said, with a confident nod of his head.

'I'm sorry, Jesus,' I told him. 'Your memories are wrong. I shouldn't have kept indulging you. When we get back to Germany, we'll get you some medical help.'

'I don't need medical help. I need to take you to the United Kingdom. This is my purpose.'

'We're not going to the United Kingdom, Jesus. And you don't have a purpose. None of us do.'

I expected him to be upset by this sentiment, but I did not expect him to get so angry. I did not expect him to jab me in the chest with the stub of his missing index finger.

'Do you know what I want, more than anything?' he asked.

'No, Jesus. I don't. I don't know what you want.'

'You probably want to have a drink,' Mohammed said. 'That's my guess.'

'Mohammed!' I hissed. 'You're being cruel. There's no need—'

Jesus cut me off by jabbing me in the chest a second time. His voice had risen to a shout. 'Mohammed is correct! I want to have a drink. This is what I want more than anything else, every single day. And every day I do the impossible. Every day I refuse to yield. I need to stay sober, if I am to help you.'

I absorbed this information like a punch to the stomach. I knew about his ongoing struggle, of course – I knew only too well. But to have it laid out like that, in those terms, was still a shock.

'I'm sorry,' I said eventually. 'I'm sorry, Jesus, but it doesn't change anything. I don't want to stay here anymore. We *can't* stay here anymore.'

He considered this for a moment, then turned to Mohammed. 'And what about you? Are you going to run away too?'

'We're not running away! We're—'

Jesus cut him off as well. 'You can forget I asked. You're a child. You don't get a say in this.'

Mohammed's mouth fell open. In other circumstances, I might have smiled. As it was, I just felt hollow.

Jesus turned to me, and I stepped back before he could jab me again. 'You don't have to make a decision now. Give it one more night.'

'I don't want to go back to the train tracks,' I told him. 'I never want to see them again.' I looked to Mohammed for support, and was surprised when he shook his head.

He held my gaze for a few moments, his eyes full of fire. 'Well, what else are we going to do? I'm not going to hang around here all night, feeling like shit.' He glared at Jesus. 'I'm not a fucking child and I *do* get a say.'

That was how the decision was made. I was too deflated to argue. And I thought, stupidly, that it would be a way to honour Firas's memory. With a final hopeless attempt.

I didn't see the danger. I didn't know it was a night set to erupt. I just thought we'd try our luck once more, and it would be pointless and futile. And in the morning, we would go to Germany.

Riot

We got in through a gap in the fence, and we got thrown out again. We tried closer to the tunnel entrance, as part of a larger group, but the police pushed us back within minutes. They were more aggressive than usual; I saw an African man go to the ground after being struck on his shoulder by a baton. His friends responded by hurling rocks. It was a scene I'd witnessed many times over the past month, but tonight felt subtly different. There was an atmosphere, violence in the air. I can't explain it better than that. I just knew, in my gut, that it was a bad night to be there.

Later, we sat in one of the fields to the southwest of the terminal, eating chocolate. I still wasn't hungry, despite having skipped a meal, but I knew I'd need the energy for the walk back to The Jungle. It had only just gone one, but already I thought it might be time to call it a night. The atmosphere hadn't changed; it still felt tense. And if we left now, we'd be back at the camp in a couple of hours. We'd be able to sleep until mid-morning, then head to the bus station in town. This time tomorrow, we might already be in Munich.

I don't know if I expected an argument from Mohammed or Jesus, but I got none. Mohammed just nodded, and Jesus hardly reacted at all. He looked troubled, but that was how he'd looked all evening. I suppose he was having a hard time adjusting. It's not easy, giving up on a dream.

We walked along the narrow road that ran parallel to the perimeter fence, passing the hundreds who had not yet given up. People were still waiting patiently for their next opportunity. In one spot, several dozen had made it through a freshly cut hole, but it looked like the security guards were already onto them; I could see torch beams slicing the darkness at the rail-side. If the riot police weren't in position already, they'd be there soon enough, ready to push back the intruders and disperse the crowd on this side of the fence.

Our plan was to cross the train tracks at the bridge nearest to the tunnel entrance – or, technically, entrances. There were two of them side-by-side, each with a single track carrying trains in one direction. The bridge was the most direct route back to the camp, and, usually, it would have been the quickest. But not tonight.

I could hear that there were a lot of people on the bridge before we got there. This was normal, since it was one of the few places where you could cross the tracks. But it wasn't really a viable place to attempt an incursion. Security was far too tight there. There were cameras and guards everywhere, and the fences were tall and ran the full length of the bridge to prevent people from jumping onto the train roofs. You'd have been crazy to try, since the drop was at least ten metres. But without the fence, people *would* have tried, nevertheless.

Tonight, a huge crowd had formed at the far side of the bridge

– several hundred, at least. There was a lot of shouting, and people were rattling the fencing and throwing projectiles down the steep embankment that led to the tracks. I didn't really want to know what was happening there, much less get caught up in it, but neither did I want to backtrack. Now that we'd made our decision, I just wanted to get back to the camp as quickly as possible.

I told Mohammed and Jesus to stay close to me, then started to push my way through the crowd. But when we made it to the front, I saw immediately it had been a wasted effort. No more than fifty metres down the road, illuminated by van lights, stood a line of riot police. They'd formed a solid wall with their shields and had the visors on their helmets lowered. I knew at a glance that they were preparing to move forward. I'd seen it enough times before.

'We need to go back,' I shouted at Mohammed. 'Right now. We'll find another way round.'

But going back was almost impossible. Now, the current of the crowd was against us; everyone else was surging forward, either to get a better look at what was happening or because they *wanted* to fight. I could feel the anger, the frustration, the desperation in the air. It was like the first crackle before a thunderclap. People were yelling in half a dozen different languages. People were hurling themselves against the fencing. Then everything happened at once.

The riot police started to march forward, not quickly, but in unison, with shields and batons raised. There was the sound of metal ripping, a grating screech as a whole section of the fence gave way. I don't know if it had been weakened first, with bolt cutters, or if it was the sheer weight of all those bodies pressed up against it. All I know is that it was like a dam breaking. People started to scramble through the gap and over the fallen fence, a dozen at a time, and in the same instant, smoke began to rain from the sky. There was a flash of pure white light, and a concussion so loud it made my ears ring.

My only thought was to run, and there was only one way to go. I followed Mohammed and Jesus through the gap, holding my breath so I didn't choke on the tear gas billowing from the road. Something grabbed at my ankle and I felt a sharp sting, stumbled, fell. I tried to roll, to avoid getting trampled, but my leg was caught in a coil of razor wire that had topped the fence. I pulled against it, biting back the pain.

A moment later, Jesus was there, kneeling beside me. He didn't hesitate. He thrust both hands into the razor wire and managed to free my leg. Then we were up and running once more. Most of the people who'd made it through were already charging down the embankment towards the rail line, but Mohammed was waiting for us on the flat space at the top, illuminated by the overhead security lighting that ran all the way to the tunnel. I stooped next to him, with my hands on my knees as I struggled to catch my breath. My lungs burned and my eyes stung, but I thought I'd be okay in a minute or two. I forced myself to breathe deeply, drawing in lungfuls of cool clean air.

It was then that Mohammed started swearing. 'Shit, Jesus. Your *hands*!'

I looked up and saw that Jesus was holding his palms flat and facing upward, level with his chest. He was regarding them with a small, puzzled frown, when by rights he should have been screaming. They were literally dripping with blood.

'It's okay,' he said. 'It doesn't hurt.'

'We need to get you to a hospital!'

'There's no hospital,' he told me. 'It's okay. I know what happens next. I have seen it many times.'

There were no words. How could it not hurt? It was impossible. And yet, there was no hint of pain in his expression. For the first time that night, he looked calm and certain. He lowered his hands, nodding in the direction of the tunnel. 'We need to go now. This will be our only opportunity.'

As if to punctuate this statement, another stun grenade exploded somewhere on the bridge. There were fewer people getting through now, fewer racing down the slope. From below came shouts and screams, and the wild barking of dogs.

'Jesus, we don't have to do this,' I said. 'It isn't worth dying for!'

'You're not going to die,' he told me. 'You're going to follow me. Now.'

And with that, he darted over the cusp of the embankment and disappeared from view. Mohammed glanced at me for only a moment, his eyes wide, before running after him.

I had no choice. I followed.

Below, it was a battlefield. Everywhere I looked, pockets of men were fighting the police. Some had already been subdued, and were being held to the ground, and some had clearly been incapacitated by pepper spray. But others were keeping the police at bay by throwing rocks from the rail-side. More were simply sprinting for the tunnel, some five hundred metres distant. It was impossible to tell if anyone had made it yet, but for the moment, we did have numbers on our side; even with their dogs and pepper spray, the police would be hard pressed to stop everyone. But it was a situation that could not last. Once the

crowd on the bridge was under control, the area would be flooded
with riot police. Jesus was right: the path before us would not
stay open for long.

We didn't sprint. We moved at a fast jog, following a zigzag
path to avoid the fighting. At this point, I wasn't really thinking
about anything other than staying with Jesus and Mohammed.
I didn't believe we had much chance of reaching the tunnel; I
only hoped I could protect my brother. But luck must have been
on our side. Or else, we were put at a strange advantage by not
being the fastest runners, or the strongest, or the bravest. Several
times, we were overtaken by our fellow invaders, and every time
they were intercepted ahead of us, giving us the chance to push
on a little further. Five hundred metres became three hundred,
became one hundred. And suddenly, one of the tunnel entrances
was rising before us, gaping like a huge black mouth. Like the
gates of the underworld.

There was a single policeman blocking our path. He had a
dog – a huge Alsatian that was barking furiously, straining at its
leash. I grabbed hold of Mohammed's shoulder. I didn't think
he'd do anything stupid now, but I wasn't willing to risk it. The
policeman was shouting in French, and the dog was still barking.
Jesus took a step forward, with both hands held before him. Not
in surrender, but bracing himself, as if to hold back an avalanche.

'These boys are going to the UK,' he shouted. 'You are not
going to stop them.'

The policeman couldn't have known what he was saying – I
doubt he was an Arabic speaker – but it probably made no
difference, anyway. His eyes were fixated on Jesus's hands. The
pouring blood, the missing fingers. I saw in a flash how it must
have looked to him. He thought he was looking at a man who

had just suffered a major amputation. A man unaffected by this, and in no way intimidated by the threat of further violence.

Jesus took another step forward, and I saw the policeman's hand dip to the Alsatian's collar.

It took the dog only seconds to cover the ground between us. But Jesus didn't even flinch. He kept his body rigid and his hands outstretched.

What happened next made the French policeman gasp. His hands went to his mouth, and he began to back away.

The attack dog did not attack. It juddered to a halt, no more than a metre from Jesus's outstretched hands. It leapt and snarled and snapped at the air, but it came no closer, as if some invisible force were holding it by the collar. A moment later, it had stopped barking. It sat, then lay at Jesus's feet, its tongue hanging from its mouth.

Jesus knelt and scratched the dog behind one of its ears.

Later, I would try to make sense of what I'd seen. I would tell myself that this animal could not possibly have been trained to attack in such circumstances. It would have reacted to aggression. It would have reacted to fear. It would have reacted if Jesus had run, or if he had shown any sign of submission. But he hadn't. He'd just stood there, not giving an inch. He'd acted as if he were in complete command of the situation, and the dog had responded to this cue.

These were the explanations that came to me eventually. But at the time, there was no explanation. There was only a miracle.

Jesus gave the dog a final pat on its side, then turned to me and Mohammed. 'We should go now,' he said.

This time, none of us waited. We ran into the tunnel.

The Underworld

I expected immediate pursuit, but for the moment, it did not come. There was a narrow walkway to one side of the track, which we ran down in single file. The tunnel was already sloping, and it made running seem effortless. Or maybe it was adrenaline, or simply the feeling of release after a month of going nowhere.

There were safety lights affixed to the near wall, every ten metres or so, and there were what looked to be emergency evacuation doors, which we passed every couple of minutes. But aside from this, the tunnel was featureless and unchanging. There was little by which to judge how far we'd come, or how long it had taken. But I knew we couldn't keep running indefinitely. I was conscious of the meal I'd skipped, not to mention the blood that Jesus had lost. I shouted for a halt near one of the evacuation doors, where the lighting was slightly brighter.

I put my finger to my lips and listened for any sound, but all I could hear was the air rushing through the tunnel and the blood throbbing in my ears. I gave it a count of twenty, then said to Jesus and Mohammed: 'I don't think anyone's following. Or if they are, they can't be very close.'

'Why aren't they following?' Mohammed demanded, sounding almost angry that they weren't. 'Surely they'll send someone after us?'

'I don't know. You saw what it was like up there. It was chaos. I expect their priority will be getting that under control. If we're lucky, we might have a decent head start.'

'Then we need to keep running! If we keep running, there's no way they'll catch us.'

'Mohammed, we can't run to the UK! You might be able to keep going, but I can't. And neither can Jesus. From here, we walk.'

'How far is it?' Mohammed asked.

'The tunnel's about fifty kilometres.'

'Pah! It's nothing. We've been walking twenty-five every night for the last month.'

'Not all in one go, we haven't. It's going to take hours and hours.'

'Then we should get moving. I'm not going back now.'

'Of course we're not going back! But we're not going to make it unless we pace ourselves. Jesus, show me your hands.'

They were almost black in the dim glow from the safety lights. It was difficult to tell if the bleeding had stopped. I used the torch on the phone to take a better look, and saw darker patches where the blood had perhaps started to clot. Perhaps . . . At the very least his palms were no longer dripping.

'Are you okay to go on?' I asked him.

'Of course. I have never felt better.'

'What the hell happened up there?' Mohammed hissed. 'It

was . . . well, it was impossible, that's all. Completely fucking impossible.'

'It was not impossible,' Jesus said. 'The path opened. We were there at the correct time. I led you through, as I knew I would.'

Mohammed sputtered for a moment. He sputtered, then threw up his hands in resignation. It was the only time I'd ever seen him genuinely lost for words. I stayed silent as well. It was all too much to process. Impossible, improbable, miraculous – I just didn't know anymore.

'Who *are* you?' Mohammed said eventually. 'How did you do that . . . ? Fuck, Jesus! That dog. I thought it was going to rip your throat out.'

Jesus shrugged. 'I am not afraid of dogs.'

My brother started to laugh. His laughter was almost hysterical, and far too loud. It was this that brought me back, like a slap across the cheek.

'Mohammed, we don't have time for this now,' I said. 'Jesus, are you certain you're okay to continue?'

Jesus simply gestured down the tunnel with one mutilated, bloody hand. 'The UK is waiting for us, my friends.'

'Then let's get moving. Now.'

We walked and we walked. At first I checked the clock on the phone frequently, marking off the minutes, then hours, we'd managed to keep going. But it was not helpful. It seemed that the intervals were getting smaller and smaller; I'd turn on the screen expecting an hour to have passed, and discover it had been less than half that. Just after five a.m., I stopped looking altogether. It was enough to know that we were still going, with no sign of pursuit.

Now time and distance lost all meaning. It was as if we were walking through some dark abstraction, a hole in the fabric of reality. The tunnel flattened, rose, and then started to fall again. It curved back and forth. I had no idea why. On the map, it was shown as a perfectly straight line from France to the UK.

We stopped only once, to share the small amount of food and drink we had with us. It was hardly anything – just what we'd carried to the terminal in our coat pockets. I had a little bit of chocolate left, and Jesus had some peanuts. Mohammed had a can of energy drink. Once it was gone, there'd be nothing else to sustain us, and I didn't know how much further we'd have to walk. But there could be no thought of slowing down now. As long as Jesus and Mohammed could keep going, I would too.

And so we trudged on through the darkness, on and on. We barely talked. It was difficult, walking in single file, and I think we were all just focused on the task before us, on putting one foot in front of the other. After a while, my thoughts became skittish. I don't know if it was the tiredness, or the monotony of the walk – the complete lack of external stimuli. Or maybe it was the see-saw emotions of the last day, finally catching up with me. In any case, my thoughts hopped, and soon the memories started to come of their own accord, rising like apparitions to greet me.

I saw again the mountains of Samos under the blazing Greek sun. I saw Effie, the bargirl who'd stopped to help us when Jesus collapsed in the road. I saw all the people who'd helped us: the policeman in Samos Town, whose name I'd never discovered; Dr Polgár, the Hungarian neurologist; all the volunteers and charity workers who'd distributed food in shelters and at train stations.

I saw Firas, smiling in his US Air Force hoodie.

I saw my parents, and they gave me the strength to carry on.

Some unknown time later, the first train thundered past. There was a rush of air that became a sudden gale, then lights cutting through the blackness like knives. I had a few seconds to flatten my back against the tunnel wall, and saw Mohammed and Jesus do the same. It passed barely a metre from my face, carriage after carriage, and when it was finally gone, the silence was overwhelming.

Mohammed was the first to speak. 'If the trains are running, does that mean . . . they're not coming for us?'

'I don't know what it means,' I said.

'They must know we're in here! Why are they letting the trains through again?'

I thought about this, re-evaluating. 'Maybe they *don't* know. Maybe they thought they'd cleared everyone out.'

'But we were seen! It must have been reported. That policeman . . .'

Mohammed trailed off. He was probably thinking the same thing as me: that policeman would have had some reason not to report what he'd witnessed. It was not credible.

We both looked at Jesus, who shrugged. 'They'll know we're here soon, I think. The train driver would surely have seen us.'

'Maybe . . .' I didn't know if we could be certain of this. I didn't know if we could be certain of anything, anymore. 'We'll just have to keep going,' I said. 'That's all we can do.'

There were two more trains, and then nothing. We walked on in silence, and I didn't even try to understand what was happening. All my effort went into walking, into keeping my body moving forward. It seemed to be getting harder with every step. My feet felt as if they must be swollen to twice their usual size. My stomach hurt and my head hurt, and I was so thirsty it felt as if my mouth had been packed with sand. But I couldn't stop, even for the shortest of rests. I knew that if I stopped, I would not be able to start again.

How long had it been now? Six hours? Seven? Time felt so strange down here, with nothing but pain and darkness and memories. It was like walking down a tunnel in a dream, with neither beginning nor end in sight. Just this everlasting walkway and the empty track below us.

The quiet was eerie. There was no sound but the echo of our footfalls. I kept my head down now. I kept my eyes on the backs of Jesus's flip-flops, which rose and fell in slow motion. Had our pace dropped? It seemed likely, but that didn't matter anymore. We were still going.

Still going.

I repeated it over and over to myself, until my mind could no longer retain even that simple thought. I was aware of pain, and need. Nothing else.

I kept going, step by step by step.

It must have taken some time for me to register that the tunnel was sloping upwards once more. I didn't want to believe it at first; I didn't want to get my hopes up. But finally, I risked a look at the phone. It was astonishing. The clock showed that it had gone midday. We had walked all through the night and the following morning. In the state I was in, I couldn't work out how many hours that was, but the exit had to be close. It *had* to be.

I didn't know what would happen if we were intercepted at this point, so close to the UK. Would they take us all the way back to France? I had a memory that I could not place, of floating on a dark sea with dozens of other people, of being told that we could go no further. We had to go back.

I had no hope at this point, only fear. And it was fear that kept me going for those last desperate strides.

There was light in the distance, a slit of light that grew wider and brighter. Before long, it was painful to look at. Painful and wonderful at the same time.

The ceiling opened out into a blazing white sky. I stumbled and held my hands across my face. Mohammed was laughing, and I think I was probably crying. There were two blurry figures waiting for us just ahead. I thought they must be policemen, come to intercept us, but it was impossible to be certain. The light was so bright it was making spots dance before my eyes.

I pushed back the dizziness. I pushed back the exhaustion, raised both hands to the sky, and shouted: 'Asylum! We claim our right to asylum!'

That was the moment Jesus collapsed – the exact moment.

His legs buckled beneath him, and he fell at the rail-side, utterly spent.

Sacrifice

It was a shot of adrenaline, straight to my heart. I sprang to help him, but quick as I was, Mohammed was quicker. He dived to the ground, just managing to get his hand under Jesus's head before it struck the concrete at the rail-side.

He was still conscious at this point. Mohammed and I managed to move him a safe distance from the track, and I remember shouting at the policemen that we needed an ambulance.

It was difficult to make him comfortable. I rolled up my coat and wedged it under his head, but that was about all I could do. I didn't want to cause him any pain, so I held his wrist rather than his hand; his sleeves were caked in dried blood. One of the policemen brought a blanket while the other spoke on the phone.

'It's cold in the UK,' Jesus said. He didn't open his eyes when he spoke; he looked and sounded very calm.

'It's a cold country,' I told him. 'It's a long way north.'

'Are you certain you want to live here, my friend?'

It might have been a joke. I don't know. I thought the important thing was to keep him talking. I thought if I kept talking to him until the ambulance arrived, then he'd surely be okay.

'Yes. We're certain,' I said. 'It's cold, but it's safe. They'll look after us here. All of us.'

'I was of some help, wasn't I? In the end?'

'Yes, Jesus. You helped us. No one could have done more.'

'I don't think I've done many things I can be proud of, but I'm proud of this. Is Mohammed there, too?'

'I'm here,' Mohammed said. That was all he said. Nothing clever or sarcastic.

Jesus gave a small nod. 'I've enjoyed travelling with you. You know many interesting curses, for one so young . . .'

'Thank you,' Mohammed said. 'I try my best.'

I didn't know why his voice cracked when he spoke. It made no sense. Jesus would be taken to a hospital, but we'd see him again after that. We'd be together again. Why did they both sound like they were saying goodbye?

'You must look after your brother,' Jesus told him. 'Don't let him feel guilty about this. It was my choice to make.'

'Jesus, you don't need to worry,' I said. 'An ambulance is on its way. They're going to take good care of you.'

'There's something I didn't tell you,' Jesus said, after a moment. 'It's about my dream. I wasn't completely honest.'

'You don't need to say anything. Whatever it is, it doesn't matter anymore.'

'It does matter. It may help you to understand.'

He didn't wait for me to argue against this. He spoke rapidly, but was still calm. Despite everything.

'In the dream, I saw the three of us walk into the underworld together. But I only ever saw you and Mohammed come out the

311

other side. I was no longer with you. I always understood what this meant. I understood this was how it had to be, in the end.'

'You were wrong,' I told him. 'You're here. You *did* come out the other side.'

'Yes, I did. But only for a short while, I think. The meaning of my dream was very clear.'

'You need to rest, Jesus. You need to give yourself a chance to recover.'

This caused the barest flicker of a smile. 'Yes. I think I can rest now. This is a good idea.'

There was silence. I kept holding his wrist.

'I don't feel any pain,' Jesus said, after a short time had passed. 'I just feel cold, that's all.'

He opened his eyes then, very briefly. He opened his eyes, he closed them again, and I could find nothing more to say.

When the paramedics arrived, he was still breathing, but he was no longer responsive. They put him on a stretcher and lifted him into the back of the ambulance, and that was the last time I ever saw him. I remember that he looked very peaceful, as if he'd fallen into a deep and dreamless sleep.

We were informed of Jesus's death that evening, in our police cell, but, by then, I already knew. I can't explain how I knew, but I did. I woke from several hours of blank, exhausted sleep, and the first thought in my head was that he was gone. Not a belief, but a certainty.

The policewoman who told us was extremely nice. She made us cups of tea and sat and held my hand while I wept. There wasn't an official cause of death at that point. I don't know for certain that one was ever established, though I assume it was.

In any case, I never found out. The closest I came was reading the speculation on the British news sites.

It's possible that you read some of those stories too. There were several, in the days following our arrival in Folkestone. They all reported the riots in Calais, and how Eurotunnel had been forced to close down operations for almost twelve hours, costing them hundreds of thousands of pounds in lost revenue. Apparently, a few dozen invaders made it into the tunnels, but we were the first, and the only ones not cleared out by the police. There was some brief interest in me and Mohammed – the 'two Syrian teenagers' who made it all the way to the UK – but most of the stories focused on the failings of the French authorities, who were not doing enough to manage the crisis. Several commentators suggested that the British army should be sent in, to bring order to the chaos.

Amidst all these wider issues, Jesus was little more than a footnote: an older Iraqi man, name unknown, who'd died shortly after arriving in the UK on foot. His injuries – 'sustained in the night's violence' – were mentioned in brief, as was the fact that he was dehydrated, and in 'generally poor health'. But his death was not being treated as suspicious.

I have no complaints about the Folkestone police. I realised, some time later, that they must have been in a difficult position, what with the coverage in the newspapers, and the disruption caused to Eurotunnel; not to mention the inevitable anger from the Calais police, who probably didn't like having rocks thrown at them. And under UK law, Mohammed and I *were* border criminals – it was an indisputable fact. Nevertheless, the Folkestone police made us as comfortable as possible, all things considered. I got the impression, from the start, that no one had any desire to see us prosecuted. Perhaps it was in light of Mohammed's age, or the circumstances in which we were brought in. Or perhaps the police realised something that I, too, have come to understand: that in some situations, it's no simple matter to separate right from wrong.

Mohammed and I were interviewed the following day, separately and at length. Sergeant Howard, who was leading the enquiry, told me beforehand that I was not to worry about this: it wasn't an interrogation, and Mohammed would be well looked after while we were apart. He would have an Appropriate Adult with him at all times, to ensure his welfare, as well as an Arabic translator for his interview. I was also offered this option, but I declined, and Sergeant Howard agreed that it was probably unnecessary. I did, however, get to talk to the translator briefly, when she came to our cell to introduce herself to Mohammed. She was called Mona, and she taught Arabic Language and Literature at the University of London. She smiled when I told her that my father was also an academic, and I hoped to be one too, one day.

I suppose my own interview must have lasted a couple of hours. Sergeant Howard was very patient, and encouraged me to tell my story in my own words, including anything I felt was relevant. He asked for clarification a few times, and made me repeat certain details that he deemed important – regarding what had happened on the night of the riot, how Jesus had got his injuries, how we'd evaded the French police. He asked to see Jesus's medication, when I got to that point in the story, then bagged it in case it was needed as evidence. But mostly he just listened, interrupting as little as possible.

I told him almost everything. I told him how Mohammed and

I had fled Syria, and about what had happened to our parents – what I knew and what I suspected. I told him about swimming across the sea to Samos, and meeting Jesus on the beach. I told him about Jesus's alcoholism, and his estranged daughter in Germany. I told him about the hospital in Hungary, and Dr Polgár, and the journey to Berlin, and then on to Calais. I told him how Jesus had wanted to help us – how he wanted to see us safely to the UK.

I did not talk about the calming of the storm, or the prophetic dreams, or the guard dog at the tunnel entrance – and my assumption was that Mohammed wouldn't either. I found out later that I was correct. Neither of us thought it sensible to mention details that we knew would not be believed.

After I'd given my formal statement, after the recording equipment had been turned off, Sergeant Howard told me only one thing. 'You know, Zain,' he said, 'I have two sons. They're twelve and fifteen, a little younger than you and Mohammed, but . . . well . . .'

That was all he said, and I suppose that was all he could say in the circumstances. But it was enough. I understood what he was implying. That he could imagine some terrible alternative universe, where it was *his* country that had been torn apart by war, and his children who had to flee. He was saying that he hoped our asylum claim would be successful. He hoped that we would now have a future.

I regret that I was unable to tell Sergeant Howard the full truth, but ultimately, it's a decision I have to stand by. It wouldn't have done either one of us any favours, if I'd insisted he write a statement that no court would believe.

*

There is not much left to tell.

From the police station we were transferred to an immigration centre in West Sussex, where we stayed for almost a month. It was a secure unit, which meant we were still locked up, and could only leave the premises in special circumstances and under staff supervision. But for all that, it was not such a bad place to be. We had a small room with twin beds and a desk with a kettle on it. There were clean toilets, and the tap water was not contaminated with E. coli. So, compared to The Jungle, it was very nice indeed.

Nevertheless, it was a difficult time for us. In a certain sense, I think that month spent in detention was as hard as anything we'd had to face before, in Turkey or Hungary or Calais. It's a strange thing, being confined in a place of safety after so much movement and doubt and danger. When you have an impossible task to complete, when you have daily obstacles to overcome, it doesn't leave room for much else. You worry about finding food and shelter. You worry about the men with the guns and the batons and the tear gas. Mohammed and I had spent a long time worrying about these things, but I think it insulated us from the larger shock of what had happened to us. What had happened to our family.

In the UK, in the immigration centre, we finally grieved. It wasn't that we'd given up all hope, and yet we had to face reality. It wasn't likely that we would ever see our parents again. We had to acknowledge this, together, so that we could move forward with our lives.

When we got out, I would try again to track them down. Eventually, I would manage to contact a neighbour in Latakia, and she would confirm what I already suspected. That Mum had been taken by the police shortly after we left, and she had not been seen since.

That was all anybody could tell us, for now. There was no further trail to follow, and it was unlikely that this would change in the near future.

Our neighbour was extremely teary on the phone, but when she calmed down, we talked a little about what was happening in Latakia. The Russians had arrived, shortly after Mohammed and I left, and their planes were now a constant sight in the skies above the city. The rebels were being bombed in the north, moderates and Islamists alike, and after four years of stalemate, the war seemed to be turning in the regime's favour.

Had it been otherwise, had the opposition prevailed, then there might have been the chance of answers in the future. There might have been investigations into Syria's military prisons, trials for war crimes. But as things stood, the likelihood was diminishing. Like so many others, my parents had been swallowed by a conflict in which they wanted no part. My father's crime was that he wanted to save those who could not save themselves – the young men who would otherwise have been forced to fight. My mother's crime was that she loved her husband, and wanted to save *him*.

It hurt, and it would not stop hurting, but they were both heroes, in their own way. This was the thought that Mohammed and I tried to cling to, when the grief became too much to bear. They had been so brave, and we would be brave too.

We would give their sacrifice meaning.

The time passed slowly in the immigration centre. I spent most of my days in the on-site library, and Mohammed spent his every opportunity playing football in the yard, with the other inmates. There was also a small gym that we both used every evening. I've never been a sporty person, but I found that my body had become accustomed to a certain amount of exercise over the past couple of months – what with all the walking, running, climbing, crawling, wading and swimming we'd done since leaving Syria.

In the mornings, there were English classes, but after attending the first, I realised that it was going to be too basic for Mohammed, so I took it upon myself to start improving his language skills. He was surprisingly amenable to this. Perhaps it was because we were now in the UK, and he had a clearer motivation. In any case, I spent at least half an hour every morning speaking to him in English, and in the afternoons, I had him practising his spelling, grammar and tenses. When he did well, I rewarded him with extra phone time. I also encouraged him to make use of the TV room. The quality of the programming was not great – it was mostly shows about antiques and home renovations – but it at least provided additional language exposure, and some interesting regional accents for us to study.

That was our day-to-day existence, but on a larger scale, nothing of note occurred. We lived in limbo, waiting every day for news of our asylum claim. We were told, when we arrived, that given Mohammed's age, it would likely be fast-tracked as a priority case. But it turned out that the fast track was not all that fast. If we'd had a safe address to go to – friends or relatives – then things might have been different; we'd probably have been released while our application was being processed. But as things stood, we would remain in detention.

Our salvation came from two perfect strangers, who decided to give us more than just a safe address. They gave us a home.

They were called Sarah and Douglas. They were fifty-eight and fifty-six, and both worked as academics at the University of Cambridge. They had three grown-up children, the youngest of whom had recently left home. They decided that they didn't like having a half-empty house, and had been considering for some time how they could rectify this situation.

Sarah read about us in one of the national newspapers – about me and Mohammed and our long walk through the tunnel. She was a Professor of Law, and had a good knowledge of the rules regarding the asylum process. She wrote emails to the Kent Police, and to her contacts in the Home Office.

Because, sometimes, human beings can do incredible things for each other. Sometimes, all they want to do is help.

A year has passed since then, and much has changed.

Mohammed restarted his education as soon as our asylum claim had been accepted. He attends a local comprehensive school, with modern facilities and excellent exam results. Since he is the only Syrian, and the only refugee, in his class, I was anxious at first that he would have a hard time adapting. But I needn't have worried. His advanced football skills and extensive knowledge of English swear words have served him well. He has made several friends. He even has a girlfriend! She is called Alicia, and she is very pleasant and polite – too polite for Mohammed. For this reason, I have my doubts that it will last, but who knows? Mohammed *has* matured a lot in the last year. He's matured, and his future looks bright.

Three times a week he practises football with the Cambridge

United youth team. As you know, my knowledge of football is not great, but I did some research and Cambridge United seem to be a reputable, professional team. They may not be the best team in English football – as far as I can work out, they're the seventy-eighth best team – but it's a start, nevertheless. I spoke with the coach one evening, and incredible as it seems, he believes that Mohammed may be able to turn professional in a couple of years' time. He might get *paid* to play football.

Secretly, I'm very proud of him.

As for me, I resumed my studies last September, at the University of Cambridge. Sarah and Douglas were extremely supportive here. They helped me complete my application, and took me to my interview in the Department of English Literature. To be honest, it didn't feel much like an interview. We talked about Syria and my journey to Europe. The interviewer asked about my previous studies, and when I'd started learning English. She cried a little when I talked about my mother, and I had to pass her a tissue. When she asked what my favourite books were, I told her without hesitation: *Great Expectations* by Charles Dickens, and *The God Delusion* by Professor Richard Dawkins.

'You're an Atheist?' she asked, clearly somewhat surprised.

Of course, it was the first time anyone had ever asked me that question, and the first time I could have admitted to it in a public setting, with no fear of censure. But I waited a couple of seconds before answering.

Am I still an Atheist? The short answer is yes; despite everything, it's the position that makes the most sense to me. I'm still aware that there are mysteries and there are miracles, and these are not the same thing. Obviously, though, I have questions – many questions – about what happened.

I think about Jesus most days, and Mohammed and I talk about him often. What, exactly, did he know? Were the things he *foresaw* the things that actually happened? I've driven myself half crazy trying to remember *precisely* what he said, and when, but it's proven a fruitless task. Ask any psychologist, any policeman, and they'll tell you that memory is notoriously unreliable. At best, it's a sketch, shaped and coloured by everything that came before and afterwards. If you're trying to remember the words used in a conversation six months ago, you might as well give up.

Nevertheless, there are broad brushstrokes that Mohammed and I agree upon, even when the details become a point of contention. We agree about the attack dog, and how its behaviour seemed to defy all logic; you don't forget something like that. We agree about the storm, how it was there one minute then gone the next, as if it had never been. We agree that Jesus believed he had visions of the future, and that, in the end, he believed these visions fulfilled.

We agree that he was a strange and remarkable man, who did strange and remarkable things.

And maybe that's *all* he was. The problem, when you start dwelling on other possibilities – the supernatural, the divine – is that they don't solve anything. They raise far more questions than they answer. Or, as Mohammed puts it: 'If God wanted to help us, couldn't he have found an easier way to do it? Why send us a drunken Iraqi?'

I don't know the answer to this. If God does exist, then he surely has a strange sense of humour.

*

A final thing.

I came out to Sarah, and later Douglas, soon after we'd moved into their home. You might think this was no big deal – not after everything we'd been through – but you'd be wrong. Some anxieties are so deep-rooted and long-standing that confronting them can take more courage than swimming across the Mediterranean Sea. But after much soul-searching, I decided that I did not want to begin my new life with a lie. In part, it was because I felt I owed it to Sarah and Douglas, who'd shown themselves to be such incredible, generous people. But even more than this, I thought I owed it to myself. When you're given the chance of freedom, you have to grab it with both hands.

I waited for an evening when Mohammed was at football practice and Douglas was working late. I sat with Sarah in the kitchen and I made my confession, staring at the wooden table top the whole time. I had rehearsed what I was going to say: that I had known since I was thirteen, but had told almost no one, not my own parents, and certainly not Mohammed. I finished by saying that I hoped it would not make a difference to her or Douglas, because I'd hate to put them in a position that made them uncomfortable.

Sarah waited until I'd finished, then put her hand on mine. 'It doesn't change anything, Zain. Of course it doesn't.'

That was all.

'Do you think I should tell Mohammed?' I asked, after a few moments of silence.

She smiled at this – a small complicated smile. 'That's *your* decision, Zain. It has to be. But I will say this: sometimes you have to have faith in people. I don't know what Mohammed's prejudices are, but . . . well, maybe you just have to trust him to overcome them.'

I nodded. And, of course, I'd already made my decision; I'd made it before I'd asked the question. It was just a matter of *when*.

I picked a day at the beginning of spring. It was the first warm day we'd had since coming to the UK. Not hot, obviously, but very bright, with a deep cloudless sky that made me think of home. Home in Latakia.

We took a walk down by the river, and I told him. I'm not sure how, exactly. It wasn't like with Sarah; there was no possibility of rehearsing this. I just had to get it out, in whatever way I could, with no idea of what might come next.

Mohammed was silent for quite a long time – long enough to make me extremely nervous. Then he said: 'Well, it's not like in Syria, is it? I mean, you'll probably be okay here. There are lots of gays in the UK.'

That would have been enough – more than enough. But it turned out Sarah was right. Sometimes, you *do* have to put your faith in people.

Mohammed closed his eyes and took a breath. 'You're my brother,' he said. 'You'll always be my brother.'

So that was it. We walked on for a while in silence, past the bridges and the first spring flowers and the people pushing their boats on the river. The sun warmed my face, and I remember the most incredible sense of *lightness*, as if I might float away any moment.

I knew, then, that Mohammed was right. I was going to be okay. We both were.

Author's Note

Dear Reader

This novel has its origin in 2012, when I was helping to run an English-conversation class for refugees and migrant workers. It was an informal drop-in, and most weeks a dozen or so people would turn up. We'd drink tea and chat. I'd answer questions about vocabulary and bus timetables and accessing one-to-one tuition. Sometimes, people would bring in letters they needed help reading, from landlords or the Council or the Home Office.

One week, a new student showed up ten minutes before class was due to start. We got talking.

His name was Zeyn. He was Iranian, very intelligent, and spoke excellent English. I never found out how old he was, but probably mid-to-late twenties. He'd got into trouble with the Iranian government the previous year, after taking part in the pro-democracy street protests. Facing imprisonment, he'd had to leave his home with nothing more than a rucksack full of clothes. He didn't have much money, so he travelled west however he could, hitch-hiking or on foot. He made it all the way across

Turkey and reached the shore of the Mediterranean Sea. He swam from Turkey to Greece. That was how he put it – 'I swam from Turkey to Greece' – as if it were just a footnote in his journey to the UK.

I had many questions, but at this point the other students had started to arrive. I had to welcome people, put the kettle on, finish setting up the class. So I didn't get to find out what happened next. I never found out. This was the one and only time Zeyn came to the class. But I kept on thinking about what he'd told me, for weeks then months afterwards.

There's something very compelling about an unfinished story – especially when the scant details you have are so evocative. It's like an itch you need to scratch.

I went online and started looking at maps, checking for the places along the Turkish coast where it would be feasible to swim across to Greece. It turned out there were several. A number of the Greek islands are only a few kilometres across the sea, and easily visible from Turkey. It's still a terrible risk, of course. If you're a kilometre from shore and you get cramp, you're going to be in a huge amount of trouble.

At this point, I had no idea that I was going to turn this fledgling story into a novel. I was just curious. I wanted to scratch that itch. But, in hindsight, this is how each of my books has started – with a question I didn't know the answer to, or a single idea or scene or image. In this case, it was the idea of that swim, and everything it suggested: the desperation and determination, the willingness to risk everything for the hope of a better future.

When the 'migrant crisis' began in the summer of 2015, our screens were suddenly flooded with images of all those desperate, determined people. The reaction was mixed. David Cameron warned of the 'swarm' of migrants about to descend on our borders. The Refugee Council immediately responded, calling the Prime Minister's language awful and dehumanising. Meanwhile, professional bigot Katie Hopkins was screaming for gunships to be deployed in the Mediterranean. It was like Jonathan Swift's 'Modest Proposal' (can't we just *eat* the poor?), but non-satirical.

I don't think many people shared David Cameron's assessment of the migrant threat, much less Katie Hopkins's. I think most people saw human beings rather than a swarm. They saw families displaced by war, and young men fleeing poverty and the threat of military conscription. For every person spewing bile on social media, there were probably ten using the #RefugeesWelcome hashtag. And there were many thousands of people, all across Europe, donating time and food and money and clothing to those in need. The problem, of course, is that compassion tends to be much quieter than anger and ignorance and prejudice. Compassion often takes place behind the scenes, while prejudice stands centre stage and grabs the headlines.

Sometimes my books are topical, broadly speaking, but in all honesty, I don't write them with a higher purpose in mind, some central theme or message. I just try to tell a compelling story about a subject or group of characters I care about (and I suspect this is the same for most fiction writers). Nevertheless, if I had to name a secondary aspiration, it would probably be to shout about compassion. I'd like to shout as loudly as I can about compassion and understanding and empathy. I hope that's one of the things this novel does.

We live in divisive times. Parts of the world are becoming more and more insular, and there's an 'us and them' narrative that's been gaining strength for at least the past decade. My belief – my hope – is that novels can offer an antidote to this. More than any other medium, novels allow us to see the world through different eyes, from someone else's point of view. To paraphrase Atticus Finch, they encourage us to climb into someone else's skin and walk around in it. This, too, is something I try to do in my books. It's one of the things I love most in both reading and writing fiction.

Thank you for taking the time to pick up my book. I hope you enjoyed it. Or enjoy it, if you're the sort of reader who skips straight to the author's note. I've never met one, but who knows? The world is a strange place, full of wonderfully strange people.

I'm feeling anxious as I write this, so I'll sign off as Kurt Vonnegut sometimes did, with the loveliest word in the English language.

Peace.

Acknowledgements

First and foremost, thanks to everyone at SAVTE, past and present, for transforming so many lives for the better, my own included. Special thanks to Zeyn for inspiring this story, and to Mohammed and Ailin for being such good friends over the past eight years.

The research for this novel was extensive, and it would be impractical to list every source consulted. But I feel I should give special mention to *Samos Chronicles* (www.samoschronicles.wordpress.com), which documented life on the island during the refugee crisis, and also inspired a chapter title ('A Walk in the Sun'). Likewise, I'd like to express my gratitude to the many bloggers and YouTubers who shared their first-hand experiences and painted such a vivid picture of the journey from Turkey to Western Europe.

Thanks, as always, to everyone at Hodder, London's friendliest publisher. I visit seldom, but when I do, I feel part of a very wonderful, very extended family.

Additional thanks to Charlotte, Lily, Maddy, Sarah, Simon, Steven and Thorne for all your personal contributions – your energy, enthusiasm, kind words, creativity, attention to detail, patience and professionalism.

Emma: thank you for being such a dedicated, sensitive and insightful editor. You understood what the story needed in the places where I didn't, and it's a warmer, richer book for your considerable input.

Stan and Kate: thanks for your unflagging support, advice, faith and encouragement.

Thanks to my family, even the ones who keep me up at night. I'm lucky to have you.

Finally, thanks to every reader who has contacted me to say nice things about my books. There are days when this makes all the difference.